Clipped By You

Chicago Steel
Book 3

Jessica Buss

Clipped By You
Chicago Steel Book Three
First Edition
Jessica Buss

This book contains mature content

Developmental Edit by Emerald Edits

Copy Edited by Ink Machine Editing

Cover Design & Interior Formatting by Feed Your Dreams Designs

Ebook ISBN: 979-8-9863903-4-5

Paperback ISBN: 979-8-9863903-5-2

Dedication

For Bob & Betty
My examples of love.
Forgiving. Sacrificing. Faithful. Selfless. Forever.

Chapter 1

Monica

August 2014

"Monica, what did you pack in this, rocks?" my brother, Josiah, drawls as he carries my biggest duffle bag up the six flights of stairs to my home for the next nine months. My dorm room isn't much, but to me, it's everything. Next week, I start my freshman year at NYU, and I'm so excited. It's something I've been dreaming about for a long time.

"Why don't you use those big muscles you got from working on the farm all summer? You know... the ones you love to flex for all the ladies in town," I holler down at him while I lug my own overstuffed duffle up the cement staircase.

"Shut up!" he grits out through clenched teeth. Glancing over the handrail, I see he's only a floor below me, but he's bent over and panting. He looks completely out of shape. Which is odd because that is the exact opposite of what Josiah is. He's one of the fittest guys I know. Farm life is not for the lazy or weak. In fact, all three of my older brothers are in phenomenal shape. Josiah, however, also runs track for Penn State, so he's in much better shape than most. Seeing him like this is definitely confusing. *What is going on with him?*

"Are we almost there?" he groans.

Noticing the placard on the landing above me shows this is the sixth floor, I squeal. "Yep, it's the next floor." The last few stairs take me no time to ascend, as I'm feeding off all the adrenaline pumping through my veins.

Propping the door open, I hold it for Josiah, who breezes through seconds later, as if the bag he's carrying has gone from filled with bricks to stuffed with feathers. He is absolutely ridiculous. Here I was worried about him and he was just giving me a hard time. *Brothers.* I know I'll miss them while I'm here, but for now, I've had my fill. How does the proverb go? Absence makes the heart grow fonder? We'll just see about that.

Turning down the hallway toward my room, I see it's stuffed with other freshmen moving in. Scooting around boxes and suitcases, we finally find my room, and the door is open wide.

I know from the paperwork NYU sent me that the room houses two. Peering in, I see most of the furniture has already been covered by boxes and suitcases.

Immediately, I wonder if I have the wrong room. It looks like two people have already moved in. Looking at the number on the door and then my phone, I confirm I'm in the right spot. Flashing my brother a panicked look, he steps up to help me.

"Monica, what's wrong?" he asks in a hushed tone.

"Everything says this is my room, but it looks like two people have already moved in." Making my point, I motion to all the covered furniture.

"Let's see," Josiah says as he raps his knuckles on the metal door frame. Surprised, three people spin around with wide eyes. A girl my age steps forward with her hand out. "I'm Samantha Fox. Are you Monica, my roommate?" Her smile is welcoming and friendly.

Nodding my head, I answer, "Yes, I'm Monica, and this is my brother, Josiah. He's helping me move in." I don't miss Samantha and my brother checking each other out.

The older gentleman next to Samantha clears his throat. "Samantha, dear, shall we move your stuff out of the way so Monica can get settled?"

Samantha laughs. "Sorry about that. My brother Christian, who's going to be a junior, was helping, and he needed to run back to the car for something. He just left everything scattered."

Totally understanding how unhelpful brothers can be, I just wave it off. "I totally get it. Which furniture do you want?" After we both pick, Samantha introduces me to her parents, George and Susan. They're terrific, both welcoming and kind.

After unloading my bags onto my bed, Josiah reminds me he needs to get on the road back to his school before it gets too late. He says goodbye to the Foxes and I walk him back out to his car. On our way out of the building, I run into something that feels like a brick wall. Shocked, I stumble back. A large hand reaches for me and steadies me. Warmth pulses through my body from where our hands touch. My eyes trace up the tanned arm holding me still and I find the most handsome man I've ever seen. "S-sorry 'bout that. Wasn't w-watching where I was going," I stutter out nervously.

Heat radiates from where he's still gripping my hand. It feels like my knees are weak and I'm going to faint. My body sways, and the handsome Ryan Reynolds look-a-like pulls me into him, causing me to gasp. Hints of leather, musk, and amber swirl around me, making my heart pound in my chest. My brain feels foggy and confused. Dreamily, I look up at the sexy stranger and mumble, "Thanks."

Josiah, who's nearby, lets out a loud laugh, knocking me out of the dreamy haze I'm in. Pushing back from the warm embrace of the god in flesh is painful. Within his hold, I feel safe and protected. Now I'm vulnerable. And even though I'm a new transplant to New York City, I know that's the last thing you want to be.

Checking to make sure I'm okay, the stranger pushes a few strands of stray hair behind my ear and nudges my chin up, making eye contact. His crystal blue eyes are piercing and penetrating, making me feel naked before him. Suddenly uncomfortable, I look away. I feel my brother step up next to me and have a conversation with the unknown sexy man. I stand there stupefied, unable to concentrate on what's actually being said between my brother and this god of a man. It's only when I finally go to open my mouth and contribute *something* to the conversation that he walks away without looking back.

"Mo, you, okay?" Josiah elbows me, breaking me from my still hazy thoughts.

Nodding my head, I reply, "Yeah, I'm fine. Don't you have to get on the road or something?"

Josiah wraps me in a warm embrace, setting his chin on the top of my head. "I do. Just want to make sure you're fine before I leave."

Hugging him back, I move my head to the side and answer, "I'm okay. Thanks for all the help. Text me when you get there, okay?" I sound like our mother. Hugging him extra tight, he squirms with discomfort. It's going to be a long day for him. After he leaves the city, he's heading to Penn State, where he'll finish his degree in Agribusiness Management this spring. When he graduates, he plans to return to the family's farm to help our older brothers, Mike and Will, run it. I am the only Fields child who isn't planning to make farm life my profession. Unlike Mike and Will, I'm attending college to obtain a degree that will take me far from farm work. Although, I suspect there will be days when I am surrounded by animals and have to deal with my share of shit, literally and figuratively.

The decision to not return to the farm for my career was one that I'd struggled with repeatedly. Over my lifetime, I've gotten enough of the hours, animals, chores, and constant wariness. Now I'd rather have a bit more freedom, even though I love our family farm. My plan at NYU is to earn a teaching degree and eventually teach in Chicago, which is only a few hours from our dairy farm. I know I'll miss my parents and brothers and Maribel, my favorite cow, but I'm excited about this new adventure.

Heading back up to my room to get unpacked, I run through the list of things I need to do before classes start next week. Things like visiting the campus bookstore, familiarizing myself with the subway and campus, and getting groceries distract me. As I weave through the still-packed hallway, I stare at the floor so I don't trip over all the clutter. When I reach my room, I turn sharply, trying to avoid a collision with a co-ed who has their arms overfull, and again I run into something hard.

"Oof!" a deep, masculine voice groans out.

"Not again," I mumble as I rub at the sore spot on my sternum that I gained from my earlier crash. This must be a record. Running into someone while not paying attention twice in less than a half hour. What are the chances?

"Hello, again," the deep, sexy voice comments, startling me. Flinching, I glance up slowly and freeze. Before me is the god from downstairs, and apparently, because Karma hates me, I've run into him... again. I grit my teeth. *This is not my day. He must think I'm an idiot.*

"Hi," I quietly answer as my face grows hot from embarrassment.

"How do you know each other?" Samantha asks while motioning between us with the curling iron in her hand.

The stranger snickers and a sly smirk stretches across his gorgeous face. His response makes me feel strange. Off balance and jittery. Uncertain of what I'll say, I let him answer. "We ran into each other outside, right?" He flashes his brilliant blue eyes at me, rendering me stupid, and all I can do is nod my agreement. *Great. Within half an hour of meeting him, I'm already looking and acting like a dopey bobblehead.*

Then he surprises me by stepping forward. His long fingers touch my arm, sending needy surges through my body. Before I can do anything else mortifying, he remarks, "We briefly met, but I didn't catch a name." Panicked, my eyes shoot up and focus on him. Just as I'm about to introduce myself, Samantha takes care of it for me. Unknowingly, she's probably saving me from some embarrassing response.

"Christian, this is Monica, my roommate. Monica, this is Christian, my brother, the one I was telling you about." Samantha handles the intros, gives a smirk to her brother, then strolls back over to their parents to finish putting away her clothes.

Christian sticks out his hand and lowers his voice. "Good to meet you. I'm Christian, her older brother, who she needn't warn you about. I'd prefer you get to know me on your own." He follows that with a wink while still holding my outstretched hand.

"Nice to meet you too. I'm Monica, officially," I respond shyly.

Just as he's about to speak again, his cell phone rings. Glancing at it, he says, "I have to take this. Excuse me." He steps out into the hallway. Giggles from girls who are stopping to flirt with him cover his muffled conversation. When I hear his deep voice say, "ladies," my heart drops. I thought he was flirting with me because he was genuinely interested. Realizing he's nothing but a gigantic flirt, I move back to my bed and begin unpacking my duffle bags. *It meant nothing. Okay.* This was obviously lesson number one in college, flirting and dating. I'm sure the next few weeks will be a whirlwind introduction for me, as I've literally had zero experience with guys. *Hopefully, I won't crash and burn.*

A few minutes later, Christian steps back into the room and over to his parents and sister, telling them he has to go. Assuming he won't say anything to me—

because why would he?—I continue unpacking. But when a warm body steps up close behind me, shivers cover my body. His cologne smells amazing. With nods of amber and leather, it's both warm and spicy. Pulling back some of my loose hair, he leans into my ear like he has a secret he only wants to share with me.

"Monica, I have to go, but it was more than nice to run into you twice today. I look forward to our future run-ins." His voice is like honey, smooth and sweet. Dripping with suggestion. He returns to his normal height above me and I swear he inhales before he leaves. Frozen in place, my body is overheating, my heart thumps wildly, and my stomach swirls like I've just ridden the tilt-a-whirl too many times in a row. *Why did having him so close cause my brain to shut down?*

Chapter 2

Monica

November 2014

"**A**re you sure your parents are really cool with this?" I hesitantly ask Samantha for the tenth time this week. While I wait for her answer—already knowing it—I fold various clothes for the weekend bag I'm packing. My plan is to spend Thanksgiving break at Samantha's parents' house outside the city. Since school began, I've met her parents a handful of times They were always nice to me and had many times invited me to dinner with Samantha and Christian. Even though they weren't my parents, they showered me with attention, asking how school and life were going. Being from a large family, I missed that sort of personalized attention from my parents. Not that my mom and dad weren't interested, they were just incredibly busy with running the farm and the shenanigans my three older brothers were constantly in. It was easy to be overlooked.

* * *

About a month before Thanksgiving, Samantha and I had been talking about our holiday plans and I shared I didn't want to head back to my family's farm. Adjusting to college had been tough for me, and the idea of going home and being expected to hit the ground running sounded stressful. Jumping back into farm chores or helping a family friend harvest their Christmas tree crop sounded overwhelming. Granted, I wouldn't have been expected to be doing the manual labor, but I know I'd be plenty busy doing other things. I'd probably be canning the last items pulled from the garden or making jam with the berries I'd picked this summer and frozen before heading to NYU. I felt bad about leaving all that to my mom, but my two oldest brothers were finally married and their wives were still trying to earn my mom's favor. They'd be eager to help her out, right?

When Samantha invited me to go home with her, I jumped at the opportunity. I wanted to see how the other half lived. The Fox family was uber wealthy compared to my meager upbringing. As thoughts of their lavish lifestyle swam in my brain, I wondered about many things. *Did they have a butler or maid? Maybe a personal chef? How big was their house? Did they have a pool?* Every time I tried to extract information from Samantha, she waived it off as unimportant.

From my experience so far, none of the Foxes came across as snobby or pretentious.

* * *

Samantha finally pulls me from my thoughts by answering my question. "Yes, Monica, you are definitely invited. I think my mom was more excited than I was when I told her you were coming home with me. She's been talking for weeks about the plans she's made for us. I need you there to help me handle all the crazy." She smiles and laughs before going back to throwing random things in her fashionable Louis Vuitton duffle bag.

I sigh and study my well-worn and stained polyester duffle bag. I couldn't even recall what color it had been originally. My bag is the exact opposite of luxury. I bet even the secondhand store wouldn't entertain reselling it. In elementary school, right before sixth grade camp, I'd gone with my mom to Walmart to pick out something that was not only practical but thrifty. Growing up on a dairy farm, I'd had nothing that could be considered luxurious. Having three older brothers who were always growing ensured we lived on a tight budget that afforded a simple life where our basic needs were met. Honestly, I'd never really wanted for anything, but I noticed we had nothing extra for fancy back-to-school clothes or birthday parties at the Fun Zone in the next town over.

Living on a farm afforded you a variety of experiences, even if it didn't provide much in the areas of money or material possessions. I'd learned so many valuable things like lending a hand where you could, helping your neighbor, and that hard work is invaluable. My parents had led by example, which spoke volumes. They were up before the sun, got their hands dirty, and worked hard for what we had. My entire childhood helped me to become a strong, independent, driven woman.

Even though I'd had a lot of significant memories and life lessons, I had some unpleasant experiences that colored my development. Life with my older brothers wasn't exactly easy. Don't get me wrong, I usually loved my brothers and their protective tendencies, but sometimes it was suffocating. I'd missed out on some major milestones, like dating. Because of them, I didn't even have my first kiss until I started college.

Coming to college allowed me to escape the farm in so many ways. During those first few weeks of school, I took full advantage of my freedom. I went to too many parties, had a couple of shady hookups, and suffered a major hit to my grades. Thankfully, after watching me go off the rails, Samantha talked some sense into me. If I'd continued down the path I'd been on, I'd probably have to return to the farm a college dropout or worse, pregnant with a stranger's baby.

Once I got myself back on track, I focused on why I was in school, on getting the degree I wanted. My chosen area of study, elementary education, was all mine.

Back home, my brothers had committed to taking over the farm when my parents retired. Our parents had always stressed the importance of schooling, but carrying on the family farm was a priority too. All of us had had a choice: go to school or work on the farm.

When it was my time to choose, my mom and dad encouraged me to pursue something I was passionate about since I hadn't needed to help run the farm.

Wednesday afternoon after classes, Samantha and I take a car service, sent by her dad, out to their family's house. Only it isn't a house like she'd said. It's an estate. We drive past an ornate metal fence and down a long driveway surrounded by a well-manicured lawn. The car pulls up to a large contemporary-style mansion that takes my breath away. It's gorgeous. The mansion looks like they could feature it as the cover story on an archi-tectural magazine.

Flowers and bushes decorate the front walkway. The house sits at the forefront of acres and acres of lush green lawn. Looking around quickly, I also spot a four-door detached garage that I'm sure houses a few luxurious vehicles. The Foxes' estate is enormous. Growing up on a working farm, I'm comfortable with a lot of land. Acreage did not intimidate me. I am, however, rendered stupid, taking in the opulence of it all.

"Wow!" I blurt as I gape at the luxury in front of me.

Samantha giggles.

I close my mouth and look over at her, knowing I probably look ridiculous.

"It's just a house, Monica. I promise. Come on inside. I'll show you around and then we'll find my mom." She pulls me from the car and we grab our bags from the driver before walking into the most beautiful house I've ever seen.

My well-worn Chucks slap on the marble tile that stretches across the entryway as I shuffle behind Samantha. My eyes dart back and forth, trying to take everything in. The artwork, flowers—everything, really —paint an idyllic picture of a well-loved family home. I know from conversations that even though her dad works long hours in the city, he still comes home to this sprawling estate every night. I could not imagine making that commute every day. According to Samantha, her parents had entertained the idea of getting an apartment in the city for her dad to use on long days, but they'd decided against it because they wanted to be together every night. In fact, the only time her parents were ever apart was while they were growing up and her dad had a business trip away. Now that she and Christian are grown, her mom tags along with her dad. In fact, Samantha even shared that they often turned those business trips into mini romantic getaways.

We wander through the entryway and Samantha shows me where the family room, kitchen, and dining room are. Then she takes me up a wrought iron u-shaped staircase that leads up to the mansion's six bedrooms and six of the eight bathrooms. I'd definitely get lost if Samantha wasn't escorting me.

She shows me to the guest room I'll be sleeping in all weekend. The room rivals what you'd find at a five-star hotel and leaves me completely speechless. Samantha then ushers me around the room. It looks nothing like mine at home. Decorated in subtle champagne and pink colors with accents of gold, it is breathtakingly beautiful. A small but classic chandelier hangs above the bed and a set of french doors reveal a small but private balcony.

The private en suite bathroom is the definition of luxurious. In my entire life, I have seen nothing so fancy. I gasp. Sam explains that each room has a gorgeous tiled shower and a large stand-alone bathtub that promises relaxation. They also carried over the colors from the bedroom into this room in understated ways with the use of candles, flowers, and linens. "Wow." I sigh as I spin around, taking it all in. Again, Samantha laughs at me. I feel foolish until I see that her response isn't critical at all.

"You know, you have this bathroom all to yourself, all weekend long." A smile dances on her lips.

"I do?" I squeak, trying to mask the excitement in my voice. *Yeah, I'll definitely be taking a long relaxing soak in my tub later tonight.* The thought of that makes me feel warm and relaxed already.

She nods. "Let's go find my mom and see what the plan is for the weekend. Okay?" We find Mrs. Fox in the kitchen with their personal chef, Jacque. *Really? Personal chef?* I could really hate these people if they weren't some of the nicest people I've ever met. They don't flaunt their wealth or rub your face in it either. In fact, they are incredibly generous, and I can't help but admire them.

As I look around their enormous kitchen, I wonder, since they have a personal chef, if they ever cook for themselves. Growing up, I learned everything about cooking, baking, canning, and preserving from my mother. She armed me with a wooden spoon at three years old, putting me to work stirring everything from hand-squeezed lemonade to every cookie and cake concoction you could imagine. When I was ten, I was in charge of meals on the regular. I could probably operate the instant pot or make a loaf of bread in my sleep. Living far from the local supermarket, we made most things from scratch. My favorite times of the year were all the special foods we made during the holidays. Things we only had during those times, like the pies at Thanksgiving.

Just as I'm imagining all the yummy goodness,

Jacque pulls out a mixer and what appears to be the ingredients for a pie crust.

Excitement bubbles up within me. "Are you making a pie?" I ask.

"I am," Jacque answers with a kind smile.

I lean over the counter, completely fascinated. "What kind?" I inquire, wondering what their normal Thanksgiving menu is. Will it be pumpkin, or is that not sophisticated enough, seeing that they have a personal chef making their meal?

"I'm making a few different kinds. Would you like to help?" she offers.

I smile widely at her invitation. It's been months since I've made a pie. Before I left for college, I'd been busy with my senior year of high school and working on the neighboring farm doing administrative tasks. Baking had taken a back seat to it all. Nervously, I look at Samantha and Susan for permission to help. Instead of seeing disapproval, I'm met with the kindest eyes and smiles from both. Relief washes over me. I don't want to be the odd duck that doesn't fit in all weekend, and here I am letting my farm-girl flag fly.

Susan clears her throat. "Actually, that was my plan. Jacque and I decided that we'd add a few new pies to our menu, and we thought it might be fun for you girls to help. What do you think?"

Samantha and I glance at each other and nod our heads in agreement. Jacque pulls three aprons out from their enormous walk-in pantry and hands them to us.

Three hours later, six different pies cover the island of their kitchen. We made pumpkin, pecan, apple, berry, chocolate cream, and a turtle pumpkin cheesecake. The smell of the kitchen is heavenly and I can't wait for dessert the next day.

As we're cleaning up the kitchen, Christian saunters in, looking incredibly attractive. He's just wearing a pair of faded blue jeans, an NYU sweatshirt, and Chucks, but he's as gorgeous as I've ever seen him. I've been crushing on him hard since his parents took us out for Chinese food a few weeks into the semester. He probably hadn't even noticed I was there. Seeing him again, I freeze like a deer in the headlights and hope he'll move right past me, letting me gawk in silence. I knew I'd see him this weekend, but I had hoped to look better when it happened. Knowing I'm likely covered in flour, I grow embarrassed. My cheeks flush hot, and I want to hide behind something.

"Ladies," is all he has to say to make my knees go weak. Even though he's young, his already deep voice is so sexy and commanding. I know that one day, because of that, he'll go far in business. He'll most certainly be able to silence a room with his presence and voice. Shivers break out all over my body and I try to hide my nervousness by fidgeting with my hands.

Susan breaks the silence first. "Christian, I figured you wouldn't be joining us until tomorrow. I imagined you'd be staying in the city tonight to celebrate the break from classes. To what do we owe the pleasure?" She grins at him.

He gives her his thousand-watt smile and then looks directly at me before answering her. "I didn't want to miss out on all the festivities. Samantha said you were planning some extras since we had a guest." He drags his eyes off me and focuses back on his mom. The air in the room suddenly changes and feels more electric. Has something shifted in the atmosphere? Perhaps something notable was happening in the cosmos?

Samantha snort laughs, then asks, "When have you ever wanted to take part in holiday extras with your family?"

He rolls his eyes at his sister dramatically, then pushes off the white granite counter. "Whatever, Sam! Mom, I am all in this weekend. For all the Thanksgiving fun. Let me know the plan and I'm down with it."

Before I can drool over his fine backside as he strolls out of the kitchen, Samantha pokes at him one more time. "Christian, shall we count you in for Black Friday shopping, lunch, and afternoon pedicures in the city?" Just imagining him at the spa with his jeans rolled up, feet soaking in hot water, waiting to have his soles scraped and rubbed before his toenails are trimmed and painted, makes me laugh out loud. Mortified by my reaction, I try to cover my mouth with my hand, but it's no use. Everyone already heard me.

Christian stares at me before he shoves his hands in his pockets, grumbles, and strides out of the kitchen. Shrugging, I go back to listening to Jacque, Samantha, and Susan talk more about the menu for Thanksgiving Day.

Lounging in the soaker tub after an exquisite dinner of brisket, roasted vegetables, gravy, and light-as-air rolls, I let my body unwind. Throughout my life, baths have always been a luxury. Hot water was a commodity on a farm with five other adults. Even though baths were rare, they'd always been able to completely relax me and allow me to tap into my emotions. Which could be either a good or bad thing.

During one of these rare indulgences, I weighed the pros and cons of going to college versus staying on the farm. The warm soak had ended well, with me deciding to apply to NYU. I also remember taking baths to console my aching heart when my memaw died. And when Janet, my best friend since elementary school, slept with the guy I had been crushing on since junior high. During those baths, I'd cried and cried. The hot water had felt like a hug holding me tight as I grieved my losses.

But this bath, here and now, offers me some much-needed mental clarity. This semester has already taken me on an emotional rollercoaster, and I need to make sure my mind is clear and focused. My first weeks at NYU, I'd behaved completely out of character for myself. I had freedom for the first time in my life and I embraced it fully, doing things I'd always been curious about. It had been a self-discovery of sorts, and I'd learned a lot about who and what I wanted to be. Now I was focused on achieving that.

Following the divine, vanilla-scented bath, I wander over to Samantha's room to see if she's still awake. Maybe we could watch a movie. I'd thrown on a pair of black yoga pants and a tank with a built-in bra, just in case I ran into Christian or Mr. Fox. There is no response to my knocks, so I turn back down the hall, deciding that a cup of peppermint tea will help me get to sleep.

In the kitchen, I grab a mug from the cupboard before heading into the spacious walk-in pantry. Either Jacque or Susan is type-A because everything is labeled. Tea is easy to find, and I pull a Stash Moroccan Mint satchel from the tea tin. Not looking where I'm going, I flip off the pantry light and head back into the darkened kitchen and right into a naked, muscular chest.

I squeak and drop the tea bag. *Not again.* Flashbacks of months ago flood my brain. Move-in day at the dorm. Only this time I can't get past the naked chest in front of me. *Holy hell.* Cue the drool. My embarrassment only grows when I realize one of my hands is planted on the well-defined pectoral muscles of a very unamused Christian. *He is so warm.* He grunts at me as if my touch offends him. I withdraw my hand slowly, as if he were a coiled snake ready to strike. "Sorry," I mumble as I sheepishly back away. My heart races and my eyes desperately try to focus on seeing Christian's expression. An intimidating scowl covers his gorgeous face, and I shiver. Is my touch, my presence, really that repulsive? I take another step backward, preparing to make my escape.

Chapter 3

Christian

I couldn't sleep. After everyone turned in for the night, I found myself in my room, completely bored. I did a light workout with my weight bench and free weights. After my workout and shower, I pulled on my favorite gray joggers.

Needing something to entertain me, I grab my phone and play a few levels of Candy Crush. Even that doesn't work. I still feel edgy and restless, and I don't know why. Maybe I'm hungry. Rolling out of bed, I head toward the kitchen, ready to raid the fridge for leftovers.

Walking into the kitchen, my gaze falls on the delicious pies that my mom, Samantha, Jacque, and Monica made. Memories of the afternoon invade my mind. Sounds of unrestrained laughter; tantalizing smells of cinnamon, butter, and sugar; and the sight of a beautiful, petite blonde with flour dusting her gorgeous face. It was sensation overload.

This afternoon, when I'd entered the kitchen, my breath had been sucked from my lungs. My parents told me that my sister was bringing a friend home for Thanksgiving break, but I never imagined it would be Monica.

Since meeting her months ago, Monica has stolen my focus and attention. Shortly after the school year started, my parents took my sister, Monica, and me out for dinner. That night, I'd hung back and watched her, studying her mannerisms, gestures, and expressions, desperate to know everything about her. Being that close that night, I came to realize she wasn't just beautiful. Monica was genuine, kind, and caring too. She was a dangerous combination for any guy who was trying to live his best life as a bachelor. She was too tempting to pass up, and I wanted her. But I wasn't interested in relationships, and after getting to know more about her, I know that's what she deserves.

Now Monica is in my house and sleeping only doors down from me. Maybe that's why I feel like I'm suffocating. She's a walking temptation I have to stay far away from. *How am I going to do that?* As far as I'm concerned, it's going to be nearly impossible to get a break from her invading my personal space. Squeezing my eyes shut in frustration, I ask myself, "Why didn't I stay in the city?" *Because you didn't know she'd be here.* I could have gone drinking and clubbing with my friends, driving out for Thanksgiving dinner, then returning to the city afterward. But, no, I'd told my mom I was staying the entire weekend. In fact, I'd insisted I was down for everything holiday and family related. Fucking Samantha and her incessant need to challenge me at everything. As appealing as it sounds, going back on my word isn't something I do, so I'm just going to learn to temper my response to the goddess in my house.

Looking up from the pies, I notice that the pantry door is open and the light is on. Who's down here? I know it isn't my parents; they're probably canoodling in their bedroom. Maybe it's Sam.

I step up to the door just as the light flicks off, shading the mystery of who is only feet from me. I stop when a petite something that smells like vanilla bean runs into my chest. Instantly, my mouth waters, and I lick my lips. Whatever she was holding drops from her hand as soon as she smacks into my naked chest. The sound of slapping skin echoes across the empty kitchen. I grunt because the contact catches me off guard. She removes her hand quickly and, in its wake, my skin feels as though it's been singed. Rubbing at the spot, I notice it feels tingly and hot. *That's weird.*

My eyes finally adjust to the darkness, and before me stands the most beautiful woman I've ever met, the one I forbid myself from wanting. And here she is, apologizing in a timid voice. Shaking my head, I tell her it isn't necessary. Even though her touch startled me, it had been welcome. In fact, I remember the weight of her hand on me and I realize I miss the contact. Internally, I fight the desire to pull her close, nuzzling her into my chest, where it feels like she belongs. But knowing that isn't possible, I scowl. The expression deepens when I realize her staying here all weekend is going to be harder than I thought. Monica begins stepping away from me. Her eyes watching me, assessing me. Her body is poised like she's getting ready to run away. Only, I don't want her to go.

"Monica. I'm sorry. I didn't mean to scare you," I say in a low, non-threatening tone. Reaching down, I grab what she dropped: a lone tea bag. When I stand back up, our eyes meet and we stare at each other, unsure of how to proceed.

Holding out the tea bag, I ask, "Thirsty or can't sleep?" Not even giving her time to answer, my brain offers a solution. If she couldn't sleep, I can offer something that might help. *Orgasms. They're supposed to do that, right?* Thinking about the possibility of that, my cock jumps to attention. *Yes, I could totally help with that.* No! I chastise myself firmly. Tugging my hand through my hair, I mentally force my cock to control himself. In that silence, I learn waiting for her response is an exercise in patience. Many moments tick by before she finally says anything.

"I... I couldn't sleep after my bath. I needed something to quiet my mind," she says in a quiet voice.

I nod my understanding. Trying to not think about

the fact she just told me she'd taken a bath, where she would have been naked, is impossible. My cock flinches, and I hope it isn't obvious in my gray joggers. I don't need her to see the reaction I'm having to her. I need to get that shit under control, and fast.

While talking, I turn away from her. "I couldn't sleep either. I came down here to raid the fridge and watch some TV before I head back to bed. Interested?" I pull open the fridge doors and pray the cool air escaping will calm down my overheated body.

Chapter 4

Monica

When Christian asks if I'm interested, I have to remind myself he's talking about the television and not himself. Stunned, I ask, "What do you want to watch?"

Shrugging his shoulders, he noncommittally answers, "I could pop some popcorn and we could watch reruns or something." His vague tone makes me question if he really wants me to stay or not.

Confused and unsure how to read the situation, I offer, "I can always go back up to bed. I didn't mean to interrupt your plans." I know I sound hurt, and I kind of am, which honestly doesn't make any sense. Christian doesn't owe me his time; or anything, really. He's nothing more than my crush. I could probably make the point he holds that title for at least half of the NYU female population. I'm not anyone special.

Moving to the counter, I grab my empty mug. At

least I can pacify my feelings with a warm cup of tea while I wait for my mind to quiet itself.

Christian closes the fridge and saunters up to me. With a determined look stretched across his irresistible face, he says, "I want you to stay, Monica. I just didn't have a plan." His words take me by surprise. Right now, I don't know what to think or feel.

"Oh, okay," I reply with hesitancy. Maybe he wants to spend time with me. I shake my head at my nonsense. He isn't interested in me. After all, I'm not even close to the girls I've seen him with on campus or documented all over social media.

My eyes lazily roam over his strong, defined body. Covered with muscles, he seems unembarrassed by his lack of clothing. His confidence is sexy. I dip my gaze lower, taking in his trim waist and the well-groomed treasure trail that leads into his gray sweats. When my perusal gets to a well-endowed shape below his waistline, I unconsciously lick my lips. *Why did I do that?* I've never given a blowjob, but the thought of doing that to Christian lights me up inside, making me squeeze my legs together, hoping to ease the desperate ache I'm feeling.

Realizing my eyes are still locked on his crotch, I shake my head, forcing myself to refocus. When I pull my eyes to his chest, I see him flinch before he spins away. Christian retrieves two bags of microwave popcorn from the pantry and then pulls a large bowl from the cabinet. After popping the popcorn and grabbing water, he nudges me and playfully says, "follow me," before he escorts me through the house.

My nerves flare. Where is he leading me? We pass the family room and continue on. Passing the empty room with a perfectly good television mounted on the wall, I stop, but Christian keeps moving, so I follow.

"Where are we going?" I question.

"Movie room." Until now, I hadn't known about a movie room. Nothing surprised me about this house. They probably have a pool hidden around here too.

"Yeah? Where are you hiding the pool?" I jokingly ask.

He stops and turns to me. "It's outside, but it's too cold for a swim." Smirking, he turns back toward our destination, and I trail behind like a lost puppy.

After another minute, he leads me down a set of stairs into a basement. It's eerie, quiet, dark, and kind of scary. Quickening my steps, I move closer to him so I'm within reach if something startles me.

Christian's steps are confident as he moves through the darkened hallways. Why didn't he turn on any lights? Isn't this creepy to him too? My heart pounds in my chest, making me anxious and jittery. Then he takes a hard left. He opens the door in front of him and turns on decorative sconce lighting that brings the room into view. Before me is a large room that completely blows me away. Mounted on the far wall is an enormous screen, and a projector hangs from the ceiling. An over-sized plush gray couch is situated in front of the screen for perfect viewing. It looks like the most comfortable thing I've ever seen, and I can't wait to snuggle into it.

"Well?" is all he says before he looks at me. Then he let out a deep, soul-warming laugh. I'm sure I look ridiculous. My mouth is probably hanging open and most likely my eyes bulging out. This space is incredible.

"Wow!" is all I can manage.

"What do you want to watch? We have Netflix, Vudu, HBO Max, YouTube, and more," Christian offers. *Is he really letting me pick?*

Whenever I have access to it, which is never, I always watch reruns of *Friends*, and I know they're only on HBO Max. Nervously, I ask, "Do you like the show, *Friends*? It's my favorite." I gush like a schoolgirl.

"Never seen it, but I'll give it a try." I squeal with delight. He smiles, then asks, "Should we start at the beginning?"

I nod. "That sound's perfect. I promise you'll love it." Promising him that is stupid. Christian probably won't like my favorite show.

Chapter 5

Christian

Does she feel the chemistry that surrounds us? Before now, it was completely foreign to me. No one had ever put me on edge. She overwhelms me in the best ways. When I agreed to watch her favorite show, her giddy reaction had me hard immediately. This woman is fucking adorable. She wears all her emotions on her face. She's refreshingly honest, sincere, and genuine. She's real and so unlike what I'm used to. Nothing she does is for show or to win my attention. Every time I'm near her, I fight the urge to pull her in close and kiss her senseless. She's driving me insane, and I agreed to sit next to her for an undisclosed amount of time. *How the fuck am I going to survive this? Major blue balls are going to be my punishment for being too close to this siren.*

"*Friends* is your favorite show. Who's your favorite character?"

"Joey is the best. He's a loveable idiot. He always gets into hilarious situations." Monica laughs.

I nod my head. "Pay attention to Joey. Got it. Anything else I should know before we begin?"

"Nope," she answers with a pop to her p. *Man, I want to taste her lips.*

As we settle into the over-sized couch, we have an appropriate amount of distance between us. We start with season one, episode one, and I barely make it through the theme song before this beautiful woman captures all of my attention. Monica bebops her head and hums along. Thankfully, she's so enthralled with it, she's completely unaware I'm captivated. There's no denying it—Monica is breathtaking. Swallowing hard, I realize I'm in trouble. This woman is already getting under my skin, and that's not something I'm willing to let happen. Considering I'm only twenty, I'm too young to find my forever.

Sure, my parents married young and are still madly in love after thirty years, and maybe one day, I'll have that too. But not now. Life is too short, and I'm ready to enjoy it before I really have to grow up. For now, my cock is in charge of my dating life and he has a one-and-done philosophy that I'm totally behind. This sappy love stuff isn't for me. Unfortunately, the woman next to me, who fascinates me, is the epitome of romance and happily ever after. She'd never entertain a one-night stand.

Despite my brain warning me to stand down, I

move closer to her the longer we watch the show. We share popcorn, and every time our hands brush, I feel a jolt travel up my arm, making my entire body feel alert and energized. When Monica pulls her knees up under her, she knocks my thigh, sending my body into overdrive. Heat radiates from the point of contact and down to my groin, making me hard as steel. Shifting, I try to make my attraction to her less visible. Dressing in gray joggers had been a mistake. A mistake that will become glaringly obvious if I can't get myself under control. Pulling a nearby throw pillow over my crotch, I attempt to cover my cock, which is begging for her attention. He needs to settle the fuck down. However, that isn't seeming likely because the show only appears to energize Monica instead of making her sleepy. With all her happy little noises, I'm going to come without even being touched. *Is that possible? I hope not, because that would be fucking embarrassing.*

Chapter 6

Monica

I rapidly blink my eyes, trying to clear the haze and evaluate my surroundings. *Where am I?* Panicked, I look around the room. My eyes land on the gigantic screen in front of me, still playing *Friends* reruns. Noticing that the time on the screen shows three o'clock, I wonder how long I've been sleeping. Then I recall what happened before I fell asleep.

While watching the show, Christian and I tried to keep some distance between us, but before long, we were snuggled up next to each other. Every time we touched, a delicious heat transferred between our bodies, leaving me desperate for more.

I've never responded like that to anyone. Had he felt it too? Had he touched me on purpose? Had he felt as out of control as I did?

Pushing up to sitting, I glance over to where I last saw Christian and find him fast asleep. Taking a few moments,

I gather my thoughts, but instead of being helpful, they are jumbled and chaotic. Leaving me with more questions.

Sitting there, I notice how incredibly handsome Christian is. He was still awake when I'd apparently fallen asleep. Why had he stayed? Should I wake him? If I do, will things be awkward? From my lack of experience, I'm uncertain of how to deal with this situation. I've never slept over with a guy before. Not that that's what we did, but being unsure of his reaction, I'm nervous. What if he wakes up and is annoyed or embarrassed about what happened? I know I'll be crushed if his reaction is negative. *Avoid it. Do nothing.*

I slip off the couch, careful not to wake him. I gently lay a blanket over him, grab the empty popcorn bowl we'd abandoned on the floor, and backtrack to the kitchen, where I empty the bowl into the trash before putting it into the dishwasher. Then I go up to my room. I make sure my phone is charging before I climb into an incredibly comfortable bed. Falling asleep immediately, I drift off into pleasant dreams starring the man I just abandoned in the movie room.

Samantha wakes me a few hours later when she bounds into the room. "Wake up, sleepyhead," she calls out as she crawls up onto my bed. I sit up quickly, startled awake, and push my hair out of my face.

I rub at my eyes, which feel heavy, and ask in a groggy voice, "How'd you sleep, Samantha?"

She flashes me a brilliant smile that immediately

puts me on edge. What was that for? What does she know? Does she know I spent hours with her brother in the movie room last night?

"I slept great, thank you," she sings. Why is she so cheery?

I push my blankets down my body and eye her suspiciously. "Why are you so happy?"

She lays her hand over her heart. "You think I'm happy?" I just nod. She squeals and then falls back onto the bed.

Leaning forward, I squeak, "What?"

"Last night, when you were in your bath, Mitch and I were texting. He asked me out for next weekend," she gushes and then squeals again.

I smile. Samantha met Mitch in an intro class earlier this semester and has already developed a major crush on him. According to her, he is exactly the kind of guy she'd hoped to find at college. He is one she could date seriously and marry after graduation. The perfect man. At eighteen, my best friend has a plan, and she is adamant about sticking to it. Even though she was popular in high school, she hasn't dated much. She didn't see the point. Rather, Samantha focused on her GPA and keeping herself busy with volunteering opportunities.

So far, I've only met Mitch once when he joined us for coffee after class one day. They text often and attended a study group together. Even though

Samantha seems quite taken with him, I'm still forming my opinion. Overall, I'm glad she's excited.

"That's great!" I proclaim, genuinely happy for her.

"Isn't it?" She beams.

"Where's he taking you?" I ask. Not being from the city, I probably won't recognize the location, but I want to be supportive. After all she's done for me to help me get back on track, I want to celebrate with her.

Her smile disappears, and she shakes her head. "He didn't mention details. He told me he'd call me when he got back from break."

Giving her an encouraging smile, I say, "I bet he was nervous. You are stunning. You are incredibly smart. You are the complete package! He was probably so focused on you saying yes that he hasn't figured out the specifics yet."

She reaches out her hand and wraps it around mine, squeezing it. "Yeah. You're probably right. Are you ready to get this day started?"

I cover her hand with mine and squeeze her back. "Yes, I am. Jacque told me she was getting up at five to put the turkey in. She was going to set out a light breakfast at nine so we didn't eat too much before dinner."

Looking over at my phone, I see it's eight thirty. I slept five and a half hours after I left the movie room. I wonder if Christian woke up and made it to his room. Wanting to look my best when I see him later, I decide I need to make an effort when I get ready. I'm not sure how to interpret last night. I understand things probably haven't changed between us, but I'm hopeful they have.

"I need to hop in the shower first," I inform Samantha as I run my fingers through my messy blonde hair.

Samantha nods, hops off the bed, and heads to the door. "Me too. See you downstairs soon." She finger-waves at me before closing the door behind her. I throw off the covers and walk into the bathroom. Showering and drying off quickly, I put mousse in my hair, confident that in an hour my hair will be dry and filled with luscious beach waves. Thank goodness for genetics, because I could be totally lazy with my hair and it always looks great.

I pull on a pair of worn boyfriend jeans I found at a thrift store near campus. Pairing it with a lacy black tank and a large off-the-shoulder black sweater, I feel sexy but still respectful. My makeup routine is subtle. I apply powder, light eye shadow, mascara, and ChapStick.

Checking my appearance one last time before I tuck my phone into my back pocket, I wink at myself. *Looking great, girl.* Feeling good, I walk out of my room. Just as I'm pulling the door closed, Samantha exits her room too. We laugh. After living together for such a short amount of time, we're already synced in so many ways. Arm in arm, we head toward the stairs. As we're descending, a disheveled Christian heads up, still wearing his sinful gray joggers. I blush and try to hide my reaction to him. He notices, and a sexy smile spreads across his irresistible face. But then it quickly fades, leaving me confused. *Had I done something wrong?*

"Christian," Samantha yells. "Where have you been? Late night, brother?" Her questions are loud, and he flinches in response. Apparently, he just woke up and isn't ready for her boisterousness yet.

He stops, steps away, and runs his hand through his messy hair. Christian's just woken look is incredibly sexy. His eyes flash to me and they look troubled. Desperately, I want to ask him what's wrong. Maybe I should've woken him up? Was he upset that he'd woken up and I was gone? No, that doesn't make sense. From rumors I've heard, Christian doesn't do sleep-overs. So why would he care if I wasn't there in the morning? The reason I left was I thought I was doing the right thing and saving us from an awkward exchange. Only now, I'm second guessing that decision. Now, it feels wrong. Looking at him, I plead with my eyes. I notice a stern, disapproving expression appear across his face, and I shudder. Instead of answering his sister's questions, he grunts and pushes past us. My shoulders fall, and I feel like I've been punched in the gut. Earlier, I was happy, and now I feel utterly defeated. What happened?

Chapter 7

Christian

I've been learning in the short time I've known her that Monica's beauty is unmatched, especially when she laughs at something she truly loves. Everything on her face reacts. Her cheeks turn pink, well-earned laugh lines break out, and her blue eyes sparkle. A laugh that falls from her lips is a whole other story. The sound makes my heart beat faster and my stomach tighten.

The longer we sat next to each other in the movie room, the stronger my want for her grew. Desperately, I wanted to pull her into my lap. Harnessing willpower I didn't realize I had, I'd resisted. Instead, giving myself permission to sit close enough that when either of us moved, our bodies made subtle touches. Touches that electrified my needy body, making me crazy with lust. Unfortunately, the contact we made wasn't what I wanted, but it would have to do, considering her best friend is my baby sister and she deserved more than what I could give her. More than what I knew she wanted. I suspected she had a crush on me, but I'd always been very careful to shield my intense attraction to her. Everyone thinks I'm a flirt, and I am. But with her, it isn't just casual. With her, it's real. And something I can't explain.

At some point, Monica had fallen asleep. I must have been daydreaming about wanting to touch and kiss her and not noticed. Nestled beside me, she looked so peaceful and beautiful, and I couldn't bring myself to wake her up. Watching her, her eyelids fluttered, her breathing was even, and a small smile appeared on the glossy lips I long to taste. I tucked back a few strands of her soft blonde hair behind her ear and she sighed. Just that slight contact lit my body up like a scoreboard during March Madness. Everything in me responded. My skin tingled, my heart rate spiked, my mouth watered, and my stomach knotted. Even below, my joggers saw some stiff action too.

Carefully, I moved closer to her, taking in her vanilla kissed skin that looked so soft. Laying my head on the throw pillow next to her felt amazing. Blowing out a heavy breath, I knew this was probably as close to her as I'd ever be. My exhale was full of feelings that I'm not ready to acknowledge or deal with. My brain knew she was off-limits, but my heart screamed no.

Closing my eyes, I ran through every scenario in which I might be able to have her. I hadn't meant to fall asleep. Because when I opened my eyes hours later, I was all alone. The room felt chilly, despite the blanket I had on me. Just like my heart, the space around me felt empty and lonely without her there. Reaching over to her spot, I noticed it didn't feel warm, and I wondered how long she'd been gone.

Last night I hadn't given any thought to how the night would go, but I know I'd enjoyed every moment. This morning, I'm struggling with identifying my feelings. Yes, I'm sad she left me, but I also understand that as much as that hurt, it was probably for the best. We hadn't done anything more than sit together and share popcorn, but to me, it felt life-changing. It was more meaningful than anything I'd done with any woman before. Maybe that's because deep down, that's what I want. An undeniable connection with someone. With *her*. Even if it isn't a possibility. Wrapping my head around that is excruciating. It feels like a heavyweight champ punched my chest over and over. The pain and ache wind itself into every facet of my heart, invading it like a cancer. I hate feeling like this. It's unfamiliar and uncomfortable. *This is nothing. Seriously. It will pass. Move on.* But trying to do that proves to be a challenge.

Normally when I'm around women I'm attracted to, I feel extreme pressure to perform. I'm Christian

Fox after all. It is expected that I present myself perfectly. Being off my game or awkward isn't acceptable. I learned from a young age that if you're rich, everything in your life has to appear to be flawless. But it isn't the truth. Unfortunately, because of that, the only place I've ever been free to be me is at home. My parents hadn't forced those societal expectations on me, others had. The clubs they belonged to and the snooty people they found themselves surrounded by, did. So, I'd camouflaged the real me from everyone outside of my immediate family. Until last night with Monica. Being vulnerable like that was a first for me. Then reality crashed down on me when I woke up in the movie room this morning, all by myself. Waking up from an unbelievable dream starring the particularly sexy blonde who I'd shared a bowl of popcorn with earlier left me feeling euphoric. And then I noticed she was gone, and I felt lost.

"You knew she was off-limits. What you felt wasn't real. Before long, you'll forget her smell, laugh, smile, kindness, and beauty," I mumble to myself as I try to squash the uncomfortable feeling invading my chest.

I guess it's good that I haven't tasted her yet, because that would be a definite recipe for disaster. There would be no recovering from that. I already know she's one in a million. She's worthy of so much more than I can give her. I'm not at a point in my life to make her the priority she deserves to be. Someone who will worship her and treat her like the rare gem she is.

No matter how much I want her, I know it isn't right for either of us. If I pursue her, it would only end in heartache. I need to let her go.

Eradicating her from my life is the right thing to do. Recognizing that fucks with me, though. *How has she already wormed herself so far under my skin?* Running my hands through my hair, I sit back on the couch and growl. I have to figure out how to build Monica-resistant walls that will effectively block out the temptation she is.

My phone rings loudly in my pocket, interrupting my thoughts. Retrieving it, I see its Chase, my roommate at NYU and partner in crime.

Hitting the answer button, I croon, "Chase. My man. Happy Thanksgiving."

He grunts, then replies, "Yeah, happy Thanksgiving." Something in his voice sounds strange and immediately sets off alarm bells. He doesn't sound like the typical happy-go-lucky guy he usually is. There's absolutely no humor in his voice, only undertones of anger. And that further concerns me.

"What's going on? Not having a good time at home?" I question. Chase doesn't have the best home life. He'd told me that his parents barely paid him any attention. In fact, when they were in the same room, it was always uncomfortable. His mom nagged his dad relentlessly and his dad's reply was to snap and growl horrible things back at her. Chase told me several times he'd wished they'd just divorced after he'd left for college. Instead, they stayed together because he had a younger sister. Chase worries about her a lot. Sophie is in her final year of high school and has already been accepted to several schools on the east coast for her undergrad. She's just biding her time until she can move out, and Chase is eager to help with that. Seeing that we have an apartment that isn't part of student housing, Chase could have stayed in the city over Thanksgiving break, but he'd gone home to see Sophie and make sure she was fine. Despite being roommates for years, I still haven't met his folks, but from what I heard, their house is unbearable.

"I need to get out of here!" he groans.

Knowing I can't skip out on dinner, I tell him I can head back into the city afterward. My friend needs me and it provides the perfect excuse to leave and stay away from Monica. Because avoiding her will be impossible if I stay the entire weekend.

My parents will understand why I need to get back to the city. They aren't Chase's biggest fans—they know we aren't always well-behaved together—but they understand helping a friend out. Plus, they always squeeze a multitude of activities like family game night in during the long holiday weekend. I won't be missed. I tell Chase he can bring Sophie with him if he needs to, but he declines, saying she's going to a friend's. Making sure they are safe before I end the call makes my stomach churn with unease. My family is idyllic, and I can't imagine what it feels like to be constantly worried and uncomfortable at home.

Looking down, a blanket covers me. It hadn't been on me when I'd fallen asleep because my body had felt like it was overheating with Monica so close. So, when did I get a blanket? Racking my brain, I realize Monica must have covered me up before she left. Even though it was incredibly kind, I know it changes nothing about our situation. In all honesty, I need to get her out of my head, and the more I think about her, the more difficult it is.

Move on. Folding the blanket, I place it back in the basket with the others. After one last look to make sure the room is tidy, I flick off the lights and head upstairs to my room and to find my parents and tell them of my new plan to head back into the city tonight after dinner.

As I walk up into the main house, I wonder what will be open in the city after I get back. We could hit up a bar and find some entertainment for the night. That would get Chase's mind off his troubled parents. Thoughts about an uncomplicated hookup make me smile. Who doesn't like sex, orgasms, and avoiding feelings?

Cockily, I daydream about the lucky lady. The closing of a door causes me to look up the stairs. Before my eyes is Monica, and my heart stutters. She is beyond beautiful. My mouth waters as I stare at her.

Pushing my wild hair out of my face, I lift my eyes to hers, which are wide with guilt. *Why?*

Samantha and Monica head toward me, down the stairs, arm in arm, laughing. When my sister sees me, her eyes light up and a giant smile appears on her face.

"Christian," she shouts, her voice echoing in the open staircase. She keeps talking, but all I can focus on is Monica. Just seeing her stirs up so many emotions within me. It's difficult to identify them all: anger, lust, confusion, and curiosity, just to name a few. *What is she doing to me? What happened to getting over her? Thought you were moving on.*

Instead of responding, I scowl and push past them before I continue up the stairs. A whiff of Monica's vanilla scent invades my nostrils and my stomach rolls. Hurrying to my bedroom, I feel like I'm going to be sick. Just being close to her again makes me uncomfortable, and I hate that.

After tonight, after screwing some unknown woman, I'll wipe Monica from my memory and move on with life. "Sure, buddy, whatever you have to tell yourself," I mutter to myself. I crave everything about her, her brain and her body. When I get to my room, I shut the door harder than I intended and I hear a loud gasp. My behavior startled someone and my guess is that someone is Monica. Leaning back against the door, I hear my sister say, "What crawled up his ass?"

Then Monica softly asks, "Do you think he's okay?" *Why would she care?*

A good workout, dinner where I ignore her entirely, a night out at the bar, and hooking up with someone will get me over my intense attraction to Monica. *"You don't get over a woman like that!"* my brain warns as my cock twitches. Great, now even he recognizes she is invaluable. *What the fuck is happening?*

Chapter 8

Monica

Thanksgiving dinner at the Foxes' house was fabulous, except for how Christian treated me. During the meal, he sat at the far side of the table, refusing to acknowledge me or engage in any conversation with me. Basically pretending I wasn't even there.

His attitude toward me was beyond hurtful. I'd thought we'd gotten along great last night. Sure, we'd remained mostly quiet, but things had been easy and comfortable. Just sitting next to him had my body buzzing with energy as if there were an invisible connection between us. Until then, I'd experienced nothing like that before.

However, looking back now, I wonder if I got it all wrong. Had I misread the situation completely? Is what I'm feeling only one-sided? Do I have any effect on him? It's all so confusing. And I didn't have any other chances to test my theory, as Christian headed back into the city right after dinner. Not returning for the rest of the weekend. *Had I caused that?*

From what I'd heard from Samantha, Thanksgiving has always been a big deal in their family. Their parents fill the long weekend with lots of family activities, which I understand now, having spent the entire weekend with them. Did my presence ruin the weekend for him? For their family? If so, I would feel terrible. But seeing that both George and Susan hug me and thank me for spending the holiday weekend with them, I'm sure it hadn't.

Apparently, Christian is the only one who had a problem with me. If that were true, my crush on him is definitely idiotic. Continuing to harbor feelings toward him will only end painfully for me. Knowing I need to move on, I give myself a pep talk while I unpack my bag after we return to our dorm on Sunday night. "He's just another guy, nothing special. The connection you thought you felt was misguided. Because if he liked you, he would have never treated you the way he did. Move on, there are more fish in the sea."

Seeing that I have no plans to end my friendship with Samantha, Christian will just have to learn to deal with me. He needs to grow up and stop acting like a dick. It isn't that hard to be civil to someone you don't like. I can do it. Can he? Guess we'll see.

Chapter 9

Monica

May 2016

With the end of the school year rapidly approaching, and being frazzled with so many commitments, I hadn't successfully been able to talk my way out of a party invite. The Foxes are having a large party at their house the weekend before summer break. The party is to celebrate Christian being selected for a summer internship with the sports division of MSCBC. It sounded impressive when Susan told me about it during a phone call where she'd invited me to the party. I couldn't say no, even though I need to study for finals and I also need to continue avoiding Christian. *How would I do that by attending a party thrown in his honor?*

Since that fateful Thanksgiving freshman year, I've only seen him a few times, and each time, it's been painful. He, of course, looks amazing. His smile still makes my heart flutter, my body grows hot, and my knees go weak. But that intense attraction dies a little more when he pretends I'm not there. *Is that what people call ghosting?* I don't know. All I know about it is that it's a shitty way to treat someone. I mean, who does that? No one decent, that's who.

I think after everything, I even like Mitch better than I do Christian, and that's saying something because I think Mitch is a major douche. Unfortunately, Samantha keeps telling me she loves him. Even though it kills me, I'm trying to respect her choice.

When I told her that her mom had invited me to the party, she even suggested we ride out together. Still not wanting to go to Christian's party, but feeling like I needed to at least make an appearance, I thanked Samantha for the offer and told her I had some things to take care of first. Honestly, I don't have anything, I just don't want to be stuck in a car with Mitch. And I certainly don't want to be trapped at a party for Christian without an exit plan. Arriving late and leaving early sounds like the winning recipe for success.

On the day of the actual party, I finish some studying and catch a ride with Jackson, a good-looking guy Samantha introduced to me at the beginning of the school year. He also knows Christian. They grew up together. Their families are in the same social circles.

Even though they aren't close, they expected Jackson to make an appearance. From what I understand, Christian and Jackson aren't enemies, but they aren't friends. Jackson isn't planning to stay too long and so he offered to take me to and from the party. His offer is amazing because a Lyft or train ride would be incredibly expensive.

The ride out to the Fox estate is relaxing.

"Thanks for the ride, Jackson. I appreciate it."

"It's really no problem. It's nice to have company for the ride."

Looking ahead as the landscape flies by, I ask, "Is your house close to the Foxes?"

Shaking his head, he replies, "No, our house isn't quite as big. Our parents just belong to the same country club."

"Country club. That sounds fancy. Nothing like growing up on a farm." I laugh because, honestly, it's like a whole other world.

Jackson chuckles. "I bet. Is that where you're headed this summer?"

"Yes, and I can't wait."

"I've never been to a farm. What is the best part?" he asks.

"Everything," I gush with a smile. "The cows, the quiet, my family, and my mom's cooking."

"Sounds like you really love it there."

I nod. "I do. What are you looking most forward to this summer?"

Jackson drums on the steering wheel. "If I'm being honest, it'll probably be our housekeeper's cooking. Maria is a whiz in the kitchen."

As we near the estate, conversation drops off and I feel myself grow edgy and anxious. My palms sweat, my stomach rolls, and my heart races. Panic crawls through my body. The farther we drive up the driveway, the more I try to regulate my breathing and swallow past the bile rising in my throat.

Jackson parks his Mercedes and we climb out. Grabbing the congratulations card I bought, I grip it tighter than necessary. Jackson steps next to me, matching his stride with mine. He nudges my arm, and says, "So we're only staying an hour, then escaping, right?" He winks at me.

Being this close to him, it occurs to me I've never paid much attention to how attractive he is. I've noticed he's good-looking, but now it's all I can focus on. His dirty blonde hair is curly, giving him an adorable boyish charm. He has a pleasant smile and crystal blue eyes that are deep and dreamy. *Why hadn't I ever noticed him before?* He's definitely attractive, and I've been friends with him for most of the school year. We've had multiple classes together and joined the same study groups. It was actually in one of those study groups that Christian's party came up and he offered me a ride. Jackson has been nothing but kind, caring, and respectful. Actually, kind of perfect and maybe just what I need to finally get Christian off my brain.

As we stroll up to the front door, I finally see him in a new light. I step closer to him and our hands brush. He hooks his pinkie with mine, and even though the chemistry doesn't feel as intense as it does when I'm near Christian, it feels comfortable. My eyes find his, and he offers me a shy smile. He moves to hold my hand, interlocking our fingers. My heart gallops in my chest. I've never held hands with a guy before. This is new and exciting. I'm so distracted by it all, I don't even notice when someone opens the door, welcoming us to the party.

"Ahem." An obviously loud throat clearing breaks my attention from Jackson and I switch my focus to the rude person interrupting our moment. There stands Christian, glaring daggers at Jackson. I know they aren't friends, but I imagined everyone liked Jackson. What is Christian's problem? Oh, that's right, me! What a dick. Why did I come to his stupid party, anyway? Annoyed, I watch as Christian's eyes trace up and down my body, stopping briefly on my hand that's interlocked with Jackson's. His jaw clenches tighter, highlighting his anger.

Sensing Christian's heated stare on our joined hands, Jackson drops mine and steps away from me. My heart spasms. Yet again, Christian's screwing with my happiness. *What gives him the right?* Righteously pissed off, I shove his card at him and make my way into the house. I've been here before, I can find my way around. There's no need to stick around and take Christian's abuse. Obviously, Jackson is intimidated by him and easily cast me aside, so as far as I'm concerned, he can deal with Christian on his own.

Darting into the half bath at the bottom of the stairs is my saving grace as my nose stings and my eyes fill with tears that are threatening to escape. Looking in the silver-framed mirror, my blue eyes scream heartache. Placing my hands on the pedestal sink, I suck in ragged breaths and will myself to calm down. "Just breathe. You got this. Don't let him affect you. You don't need to worry about him." Taking deep cleansing breaths and counting to ten, I'm able to regulate my thoughts again. Once I clean myself up, I plan to find Mr. and Mrs. Fox, say hello, and call a Lyft to take me back to the city. "Damn, that's going to be expensive. I'll have to pick up some side work this summer to make up for it," I mumble to myself. Feeling slightly better, I walk out of the bathroom with my head held high.

Following incredible smells, I stroll through the kitchen and spot Jacque. "Jacque," I squeal, because she is the absolute best.

The Foxes' personal chef and friend squeezes me in a tight hug. "I was hoping you'd stop in the kitchen. How are you? I haven't seen you in ages. I've had no one to make pie with." She laughs at her own joke while she studies my face. "Monica, what's wrong? Are you okay?" she asks in a strained voice.

"I'm fine. It's just been a tough year. Actually, I'm not staying long because I need to get back and study for finals."

Jacque rolls her eyes at me, laughs, then gives me another hug. "Good luck with finals, dear. And don't be a stranger, you hear."

Nodding my understanding, I whisper "bye" to her before I head to the patio where most of the guests are. I'm careful to avoid Jackson and Christian on my hunt for George and Susan. Lifting my chin higher, I don't want to see either of them. One was a coward and the other a bully. I need neither of them in my life. Spotting Mr. & Mrs. Fox over by the pool, I head their way. I notice they're holding hands, and that immediately puts a smile on my face. Just like my parents, they truly love each other, even after all these years. *That'll be me one day.*

Seeing Jackson across the pool makes my blood boil. I thought he was a good guy, but apparently, I was wrong. We hadn't been doing anything wrong, but one look from Christian toppled any chance we could've had. I don't know why Christian cares. *He's acting like a jealous asshole.* But that doesn't make sense. He isn't interested in me. Over the years, he's shown his true colors, and I'm well aware of how little he thinks of me.

Susan sees me heading toward her and she smiles brightly. She whispers something to her husband, and he turns to me, also smiling. I absolutely love them.

They both welcome me into a warm hug that melts my residual anger at their son. How they got a dick for a son, I'll never know.

"Monica, we're so glad you made it," Susan gushes.

"Thank you for the invite. I wanted to stop by and see you, but I have so many finals to study for and I really need to get back," I rush out, hoping I'm doing a decent job of camouflaging my discomfort at being here.

George frowns. "No, dear. You just got here. Have you seen Samantha yet? Christian? Are you not staying over?"

I shake my head. "No, I can't stay. I've got several finals that are going to be tough and I want to finish strong. I haven't seen Samantha yet, but we hung out this morning, and I saw Christian briefly when I first got here," I explain. Feeling a sharp pinch to the palm of my hand, I realize I'm squeezing my fists tight enough that my fingernails are cutting me. Desperately, I'm trying to save face in front of these people I adore. Forcing a smile on my face, I'm hoping they buy it.

Just then, Christian walks up and joins us. He places his hand on the small of my back and I immediately freeze and want to pull away. Knowing I can't or it will look strange, I remain still. The warmth coming off him scrambles my overwhelmed brain. Looking at him with barely concealed rage, he flashes me a panty-dropping smile. *What the actual fuck is going on? Have*

I entered an alternate universe? Why is Christian acting like this? And in front of his parents. He's messing with me, right? Annoyed and confused, I grind my back teeth together and pinch my lips closed tightly. Unsure of what is happening, I look over at his parents for clues. They smile at us, acting as if we're some sort of happy couple. *Never going to happen, folks.*

Suddenly, I feel dizzy and off-balance. Needing to leave before I do or say something embarrassing, I mumble out, "George and Susan, thanks again for inviting me. Christian, congratulations on your internship. I do really need to get back to my dorm to study." Not wanting to give them an opportunity to respond, I quickly step away, making a beeline for the closest exit.

Just when I think I'm a safe distance away, I attempt a normal breath. Relaxing my tightly clenched fists, I know I'll have crescent-shaped, self-inflicted cuts on my palms that I need to deal with. Pulling out my phone, I select the Lyft app, just as I sense someone come up behind me. Quickly turning around, it surprises me who it is, and I gasp. *Christian.* Why is he following me? Is he going to further torture me? Like a child, I stomp my foot down. He smirks at me. I'm well aware that I'm acting immature, but I don't give a fuck. His attitude toward me over the last few years has done a number on me. All this time, I've hated that I'm still so attracted to him. In fact, if I could wish anything away, it would be that.

"What do you want, Christian?" I growl angrily at him.

He slowly runs his eyes up and down my form, making my traitorous body feel hot and needy. I feel the flush on my cheeks and I see when he notices it. His sexy smile spreads wider, becoming even cockier and foolishly more attractive. *Stupid. Fucking. Libido. Go. To. Hell.* Silently, we just stare at each other, challenging the other to make the next move. My brothers would do the same thing to me while we were growing up. Guess what? It never worked. Being stubborn and holding my ground is an attribute I've fully embraced. I could stand here all day if I need to. But, in reality, I know he won't. There is no way he would miss his party. After all, a hundred people are here to shower him with praise. Instead of basking in that, he's here, off in the side yard, attempting to humiliate me. But here we are in a pointless standoff. One that I know will end once he remembers all the people here to sing his glory. Because once that happens, he'll cave and walk away, right? And then I can head back to NYU.

But that's not what happens. Christian drops his arrogant smirk and my blood runs cold. *What is happening?* He shakes his head and I notice the muscles of his jaw tense. His eyes are locked on mine as he aggressively pushes his hands through his hair.

Unable to handle the intensity any more, I say, "As fun as this is, Christian, I have places to be. If you'll excuse me," before I escape.

What I've experienced today reinforces what I always should have done: stayed away from Christian Fox. The only thing that man is capable of is breaking my heart over and over.

Ten minutes later, my Lyft shows up, and I climb in, emotionally destroyed but determined to move on. When my ride drops me off at my dorm, I walk to the Walgreens a few streets over. Purchasing the largest package of Chips Ahoy! and a quart of milk, I'm ready to study for finals, get the school year over, and nurse my broken heart over the summer.

Chapter 10

Christian

"Welcome" dies on my lips when I answer the door to my parents' house and see Monica holding hands with Jackson Reynolds. He's the youngest son of the Reynolds family, who's close to my own. I don't know him well, but from what I do know, he is a complete asshole and entirely wrong for her. Seeing them together shifts my happy-go-lucky mood to shit in seconds. Unaware of me standing there, I clear my throat, trying to break the focus they have on each other. Angry, I glare at Jackson. Feeling my heated stare, he drops Monica's hand, and I smile in victory. He isn't good enough to touch her.

"Here," Monica growls as she slaps a card against my chest. *Damn.* I've never seen her mad and I don't like it, especially because it's directed at me. *What did I do?*

After letting them in, I return to the party. Grabbing a beer from the cooler, I take a long pull from it. Ever since Monica's hand grazed my chest, I've felt hot and bothered. The beer is refreshing, but does a shit job of cooling me down. It baffles me why my body is so reactive to her. Not only do I feel unbearably hot, but I feel edgy and incredibly horny too, and all that makes me completely annoyed.

Looking around the backyard, I see so many friendly faces representing different times of my life. When my eyes fall on my parents, I can't help but smile. After thirty-plus years of marriage, they're still madly in love. They're perfect for each other. What they have together is rare and seems entirely unattainable. Focusing in, I see they're both wrapped up in a hug. My heart stalls when I see Monica step out of their embrace. She's wearing more clothing than any of the other twenty-year-olds here, but she is breathtaking. It looks like she threw on whatever was comfortable. Her long, tanned legs are clothed in cut-off jeans. She has on a black cotton tank top that accentuates what she has without flaunting it or being obvious. Her blonde hair is tied up in a red paisley handkerchief. And like always, she has on her favorite Chucks too. Once I thoroughly enjoy roaming my gaze over her trim body, I focus on her face. Her normal peach coloring is red and splotchy near her eyes. Concentrating on them, I notice she looks dejected. Her normal bubbly personality is sullen and her posture is even hunched a bit. At the door, before I'd interrupted her and Jackson's staring contest, she'd looked so happy. *What changed?*

As my parents and Monica talk, I note how comfortable and friendly they are. My parents love Monica. To them, she's another one of their children. Initially, when Samantha and Monica first became roommates, she'd come to family dinners too. But since that one Thanksgiving, she's either politely decline or gone when I wasn't able to make it. I don't want to believe I'm the reason for it, but there is no one else to blame. And that makes me a dick. Once Samantha started dating Mitch the dick seriously, I assumed she didn't want to be a third wheel to them and didn't come at all. Despite her bowing out, she's remained close to my parents, especially my mom, and because of that, I hear about her way too often. Honestly, it's difficult to get her out of my mind when it seems my family is intent on keeping her there. I head toward them, wanting to see if everything is okay.

Shortly after I arrive, Monica politely excuses herself after thanking them for inviting her. *She's leaving already. No, she just got here.*

"That was odd," my mom says to my dad, seeming genuinely confused.

"I'm going to go check on her," I tell them before chasing after her through the side yard.

After I catch up with her, we share an intense stare-down, where Monica is defensive, angry, and pained. Then she walks away. Instead of seeing Monica's blue eyes staring daggers at me, I see her storming away. This isn't how I wanted things to go. I hang my head in defeat. I'd chased after her because I wanted to know what was wrong so I could make it better. *Fuck.* My stomach churns. Sad and angry, I walk back toward the party and into the house, leaving my guests to fend for themselves. Between the food, pool, and lawn games my parents set up, they'll be entertained for a while. Right now, I need to get my head on straight before I can deal with any more bullshit.

Chapter 11

Monica

College Graduation Weekend

Finals are done. Student teaching hours are logged and the final interviews are complete. Our apartment is packed. Yesterday was a big day. Samantha and I graduated from NYU. She received her bachelor's in Business while I earned mine in Elementary Education. Tonight, she and I are heading to a club for our last hurrah before I move to Chicago.

Over the last few months, I'd been interviewing for kindergarten teaching positions in the city. My plan is to spend the summer at home on the farm with my family before moving into the city to start my first teaching position. My brothers and sisters-in-law are especially looking forward to me being back because it means free babysitting. I love my family and I've missed them these last four years. New York has definitely changed me, but occasionally it felt good to go home.

Samantha and I are planning to have a late dinner at The Boardroom before we go to Rhythm, a newer dance club. Mitch left for Europe on a graduation trip this morning with some of his buddies. So, tonight is all about us. Two ladies on the town. We're going to live it up. And tomorrow we can sleep off hangovers if necessary because neither of us has class or work.

Over the last four years, we'd only gone out a handful of times without Mitch. Usually, he tagged along and was an absolute drag, ruining the night entirely. Even a slight buzz didn't gloss over the negative vibe he projected on everything. After a few wrecked evenings, I learned not to ask her out if he was going to be joining us.

Instead, I busied myself working a job at a yoga studio near our apartment. There were several benefits to my job. One was my paycheck, another was an unlimited punch card to classes. Taking full advantage of that, I worked out the aggression I had from classes, student teaching, and various people. The biggest benefit is that all the time doing yoga has done wonderful things for my body, and I intend to totally accentuate it in a tight, sparkly little black dress I purchased just for tonight's festivities. Besides my dress, I painted my nails to match, and I plan to wear my eyes smoky and my long blonde hair in a high ponytail. Tonight is all about freedom for me. *I am a single woman, hear me roar!*

"Ready to go, Monica?" Sam calls from her bedroom into our living room.

"I am. It's a good thing Mitch is all the way in Europe. He'd have a heart attack seeing you in that dress," I tell her with a laugh. I'm so glad we are Mitch-free tonight. "Better yet, let's send him a picture." Maybe he'll drop dead oceans away. Okay, I really don't wish death on him, but I wish Sam would see what an awful guy he is and realize she deserves better.

"Monica, put down your phone. We are not sending Mitch a picture. I don't need phone calls from him dictating what I wear. All my major parts are well covered. This dress is way less risqué than what you've got on."

Looking at my phone, I see our Lyft has arrived. "Let's go. Our ride is here. First stop is dinner and the last stop is dancing."

After arriving at The Boardroom, an older restaurant that's famous for its steaks, I order a petite filet, mashed potatoes, and grilled vegetables. Everything is perfect. The steak practically melts in my mouth while the mashed potatoes are fluffy and rich. We're careful to order mocktails so we don't get tipsy before we arrive at the club. Avoiding the dreaded hangover is our plan and we know we will have a drink or three later.

Samantha and I walk into Rhythm a little after eleven, ready to dance. We waste no time as the DJ starts spinning one of our favorite songs, "Party Rock Anthem," by LMFAO. As the song pumps and beats around us, I let myself go. My hips shake and shimmy, and I raise my hands high in the air. It feels so liberating.

"This DJ is amazing," I tell Samantha as we remain close. The beat is everywhere around us, vibrating us to our cores. Closing my eyes, the stress I've be carrying around for the last few months melts away. There is nothing weighing me down anymore. With each new song, I feel even more incredible. Nothing can touch me. This journey I'm embarking on is new. It's both exciting and scary, but it's all mine. No expectations or rules are being forced upon me. Being the boss of my life is thrilling. Unlimited opportunity sits at my feet, waiting to be discovered.

"Drink," Samantha demands of me as she grabs my wrist. Following her, I take in all the people in the club. They are fascinating to watch. Bodies move, contort, gyrate, and grind against each other. It doesn't matter if they're friends, lovers, or strangers, because they are all chasing the same release we are: freedom and fun.

"This is the best night ever!" Samantha scream-shouts at me as we make our way to the lower bar. We fight our way up to order a drink, and I notice the extremely handsome bartender. As he approaches, he moves slowly, allowing me to scrutinize every part of him. I savor his focused attention on me. The man is tall, tan-skinned, and sinfully sexy. He wears a crisp black button-up with the sleeves folded tightly at his elbows, revealing corded muscles and a scattering of colorful tattoos. *Bad boy.* His dark brown hair is expertly styled in a pompadour, and his beard is trimmed short. Everything about him screams sex, and I have to school my features and play it cool. He makes head-spinning, intense eye contact with me and winks. *Holy shit!* That has never happened before. Usually, I'm the last one to be noticed. In the game of attraction, it was like elementary school all over again, and I'm always the last to be picked. But tonight... tonight is different. I watch the sinful stranger's eyes to see if they drift toward Samantha or any other woman nearby waiting for a moment with him, but his eyes remain locked on me. Granted, he's the bartender and serving people is his job, but at this moment, I would give anything for him to service me.

"Hey, beautiful, what can I get you?" he asks in a commanding tone that sends shivers racing down my back.

I lick my lips, lean in, and, in a sultry tone, I ask, "What do you recommend?" Then I bite my lip, waiting for his response.

"That depends," he replies, tempting me to ask for more.

"Depends... on what?" I drag out my question teasingly.

"Well, if you're in the mood for something blended, I'd order a Kiss on the Lips. If you want a mixed drink, I'd choose between three: Liquid Panty Dropper, Leg Spreader, or Sex with a Bartender. Perhaps, beautiful lady, you crave a shot? Then I'd recommend a Quick Fuck or Deep Throat. Do any of those sound appealing?" He licks his lips and quirks his head seductively after rattling off the suggestions.

Swallowing hard, I look around, wondering if I imagined what had just happened. Replaying what drinks he mentioned, I blush. Is he offering the drink or the actions? Right now, I'd fully sign on for any of it. A sexy smile crosses his lips and then I notice his name tag. It reads Cristian. Instantly, I feel like my legs are pulled out from under me or someone punched me in the gut. Sucking air into my lungs is tight and painful. My body goes weak, and I get lightheaded. I try to force a smile onto my expertly decorated lips, but smiling is the last thing I want to do. The flirtatious bartender places a hand on my wrist, trying to center me.

"Are you okay?" he asks, concerned.

I nod. "Have you ever made a Lick and a Promise?" A wide grin covers his handsome face as he grabs a shot glass. He pulls a bottle of Jack out and fills the glass before me. My eyes flick to it. The reason I ordered it is that I want to forget and just have fun. Tonight, I don't want to think of Christian Fox. I'd seen him at graduation yesterday, but we'd stayed on opposite sides of the venue, never coming in direct contact. His parents had taken Samantha and me out for a celebratory graduation lunch and hadn't invited him. *Thank goodness.* Every time I think about him, my heart still aches. Even after all this time. Reaching down, I grab the shot and throw it back. And it burns. Despite being twenty-three, it's my first shot.

Setting the glass back on the bar top, I watch as Cristian mixes my drink. He expertly adds all the ingredients to his shaker and places the lid on top, then he lifts it and shakes it to the rhythm surrounding us. His arms flex, and I watch his tattoos dance across his forearms. *Why is that so sexy?* It's like a perfectly timed dance that has my entire body on fire. Transfixed by him, I observe as he pours the drink into a glass. *It's stifling in here.* The drink looks refreshing and the thought of it excites me. Months ago, I had seen it mentioned in one of Samantha's magazines and the name stuck with me. When my drink is placed in front of me, the beautiful coral color of it reminds me of a sunrise.

"It's beautiful," I mumble, and Cristian laughs. The sound echoes, coming at me from the front and the side. Do shots work that fast? Has it already affected me? Why does it seem like his laugh is traveling? Confused, I look at Cristian as if he could answer the question stuck in my head. But his uncertainty tells me otherwise.

He pushes the drink closer, licks his lips, and asks, "Are you going to try it?"

I raise the cool glass to my lips and take a long sip.

It's refreshing, just like I thought it would be. Hints of cranberry, citrus, and melon dance on my tongue. "That's amazing," I praise.

He nods and says, "It is. Plus, it has a fantastic name too." He follows his suggestive comment with a wink before he steps away to help another patron. *Holy hell. I think my panties just incinerated.*

Feeling the slight buzz of the alcohol, I turn to Samantha to see if she got a drink too. And then my world shatters. My best friend is deep in conversation with the last person I ever wanted to see. Her brother. Realizing I'm staring at them, they stop their conversation and turn their attention to me. Instead of saying anything, I just take another large sip of my delicious drink.

"Good drink?" Christian asks in a cocky tone. And I glare at him.

"Yes, it is," is all I say.

He moves closer into my personal space, making sure our arms brush. A burst of electricity sends tingles across my body. *Why does he still affect me?* My breath quickens, but I'm not sure if it's from arousal or panic. Probably both.

Lowering his voice, he asks, "What's it called?"

Not wanting to give him the satisfaction of knowing he has any effect on me, I straighten my spine and answer as clear as I can, "Lick and a Promise." Then I smugly wait for his reaction. It's slight, but I catch it. His eyes widen, he swallows hard, and he shifts his stance, adjusting himself. Nothing glaringly obvious in his movements, but I saw it. He was surprised and turned on. I'd taken plenty of psychology classes over the years, and everything he just did tells me he is as affected by me as I am by him. But before I can give that any thought, Cristian, the sexy as hell bartender, is back and his attention is again laser focused on me. His perusal of my body is obvious and unashamed. I wrap my lips around the straw in my drink and suck in another gulp of the heavenly nectar. Probably looking scandalous and not caring one bit. I'm testing a theory. Watching for Cristian's reaction to it makes my entire body feel desperate. His response is eerily similar to Christian's when I told him the drink's name. *Interesting.*

Cristian flashes me a giant smile, leans into me over the bar, and whispers, "I don't ever do this, but can I have your number? I'd like to take you out." He pulls back and looks deeply into my eyes. Right then, I wish I were staying in the city. I wish I hadn't just graduated but had months before I was moving home. I wish for more time. But no matter what, I can't change my situation. Even the pleading in his eyes won't change anything. My heart desperately wants to say yes, but it wouldn't be fair to either of us. The really shitty thing is this is the first time I've been ready to try moving on from the hold Christian Fox has on me.

I touch Cristian's wrist and answer him, my tone sad. "Cristian, I wish I could go out with you. But I just graduated from NYU yesterday and I'm moving home to Chicago in a few days." My heart sags with the heavy weight of my emotions.

He nods, forces a smile that doesn't reach his eyes, and says, "I understand. Poor timing, I guess? Can I at least know your name, or should I just call you beauty?" My heart flutters, and I giggle. His laugh is deep and smooth, making me want more. Nearby, Samantha sighs and Christian scoffs loudly, reminding me of his presence.

"My name is Monica. And for the record, I really am so sorry. I want to go out with you." I don't care how I sound, it's the truth. Cristian seems great.

Cristian wipes down the bar, wasting time, spending it with me. Other patrons try to get his attention, but it stays fixed on me as if he were trying to figure out how to make it work. His sexy mouth parts, and I suck in a breath as he says, "You're moving to Chicago? My older brother lives there and I visit him often. Maybe we could exchange numbers and get together next time I'm in town?" Excited, I sit up taller, nodding my head in agreement. Lighting fast, I whip my phone from my black clutch and open up the contacts before handing it to him.

"Yes, let's do that," I confirm with an enormous smile on my face. Still listening in, Samantha giggles while Christian growls, then stomps away.

"He's not your boyfriend, right?" Cristian asks pointing to where Christian stood.

Shaking my head, I reply, "Nope. He doesn't even like me." That earns me a quizzical look from him and a snort from Samantha.

After Cristian plugs his number into my phone and sends himself a text, we make plans to grab brunch a few hours after his shift is over. I finish my drink and head back to the dance floor with Samantha, enthusiastic about my morning date.

Hours later, I find myself in a café dining on Belgian waffles covered in strawberries and whipped cream.

"So, Cristian, how did you become a bartender?"

He takes another bite of his Denver scramble, and after he washes it down with coffee, he answers, "I'm bartending at night to pay for the college courses I'm taking online."

"I've got so many questions. What degree are you getting? Do you like doing online school? Will you keep bartending until you graduate?"

Scratching his head, he says, "Wow. I'm about halfway to earning a finance degree. Yes, I like online school because I can do my classes any time of the day. In fact, I'm most productive at six a.m. after a shift at the club. And your last question. Yes, I will keep bartending until I graduate because I make crazy amounts of money."

I nod as I spear in another bite of deliciousness. "What job are you gearing up for with a finance degree?"

"I want to work in trading, and New York City is the Mecca of traders."

Hearing that, I realize he'll never leave New York. Over the remainder of breakfast, we find that we have a lot in common, and it's sad we won't be in the same city.

After talking and laughing for hours, we promise to keep in touch. Cristian is traveling to Chicago in a few months and we make unofficial plans to get together when he's there. With a big hug, we part ways. I'm heading back to the home I've shared with Samantha for the past three years, and he's going home to sleep before his next shift. Meeting Cristian is just what I needed. He's given me confidence in myself and shown me I don't need to keep harboring feelings for someone who doesn't hold anything but contempt for me.

Chapter 12

Christian

My baby sister graduated from NYU yesterday. I'm so proud of her. She's coming to work at Fox Sporting with me and our dad. Unfortunately, her boyfriend, Mitch the dick, is coming too. The longer they're together, the more I want to pummel him. Since the beginning, I haven't disguised my dislike for him. He seems sneaky, opportunistic, and shady, but I've never seen concrete evidence to support my claims. Making matters worse is that he's won over my parents. They believe he shits rainbows, and I often have to temper my response to him, especially around them. Sam's used to it. I think she just ignores my comments. Hopefully, she'll figure it out before they get engaged. I'm sure that bullshit is just around the corner.

Sitting and waiting through the long and boring

graduation ceremony afforded me ample time to think, and I concluded that after months of logging too many hours at the office, I need a night out. Earlier in the week, Samantha asked about a new club that I haven't been to. I asked a few buddies, and they said it's amazing. So I'm heading there tonight with a longtime client whom I've been managing since I officially started at Fox Sporting. My client, Alex, just signed a huge new contract, and it was time we celebrated. *Is that the only reason you want to go to the club tonight? Yes.* It has absolutely nothing to do with the fact my sister and Monica might be there. *Nope, nothing at all.*

Seeing Monica at graduation, across the venue, was the first time I've seen her in over a year. We had a small run-in shortly after my senior year, right as her junior year started. Although it was brief, it was incredibly uncomfortable and tense. Thinking back, I'm not sure we even exchanged words.

My parents had taken Samantha and me out to dinner, and during our conversation, Sam mentioned wanting to show me something at her apartment. I didn't miss that she mentioned we wouldn't see Monica because she was working. That was the only reason I agreed to accompany her back to her place. But she'd been wrong. So very wrong.

Sam led me into the apartment, and standing in their tiny kitchen making cookies was Monica. Like always, she took my breath away. She had a dusting of flour across her cheek and her hair was in a messy braid. Monica, who had music blasting through her earphones, was completely unaware of our presence. As she read the recipe, she bebopped, singing into a wooden spoon. She was fucking adorable. I couldn't hide the smile on my face. I had never seen her look so relaxed and carefree. Then my sister ruined the moment by loudly smacking her hand on the kitchen countertop. Monica startled and jumped up, causing her earphones to fall from her ears. Her hands flew out, and she squealed. I laughed, earning me a glare from both Monica and Sam. Feeling attacked, I threw up my hands in defense.

"What?" I questioned. Sam shook her head and rolled her eyes.

Monica said nothing, but her silence spoke volumes. She turned the oven off, put the cookie batter in the fridge, then walked to her room and closed the door. It was an obvious message to me. Fuck off, Christian. Since I was already there and Monica had retreated to her room, I asked Sam to show me what she'd been talking about. Shortly after, I left, annoyed by the interaction.

Tonight, though? Tonight, I'm ready to party. After too long, I need a night out to burn off some steam. I plan to drink more than usual and find some hottie to land in bed with for the night, but my plans come crashing down shortly after I arrive at Rhythm.

Sure, my sister asked about it a few days before and I suspected I might run into her and Monica, but I didn't plan on that run-in ruining my night. But it does just that. *And why is that?*

Alex and I are headed to the bar for a drink when he's distracted by some fans. While he talks to the groupies, I continue over to the bar. When I'm about two feet from it, I spot my sister. If Sam is here, I know Monica will be too. The douche, aka Mitch, is on his way to Europe and my sister wouldn't come to a club by herself. Looking to her right, I see the back of a woman with a luscious ass tightly wrapped in a short black dress. Instinctually, I lick my lips, wanting to grab hold of her and taste what she has to offer. *Maybe I could take her home tonight?* My eyes trace up her body, hitting the curve of her waist and up to her hair, and then I freeze. The mystery goddess has her blonde hair with violet highlights in a high ponytail. There is no denying it. I know exactly who is in front of me. The woman I'm lusting after is Monica. My heart stalls. Every time I've seen her, I couldn't deny how fucking attracted I am to her. Even worse is that her personality is as irresistible as her appearance. She isn't vapid, shallow, or dumb like the women I normally spend my time with. Instead, she is caring, smart, giving, funny, and kind. She is the entire package, and she is my kryptonite.

With a pounding heart, weak knees, and feeling dizzy and off balance, I know I need to approach them. If Samantha knew I was there and hadn't said hi, she'd be mad at me. *I can totally do this. Prove to myself that she has no effect on me. No effect at all.* Ignoring what my body is feeling, I force myself forward. My feet are moving, but I still feel stuck in place. The feeling is surreal. In that short distance to the bar, I look down at my feet several times to confirm I'm actually moving.

When I get closer, I see Monica talking to someone. She's flirting with the motherfucking bartender. Am I jealous? *Fuck yes, I am.*

Standing back and watching them makes me sick. My stomach drops and dread saturates every pore of my body. It's like coming up on an accident. I don't want to see it, but I can't look away. Even though I don't know him, it's obvious he's not good enough for her. Looking closer, I spy his name tag. It's like a punch to the gut. Cristian. Sucking in a breath, I mumble, "What the fuck?" Have I been replaced? The thought of that is like a direct slice to my heart. It's unbearable. It's not like she's mine, but no man with the wrong spelling of our name should even be close enough to flirt with her. Seeing the conversation they're having stirs up so many unnatural feelings, making me edgy. Usually, when I see a man flirting with a woman I'm interested in, I just move on, unaffected. But with Monica, that's not even a consideration. I'm not going anywhere. No fucking way. I'd rather stand on the bar and beat my chest, screaming, "I saw her first! She's mine!"

Chapter 13

Monica

After returning home to the farm, I complete my final interviews and contract for a kindergarten teaching position in the heart of Chicago. My summer job is again working in the neighboring town with the kids' program. Before school begins, I move into an apartment that is not only close to my school but the iconic Wrigley Field. Go Cubs! Honestly, I'm not really into baseball, but my brother Josiah is. Since moving into my apartment, he's visited often and we've caught a few games together. I have to admit it isn't horrible. Actually, it's pretty nice spending time with my closest brother. Because Josiah's job on the farm can be completed remotely, he sets up shop in my spare room and works around the games he attends.

The last few years have been tough on him. He was diagnosed, treated, and survived testicular cancer.

Because of what he's been through, our mom tends to smother him occasionally, and that can be overwhelming. Needing an escape, he comes to stay with me. It's nice to have a little piece of home visit every so often.

Not long after I settle into my school, I get the best news: my bestie is moving to town. Fox Sporting is sending Samantha—and Christian *Ugh!*—to set up a remote office in Chicago. Apparently, their board has wanted to expand for several years, but they had to wait until both Christian and Samantha were ready for the challenge.

* * *

I can hardly believe my first year of teaching is almost done. It's been a great, but busy, school year. Mondays are the absolute worst. Earlier today, our principal called a mandatory staff meeting for after school. He wants to discuss the staff's plan for the activities we host for the students at the end of the school year. And I've been summoned to the library. I sit with a couple of teacher friends. Thirty minutes later, I feel my phone vibrate in my pocket. Trying to ignore it proves difficult when it continues on repeat. Wondering who's desperately trying to reach me, I pull the phone from my pants. When I see it's Christian, I freeze. Why is he calling me? And so urgently? What is going on? Samantha mentioned to me months ago when they moved to town that she was going to put my number in his phone and his number in my phone. Until now, I wasn't even sure she had. Guess that answers that.

Looking up, I see that the principal has finally finished his presentation and is directing staff to sign-up sheets. I rush to the front of the library and sign up for a few of the field day activities. I notice everyone else has disbanded, so I slip out of the library and into the quiet hallway. When I reach my classroom, I check to see if Christian's left any texts or voicemails. There's nothing. "Super helpful!" I groan as I shut my door behind me.

Returning his call, I busy myself around my classroom, tidying up. When he finally answers, he is both out of breath and whispering. I'm now even more confused than before. As far as I know, he'd only call me if it concerned Samantha. *Wasn't the entire Fox family in New York together?* When I spoke to Samantha a couple of weeks ago, she mentioned she was heading to New York for a long weekend. Fear creeps in and dread slaps me across the face. Is she okay?

I hadn't been listening to anything he's been saying, but when my mind presented the idea of Samantha being injured, my ears tuned in. Feeling like we're wasting time, I shout, "Christian, what's going on? Is Samantha okay? Tell me!"

"Hold on. What do you know about her trip to the city? I assumed she was here for business, but when she didn't show up for our return flight this morning, I grew worried. I knew where she was staying, and a few hours ago I forced the manager to perform a safety check."

"Safety check?" I question. My knees grow weak and my stomach rolls. *I need to sit down.* Being a kindergarten teacher, miniature chairs are everywhere, offering me respite. Overcome with worry and not wanting to cross the room, I lower myself into one of my student's chairs. I have to remind myself to breathe. My hands shake as I push the abandoned math cubes to the center of the table. *What happened to Samantha?*

"Christian. Tell me." I whisper.

"When I got there and found the manager, he let me in Sam's hotel room and... Twice in the past month, I found her curled in a ball after she'd cried for hours."

Surprised, I let out a gasp at his confession.

"Monica, she looks broken, and it doesn't make sense. I don't know what happened, but I suspect it's about a guy. What do you know?" he growls at me.

His tone immediately puts me on the defensive. "What do I know?" I angrily respond.

"You're her best friend, right? Aren't you supposed to confide in each other?" His rhetorical questions are filled with judgment and sarcasm.

Flabbergasted by his haughty demeanor, I spit back, "Yes, she is my best friend. But I haven't talked to her in two weeks. We've both been busy."

He scoffs. "Busy doing what?"

A humorless laugh falls from my lips and then I

calmly reply, "Someone brilliant said it best when they described teaching as shaping little minds. So, I've been doing my job. Ensuring future generations don't turn out to be assholes—like you."

Forcing myself to take a breath, I continue, "Instead of implying I couldn't possibly be busy, you instead meant to say *thank you*, right?" My words are daggers aimed at his stupid self. Why did I call him back? Oh, that's right, he called about Samantha.

The other end of the line is silent. I'd assume he hung up, but the incessant beeping isn't present. *Did I stun him into silence? That'd be a first. Victory!* An enormous smile covers my face. For once, I've gained the upper hand. I showed him he couldn't act like I'm less than him.

"Christian, are you still there? Why are you calling me? What can I possibly do to help from here?" I ask in a muffled tone, trying my best to disguise my annoyance while reminding myself this is for Samantha.

He mumbles something I can't hear and then clears his throat. "I'm still here. Sorry about what I said. I'm just worried about Sam. Honestly, seeing her like this is scary, and finding her this way, twice, is... unnerving. I don't know what to do to help her."

Christian lets out a ragged breath. "Thankfully, my mom was nearby, so she could help. But Samantha can't stay here forever. I don't know how I'll get her back to Chicago like this." He sighs heavily, and I feel bad for him.

"I'm sorry, too, Christian. What do you need from me?" I offer.

Another enormous sigh comes across the line. He sounds overwhelmed, which is strange because Christian is always calm and in control.

Feeling helpless, I say again, "Really, Christian, what can I do?"

I listen for clues in the background and hear Mrs. Fox talking. I'm relieved she's there to help Samantha with whatever is going on. I don't have a clue what's happening, but what Christian said about a guy makes my gut sink. Last time she was this upset, it was about a guy. Lucas. As far as I know, they haven't had any contact since the car incident months ago. But now I wonder. She was in New York and so was he. Is that a coincidence? Did they meet up? Right now, I'm just speculating. I don't know. I wish I could talk to Samantha, but it doesn't sound like she's up for it. For now, I'll take what Christian said and offer what I can.

"Monica, it's really bad," he finally confesses in a whisper.

My heart hurts for my best friend. I would do anything to take away her pain. I'll do my best when she's back in Chicago. Every turn, I'll be there, helping her through whatever she's dealing with. "When do you think she'll be ready to come back to Chicago?" I ask him.

Suddenly, the background noise disappears

completely, and I wonder if he's stepped out in to the hallway.

"That's the thing. I can cover for her at work this week, but I'd need her back in the office next Monday. Until then, she can stay at my parents' house. I plan to fly back to Chicago this afternoon so I don't miss too much. Then I plan to fly back Friday night," he informs me.

His plan sounds solid. "Okay, do you need me to go to her penthouse and get it ready for her or take care of anything while she's in New York?"

"Maybe just grab her mail, if it's not too much trouble."

Christian breathes out again before he makes his next request. "One last thing. I was wondering... if on Friday you would come with me? You know, in case I need help getting her back home," he hesitantly asks.

Surprised at his request, I shoot forward and almost throw myself out of the tiny chair. Once I'm settled again, I nervously clear my throat and squeak, "Fly on the Fox jet back to New York?"

In all the years I've been friends with Samantha, I've never been on the Fox Sporting jet.

His smooth-as-caramel laugh comes across the line, making my stomach flutter. "Yes. We'll take the Fox jet. Would that be a problem?"

"No! I've just n-n-never been on a private jet before," I admit with a slight stutter.

"It's no big deal, Monica. We'll just fly to New

York Friday night, stay the weekend at my parents' house, and fly back Sunday. Do you think you'd be available and willing to come with me?" His voice lowers, the deep, decadent timbre feeling intimate as it hits my ear. Layered with a slight inflection at the end, his tone sounds almost... hopeful?

I force myself to sit up straighter. Nodding my head, I remind myself I can do this. My best friend needs me. *But what about Christian?* Unable to deal with those feelings, I push them aside. Right now, we're working together. We can handle this, right? "Yes, I can go, but I can't leave until five o'clock because of work. That won't be a problem, will it?"

"No. That's perfect. I'll work most of the day and then come get you," Christian confirms.

Mentally, I tally everything I need to do before Friday. "Sounds great. Need anything else from me until then?"

Christian clears his throat. "I hate to ask this, but can you reach out to Sam? Find out what's going on? She won't tell me, but I think it's about a guy."

Knowing our conversation is almost over, I stand from the tiny chair and answer him. "I'll try. Hopefully she'll answer."

"Great! Thanks, Monica. I'll call you later this week." Then he's gone and I feel disoriented. Cleaning up the rest of my classroom, something occurs to me. The conversation I just had with Christian was civil and, dare I say, friendly. Maybe enough time has passed that we can now interact without hostility. Guess I'll find out this weekend.

After arriving home, I try to call my best friend to see if she's okay, but my call goes straight to voicemail. The next day I do the same, but she still doesn't answer. On Wednesday, I try again, and to my surprise, she answers, sniffling.

"Sam, I have been calling you for days. Why haven't you answered? Christian called me in a panic on Monday morning. He grilled me to see if I knew why you were curled in the fetal position for the second time in less than two months. And even if I wanted to tell him, I couldn't. Why? Because my best friend didn't tell me," I scold her.

"I know, and I'm sorry. Everything happened so quickly. Honestly, I'm still trying to wrap my head around it all. I wanted more clarity before I tried to explain it to you. Can you forgive me? I need my best friend right now more than I can say," Samantha tells me.

"Start from the beginning. I feel like I've missed so much. I'm guessing this has to do with Lucas. Last time we talked, the car fiasco just occurred, so what's happened since then?" I ask nicely.

She laughs sarcastically and answers, "How much time do you have?"

"I have all the time in the world for you, Sam. In fact, Christian and I are flying to New York after work on Friday so I can see you and get you back to

Chicago this weekend. That's if you're ready to come home."

"Oh! You and Christian? Interesting," she teases, and it grates on my nerves.

Nope! We are not talking about me and Christian. I am determined to understand what's happened with Samantha, even if it's the last thing I do. "Oh no you don't. We aren't talking about me and Christian, we are talking about you and Lucas. Now, spill," I warn her in a growl that makes most people unnerved. I may look nice, but I have bite.

My heart breaks for her. After all the shit she went through with Mitch, she didn't deserve this. She deserves to be loved and cherished, not treated like a plaything whenever it's convenient for him. Stupid playboys. Always thinking and assuming they can behave any way they want without facing consequences.

Thoughts of Christian surface, and I'm relieved to say nothing ever happened with him. After all, dealing with my feelings for him over the years has been painful enough. I can't even imagine if we added intimacy and sex to it. I'd be broken too.

"Oh, sweetie, what are you going to do now?" I ask.

Hearing her cry over the phone was torture. It didn't feel like Friday could come soon enough. Right now, I just need to be patient. Reminding both of us, I say, "I'll be there Friday night and we'll head back to Chicago on Sunday, okay?"

Sam sniffles again and then says, "Okay. Thanks, Monica, I'm feeling pretty tired and I'd like to go to bed. Can we talk tomorrow, maybe?"

"Yeah. Totally. Call me when you're free. I love you, Sam."

"Love you too," she tells me before hanging up.

Saying goodbye to my best friend, who has a broken heart, is torturous. Every time I've been heartbroken, all I wanted to do is hide and sleep too. *Wonder if I've learned my lesson yet.* In all my years, only one man, Christian Fox, has ever been responsible for my heartbreak. He is my drug, and no matter what he does, I still crave him. Because of being best friends with Samantha, he remains a constant in my life, no matter what I do or the places I avoid.

With what's going on with Sam, I've heard from Christian every day this week. He's always looking for insider information on whether she has confided in me about what happened. Until now, I haven't had much to say. Thankfully, I'm of sound mind, so if he calls tonight, I can say yes, she told me, but she wants it kept between us. As far as I know, her brother doesn't know about Lucas, and I don't intend to share that information with anyone, least of all Christian. We don't need to head to New York on Friday with guns blazing.

Laying out my yoga mat and blocks, I'm just about to do my daily exercise when my phone rings. It's Christian, and I laugh to myself. *Did he know I was just thinking of him?*

"Hello," I answer, slightly winded from bending over and raising back up quickly.

"Hey, Monica. Am I interrupting anything?" he says in a questioning tone.

Knowing this might take a while, I sit back on my couch and answer, "No, I'm good. I was just doing some yoga. My students were a little unhinged today and I'm trying to get some stress out before I take it out on a sleeve of cookies." I laugh, thinking of today and my crazy students.

He takes forever to say anything, so I clear my throat, wondering why he called. Finally, he speaks. "Sorry to hear you had a tough day. Anything I can do to make it better?"

His offer is nice and sincere sounding, totally catching me off guard. Ever since he called on Monday, he's been really nice to me. It's disconcerting and slightly alarming. After everything that's happened between us, I'm hesitant to trust him. Perhaps this is our chance to start over? Maybe be friends? Is that possible?

If we're going to be friends, maybe he can help me. I snicker at the thought of Christian with my students during arts and crafts. It's an actual war zone, but maybe he has suggestions to handle their crazy antics. "Okay, do you have any tips to encourage my kinder-garteners to use the paste appropriately? I've tried everything I can think of."

He laughs loudly. "Please tell me more about these

hooligans and the various ways they've used paste inappropriately. I haven't been in elementary school for eons. Paste is glue, right?"

I giggle. "Yes, the paste is glue, and in kindergarten we use it daily on almost everything. Seeing that the school year is almost done, I expect they will use it correctly. But today must be a full moon, because that's not exactly what happened."

"What happened?" he asks.

Where do I start? He probably needs context since he's not a teacher and I can't imagine he's ever worked with kids. "It all started when Principal Smith came to pull me out for a quick minute. Usually, he doesn't do this, but he needed to tell me something important about a kid I tutor a few days a week. It was time sensitive. So, with my mind preoccupied with that, my students took full advantage. Billy tried gluing Sally's hands to the table while Heath poured paste on the floor to see if he could get his shoes stuck. The twins in my class, Jenny and Jill, glued together all the pages of the book we use for read-aloud time. And it all happened in less than five minutes. Honestly, I'm not sure how, but it was like a well-orchestrated mini mutiny. It was insane. Hence my needing stress relief."

Christian lets out a deep, sexy laugh. "I'm so sorry. That sounds absolutely terrible."

"It was," I grumble. "But I'm sure you didn't call to talk about my day. You probably have plans to go out, right?" Curiosity hangs heavy in my words, and I desperately try to remind myself that I have no claim to him. In fact, over the last few years, I've fought hard to get out from under the overwhelming feelings I have for him.

Pointedly, he says, "I don't have any plans. I wanted to talk to you. And... see if you'd talked to Sam, if she's told you what is going on with her."

Silence clogs the line, as I'm unsure how to answer. Yes, we talked, but nothing could force me to tell him what she confided in me. I guess I could tell him that much. "Um... I talked to her earlier this afternoon, and she's okay with us coming to New York to get her this weekend. She told me a little about what happened and disclosed she needed to work through some things before she's ready to talk about it more. I told her I understood and would be there for her whenever she needed."

It's silent for a moment and then he shocks me when he says, "Monica, darling, did Sam tell you who the guy was?" His tone is low and dripping with sensuality. *Did he just say darling?* He's flirting with me to try and get me to tell, but I recognize that. I clear my voice, giving him my response. "Yes, but I'm not telling you."

Again, silence fills the line, this time longer, giving me time to question what I'm doing. When he finally speaks, he growls, "It's not Mitch, is it? Did she get back with that douchebag?" I can almost taste the anger in his voice. It's poignant and sharp. Something I completely sympathize with. I too would be livid if she ever got back together with that dick.

Hoping to put his fears at ease, I answer quickly. "No, it's not Mitch, but I can't say more." I rush through the last of my answer, hoping to move the conversation on. But Christian's like a dog with a bone. He won't give it up.

"What guy?" he asks again in a flirtatious tone.

Seriously, this man! Annoyed, I let out a deep sigh. "My day was crap and I'm not about to make it worse by breaking the confidence of my best friend. I'm. Not. Telling. You. No matter how cute you are!"

Picking up on my blunder immediately, he mocks me. "Cute, you say?" Shit. I didn't mean to say that out loud, and of course, he caught it. Cue death by mortification in three, two, and one.

"Tell me more. How cute am I?" His tone is flirtatiously happy. *Why?*

I groan loudly, obviously annoyed, and Christian just laughs. "Look, I've had a long day and I just want to grab something to eat and watch some Netflix before I head to bed. Do you need anything else from me?"

After giving my address to him for Friday, we confirm our plans. Before we end the daily call, he again tries to get information, but thankfully, I have it locked down.

"Seeing that you won't give me any more information on Sam and this guy who dicked her around, I'll get out of your hair for the rest of the evening. Let me know if you need anything from me before Friday. I hope tomorrow is better and your students aren't little assholes. But if they are, I'd love to hear about it. Those paste stories were hilarious," he tells me.

"Thanks, Christian," I sarcastically say.

He lets out a throaty laugh that I find endearing, then hangs up.

Tossing my phone on the couch next to me, I sit back and ask myself, *what just happened?* We're getting along now? At the thought of that, I smile. It would be weird to consider him not an enemy anymore. Just as I'm about to sink back onto the floor to finish my yoga, my doorbell rings. Confused at who it could be, I linger. Finally, pushing up off my black faux leather couch, I stand and walk to my door. Outside is a man I've never seen before, holding a 7-11 bag. I didn't order anything. Pulling open the door, I flash the delivery man a confused look. "I didn't order anything."

He hands me the bag, then pulls up the receipt on his phone and shows it to me. Sure enough, it's a delivery for me, from one Mr. Christian Fox. I thank the man and close the door. Inside the bag is a familiar blue package. Chips Ahoy!—my go-to stress relief. I squeal and say to the empty room, "It has to be a coincidence, right?" How would he know that these are my favorite? I don't think I ever told him. He probably sent them because I agreed to go to New York with him. Regardless, it's a very sweet gesture. No one has ever done anything like this for me. "It's just a box of cook-ies," I remind myself as I head back over to my yoga mat, sit down, and take a selfie with the cookies. When I'm happy with the picture, I text it to Christian.

He instantly replies.

CHRISTIAN

I'm drooling. Looking delicious.

ME

They are. Chips Ahoy! are my favorite! Not sure how you knew that, but thank you so much. Good night.

Christian

Remembering our upcoming flight on Friday, I tell her I need her address so I can pick her up. Technically, I know where she lives, but I don't know what unit she's in. Monica sounds like she needs a pick-me-up, and that I can do. While she rattles off her address, I pull up the Door-Dash app and order a package of Chips Ahoy!—her favorite dessert and stress relief—from the 7-11 closest to her. In no time, she'll have them. It's perfect. Thank you, technology.

After ending our call, I sit back on my couch, wondering what I should do for the rest of the night. Maybe a run? When that's all I can come up with, I head to my bedroom. Changing into workout clothes, I grab my running shoes, towel, and water, and head out to my kitchen. My phone dings and, hoping it's nothing important, I drag it from my pocket. It surprises me to see a picture of Monica. It's a selfie, and it shows how absolutely gorgeous she is. Her hair is in messy curls and she has no makeup on. She's still wearing a sports bra and yoga pants, and she looks downright divine. I'm sure she planned the picture to serve as a simple thank you, but to me, I see so much more. In the picture, she's incredibly sexy, and I'm glad I'm not in my work slacks anymore because they'd be tight as hell right now. I lick my lips and wish I was with her, enjoying her company and those cookies. In fact, if I were there, I'd push the envelope with her, wanting to have some fun and incorporate the two—Monica and the cookies. If I had my way, I'd be eating cookies off her cookie. We've never done anything physical, but I know together we'd be fire. Would she be up for something dirtier? To me, it sounds like absolute heaven. Before I continue to entertain my fantasy, I respond with, *I'm drooling. Looking delicious.* Double meaning. Win!

She replies, wondering how I knew they were her favorite, apparently not understanding my true meaning. Oh, I know Chips Ahoy! are her favorite. I also know she drinks milk with most meals, like the good dairy farm girl she is. I've paid attention over the years to what she did and didn't say. The thing I love most about her is her ability to see the good in everyone. She's never had an unkind thing to say about anyone, especially her students, who seem to be a handful, and that's on a good day.

My body gyrates with excess energy because of the high I'm riding after my conversation with her. And that picture? She is a goddess, and the picture is proof. Needing to burn off the edginess I'm feeling, I head down to the building's gym to get in a workout. While warming up on the treadmill, I decide to call Lucas and let him know I'm heading to New York this weekend in case he's in town and wants to grab a beer.

When Lucas finally answers, he doesn't sound good. He sounds depressed. I wonder what's happened. Curious, I ask, "Hey, man, how the hell are you?"

"What's up?" he mumbles.

"Not too much going on. Will you be in New York this weekend?"

"Yeah, I've got two games this weekend," he grates out, sounding miserable.

After I tell him briefly what's going on with Samantha, he sounds worse. *Why?* Despite his distraught demeanor, he offers to help me kill someone if needed.

"Not yet," I tell him. "Monica won't give me much information, but I know it's because of a guy. I'm hoping to get more details this weekend. So, about that beer? You down?"

"Yeah. We can grab one after my early game on Sunday. It'd be before you head back to Chicago. Does that work?"

It'll be great to see Lucas and escape the stress of

Samantha's heartbreak. Plus, I'll probably need some distance from Monica or I'm liable to do something stupid. She's still an enormous temptation for me, and I know she's too good for me and not someone I should pursue. In reality, I'm not ready to settle down, so getting close to her could prove disastrous for both of us.

Chapter 15

Monica

Just as promised, Christian picks me up from my apartment Friday after work and whisks me to the private airfield where the Fox jet waits. When we arrive, he parks his black Mercedes G Class near the hangar and then comes to open my door for me. *He's a gentleman.* Unloading our overnight bags goes quickly. Then he grabs a fast-food bag that I could smell the entire way here. Not wanting to be presumptuous, I hope he grabbed something for me to eat too. Saying nothing, I try to take my bag, but he waves me off. Once he's removed everything from his car, he locks it and then nods toward the open hangar. Before me sits a beautiful private jet.

As we get closer to the jet, my steps falter. Thankfully, I catch myself before doing something truly embarrassing. Looking down at my outfit, I feel severely underdressed. Should I even be allowed onboard? Maybe I should be dressed in some designer outfit or something classy that screams money. But I'm not. I'm in a pair of ripped jeans I found in a thrift shop, a distressed Central Perk shirt, and my trusty Chucks.

Christian leads me to the jet, still dressed in his work suit that's both luxurious and sophisticated. Following him closely messes with my libido and zaps my brain. This week I have seen a whole new side of him and I find it irresistible, which is impossibly annoying. That pesky crush I've had on him since freshman year of college has emerged from its deep hiding, reared its ugly head, and screwed with everything. It's entirely inconvenient and problematic.

Christian confidently walks up the stairs and onto the jet as if he owns it. Oh wait, he does. Ugh! I'm so out of his league. For years, I've tried to tell myself I could never be what he wanted, and to move on. The one thing holding me back is the insane chemistry I still feel radiating between us. Before him, a single touch from a man never lit my entire body up, but now, just a touch from Christian drives me wild. No other man has ever done that. I know if we ever did anything, it would be explosive.

We settle in our seats and the flight attendant gives us the safety briefing before taking our drink orders. Christian asks for a beer, while I'm happy with a Sprite. I haven't flown many times, but I'm aware of the possibility of getting airsick.

The flight attendant delivers our drinks and checks with the pilot to get an ETA. Once she receives word of our impending takeoff, we buckle ourselves into our seats. Then it hits. Panic hangs heavy in my gut. My mouth's filled with sawdust and it's tough to get a full breath. My leg bounces a steady beat and I close my eyes, willing my heart to calm. Suddenly, I sense someone next to me. Blinking my eyes open, I realize it is Christian. He's moved next to me.

"Are you okay, Monica?"

"N-nervous flyer," I stutter out.

Christian places his hand over mine, which is curled over the armrest. "It's okay. We are perfectly safe."

After a while, everything seems fine, and we are on our way to New York.

"You good?" His deep voice makes me nervous.

"I haven't flown much," I confess, then force a smile to show him I'm fine.

He nods, smiles back, and reaches for the takeout bag he carried on with us. He pulls out napkins first, handing me a few, teasing, "You might need these." Then he offers me one of the delicious-smelling items from his paper bag—a true Chicago dog. Poppy seed bun, beef hot dog, neon-green sweet relish, yellow mustard, white onions, peppers, tomato wedges, celery salt, and a dill pickle spear. My mouth waters.

Taking it from him, I gush, "This looks absolutely delicious. Thank you, Christian."

He smiles at me, and it's good I'm sitting because my knees feel weak. Again, he digs in the bag and pulls out an identical Chicago dog for himself. He sets it on the table in front of him and takes his napkins and makes a makeshift bib. It's both ridiculous and adorable. I laugh at him and he gives me a playful look that renders me stupid.

"What are you laughing about? Surely, it's not my bib? This is stylish. It's coming to a runway this fall, I'm sure of it," he says confidently while making sure the bib's securely tucked into his shirt. Then he smirks at me. I can't help but laugh. Again. He's crazy, but I love seeing this side of him. I know it isn't one he shows to many, and I'm lucky he's trusting me enough to share this piece of himself. It reminds me of that dreaded Thanksgiving weekend. That night in the movie room was exactly the same.

I take a bite of the Chicago dog, and it's amazing. A moan falls from my lips and, embarrassed, I cover my mouth with my hand. Quickly looking to Christian to see if he heard.

He's frozen mid-bite. That's strange. Unable to tell if he heard me, I decide it doesn't matter either way. I love how comfortable it is between us; we're truly developing a friendship. I know I'll again do something embarrassing in front him. It's bound to happen, but right now I don't care. Taking another bite, I savor the flavors that explode on my tongue. Since I was a little girl, a Chicago dog was always a treat when we ventured into the city. Some Chicagoans might claim the deep-dish as their favorite hometown food, but for me, it's this, right here. In mere minutes, I finish my heavenly dinner. Looking over at Christian, I wonder why he started acting strange. He looks uncomfortable. I notice he's barely touched his hot dog. *Why?*

Trying to ease his discomfort, I say, "You better get to work on that, or I might have to steal it from you." I smile at him, hoping to put him at ease.

He gives a slight laugh and then says, "I'd like to see you try."

Challenge accepted. "Uh, Christian, you know I have three older brothers, right?"

He nods and shrugs his shoulders.

I lean forward and warn him in a sweet, friendly voice, "I may look small, but I'm scrappy as hell. I could take that from you, easy as that." I snap my fingers.

He looks at me, surprised, and then looks at his hot dog. He lifts it to his lips and takes an enormous bite. He lets out an outrageously loud moan as he chews.

Knowing he's poking fun at me, I let out my own loud moan with overly exaggerated gestures. His eyes widen and he laughs so hard he almost drops the remaining sacred dog. Once he regains his composure, he becomes much more relaxed. Mission accomplished. Problem solved.

Christian again checks his napkin bib to ensure its secure before he finishes the last few bites of his dinner. We toss our trash in the bag and he walks it to the galley to throw away. He sits in the seat next to me for the rest of the short flight and we spend it talking and laughing. It's the best conversation I've had in a long time.

I find the more time I spend with Christian, the more irresistible he grows. Being aware of that should help me set boundaries for my heart, but even though I've tried to erect walls around it, his charm seems to be the key to bringing them down. After this weekend, I know I'm going to be even more screwed or something will finally happen between us. Just thinking about that makes my emotions go crazy. I'm giddy, nervous, confused, excited, and apprehensive.

After we land, we head out to his parents' estate via a chauffeured car, and again I'm reminded of all the differences in our upbringings. It's not that I'm jealous of how he grew up, but the discrepancy is hard to ignore. He's totally out of my league.

Christian and I grab our bags from the trunk and head into the house. We're lost in conversation when we enter the kitchen, completely unaware of the audience we've drawn. At that moment, I couldn't miss how close Christian is standing to me. I feel the warmth of his body, and I want to wrap myself up in his arms. We've had a great evening so far, and I don't want it to end. But I'm here to help my best friend through her heartbreak, I remind myself.

Ignoring the pull I feel toward Christian is critical. During our conversation, I reach out and set my hand on his arm. Just touching him feels amazing. Even though our conversation is still hushed and private, I sense multiple sets of eyes on me. I look up and see Samantha staring at us with wide eyes. Feeling guilty, I immediately drop my hold on Christian's arm. After that, I notice the surrounding air change. Sadly, I miss the connection we shared over the past few hours.

Samantha and I spend the entire weekend together. We talk, laugh, watch cheesy movies, and her mom orchestrates a spa day in their living room. Christian makes himself scarce during the rest of our visit.

On the way into New York City on Sunday, Samantha and I grab dinner before our flight. We decide to indulge in some New York style slices from Joey's pizza.

About half an hour after we consume our deliciously greasy dinner, Christian boards the jet. He enters and tension radiates around him. He's in a strange mood, and he looks frazzled. I know he was just with Lucas, so what happened?

Bewildered, I ask, "Christian, are you okay?" He looks at me, dazed, like he sees me but it doesn't fully register. Concerned, I lead him over to the couch. I've never seen him like this. Waiting for him to answer, all I can do is look at him. He finally focuses his attention on me. It's intense and I can't look away.

He shakes his head and answers my question. "Yeah. Just processing what Lucas and I discussed."

I smile, then say, "Can I do anything to help?"

He smiles back. "No, I got it, but thanks for offering." He grabs my hand and squeezes it before adding, "I appreciate the offer. I just need to get back to Chicago to take care of some things for him. Not sure I can do what he's asking."

At his touch, butterflies take flight in my stomach and my heart flutters in my chest. My hands are sweaty and clammy. This is the first time he's touched me in days, and my brain goes into overdrive. It's in front of his sister, my bestie. Why am I so nervous? This is what I always wanted. So, what does it mean?

Looking like he needs reassurance, I tell him, "You are a skilled agent, and I know you'll do everything you can to represent Lucas in whatever he wants to pursue."

Chapter 16

Christian

This morning at breakfast, I tell Sam and Monica I'll meet them on the jet because I have plans to watch the early NY Chargers game and then grab a beer with Lucas.

"You're going to the game and then to get a beer?" my dad asks, sounding jealous he wasn't invited.

"Yep. Lucas mentioned needing to talk about some business decisions he's been thinking about," I inform him, trying to convey it's no big deal and he's not missing out.

My dad nods, looking at me, and asks, "Does he still seem happy with us? I'd hate to lose him. He seems like he's not only a super-talented hockey player but a genuinely great man." I agree with everything he says, but suddenly the air in the room shifts. It feels different, negative and tense. It's almost combustive, as if we are all sitting on a ticking time bomb. *Why? What changed?*

Unsure of what might tip the scales too far, I nod my agreement before finally speaking. "He is. I don't sense that he's unhappy with Fox at all. He mentioned some changes he's been entertaining and wondered whether they were plausible. I'll know more after I meet him tonight." That answer seems to appease him, although I know he'll expect me to report back on it all later. The rest of breakfast goes smoothly and the tension in the room eventually dissipates.

After watching Lucas's game, I head over to Scythe, an obscure bar that's closer to the airfield than the arena. I figure meeting here, we'll avoid bunnies or fans. Lucas said he wants to talk, so I want to make sure we do before I head back to Chicago. While waiting for him, I grab a beer, knowing it'll be an hour because they slotted him some time with the media.

Forty-five minutes later, he strolls into the bar, looking tired and nervous. The game hadn't gone badly. Why does he look like shit? Lucas orders a beer from the bartender. After getting it, he carries it over to where I'm sitting. Sliding into the booth, I notice he doesn't just look tired and nervous but depressed too. His eyes are dark and sunken. Deep shadows sit below them. Has he been sleeping? His smile is tight and forced. His clothes are nice, but they're just pulled on without care. What is going on? This is worse than I imagined after our call earlier this week. Last weekend when I saw him, he didn't look like this. What's happened in a week?

"Why do you look like someone stole your puppy?" Lucas asks me before I can do the same to him.

Me? I didn't think I looked bad. At least not as bad as him. I take a drink of my beer, rest the bottle back on the table, then confess, "It's my sister. I'm really worried about her."

Lucas remains silent. He doesn't move for a solid minute, but then, as if the spell he's been under breaks, he aggressively rolls his beer bottle between his hands, making me nervous.

He looks at me, sucks in a breath, then at rapid speed, word vomits, "Christian, I have a confession. I'm the reason Samantha is so upset. But I think I have a way to fix things. And I'm going to need your help."

After everything is out, I try to backtrack through it, searching for the important things. A few minutes later, it all registers. No longer am I sad. I'm pissed. More than pissed. I'm enraged. Willing to make myself sit still to ensure I've heard him correctly, I grind my back teeth and tighten my fists. I want an explanation, but he isn't talking, so I do. Maybe it's more like growling? "You have five minutes to explain yourself, Lucas, before I walk out that door."

He starts slowly, telling me about his relationship with Sam and how things went sideways between them. Then he tells me his plan to make things right and asks for my help.

To say I'm blindsided by all of this would be an understatement. He went behind my back with my sister, then hurt her. But I can tell by looking at him how miserable he feels about the situation. And I can't deny that his plan to win her back is pretty incredible. So, I agree.

"Yes, I'll help you as much as I can. I'm not making any promises, because that's a big ask, but it doesn't seem impossible. I will caution you that if I make this happen, you have to do everything to make her happy. If you cause her any pain, you'll have to deal with me. Do you understand?" I tell him.

Tomorrow, when I'm back in the office, I'll start making calls to see what can be done. It isn't impossible, but it'll be tough to negotiate. I'll need to be creative about my approach.

The waitress, who's hung around the perimeter of our table while we've had this intense conversation, approaches and asks if we need another beer.

"Yes," we both answer enthusiastically. While waiting, Lucas eyeballs me strangely. He looks like he needs to ask me something, but he's remaining mute. I choose to wait him out. Knowing him well enough, I know that when he gets uncomfortable with the silence, he'll talk.

The refreshing beers arrive. We clink bottles and each take a long swig. I sit back, relaxing. Lucas again eyeballs me, then asks, "You traveled here with

Monica, Samantha's best friend? What's going on there?"

Shit! How do I explain her? Honestly, I don't even know what or who she is to me. How am I going to tell him? Maybe just sticking to the facts? "Yes, she's Samantha's best friend, and that's it." Lucas smirks at me, and my resolve cracks. "She's gorgeous, kind, and smart, man, but fuck, she's too good for me. She needs a guy who wants to settle down and start a family, and that's not me. Honestly, she's been great about helping me with Sam. On the way out here, she had me laughing the entire flight. We've actually been talking a lot recently. I guess that's thanks to you. But like I said, she is completely out of my league and my sister's best friend, so she's off-limits." Looking to confirm he agrees, I'm met with a shrug. He's questioning me.

Still knowing I have to figure out my feelings for Monica, I understand I don't have the answer. It would probably be best if I stay away from her. And now that Sam is on the road to healing, she doesn't need me aggravating her life by causing drama with her best friend. I just need to stay away like I've done for years.

Hopefully, I can do what Lucas asked, so he and Sam can get back together and I won't need to be involved anymore. And seeing Monica again won't be necessary. How does that saying go, *out of sight, out of mind?* I could only hope so. Until then, I just need to keep reminding myself that she deserves better than me. It'll hurt like hell to stand back and watch her find someone else. But it's the right thing to do. Even if my heart shouts the opposite.

We finish our beers and I tell him I need to head to the airfield and back to Chicago. I inform him I'll call him in a few days.

The private airstrip is close and my driver gets me there in plenty of time. Climbing out of the car, I'm still reeling from the conversation with Lucas. Keeping it together so I don't give anything away will be tough. But I don't want to ruin Lucas's surprise if we can, in fact, pull it off. Plus, I'm not sure I'll ever be ready to deal with my sister's emotions, knowing I discovered the truth about what's been going on. I take a few deep breaths as I walk up the steps to the jet.

The flight back to Chicago has me dealing with a barrage of emotions. Still trying to process what Lucas said and what he's asking for has my head spinning. And then there's Monica. She is so kind and thoughtful. Immediately, she sees that I'm overwhelmed and tries to support me. Her words are like honey, soothing and comforting. With them, she not only renders care, but she strokes my ego, making me feel ten feet tall.

In only a short while, I've learned she is like crack to me—addictive. Knowing that is dangerous. I tell myself I need to separate from her before I'm a full-blown addict. Because when she figures out I'm not good enough for her, it will break me. It's better for both of us to have a clean break before it gets any deeper, right? Telling myself I'm saving us both pain in the long run feels cheap but necessary. Like an addict reaching rock bottom and needing treatment, I promise myself things I'll never be able to deliver. I'm not it for her, no matter how much I wish I were. But here at this moment, I'll pretend I am. Because as soon as we're back in Chicago, I'll back away. Until then, though, I'm going to sit next to her and enjoy this time, memorizing the sight of her, the sound of her, the scent of her. Absorbing everything I can. Because after this flight, I'll never have access to her again. Especially when I hurt her, because I know walking away will do just that. I'll leave my heart destroyed if it means she can eventually get everything she deserves.

Chapter 17

Monica

The flight back to the city is quick. Before I know it, we're deplaning and climbing into Christian's SUV. Samantha climbs in the back seat and lies down, passing out immediately. This heartbreak has worn her out. I climb into the front passenger seat, trying to think of things that can distract her in the upcoming weeks. Maybe next weekend, I'll convince her to go to the Navy Pier with me. We could ride the Centennial Wheel, eat great food, and sit for a caricature. Or, we could go to the Lincoln Park Zoo. I still need to do a last check because that's where I'm taking my kindergarten students for a field trip in a few weeks.

Not long after we leave the airfield, Christian pulls up outside my apartment building. He pops the back and climbs out to grab my bag. I turn to say bye to Sam and see she's still asleep. Placing a hand on her, I whisper, "bye," before I climb out of the car.

I meet Christian on the sidewalk, unsure of how our goodbye will go. This could be awkward. He still seems off from earlier, being quiet and maintaining his distance since we landed. As he stands on the concrete sidewalk, he shifts back and forth like he's uncomfortable and ready to bolt. Why's he so on edge? I try to make eye contact, but his eyes dart around, avoiding me entirely. Over the last week, we'd become closer, and my previously buried crush had awoken from the dead. But this, right here and now, feels painful. It's eerily like Thanksgiving years ago. Will this play out like last time? Is Christian planning to ghost me again? If so, for how long? Probably until the next time he needs my help with Sam. My stomach churns, fearing the next moments as we stand in silence. Me unable to say anything, and him unwilling to.

Annoyed, frustrated, and hurt, I try again to make eye contact with him. Unable to get his attention, I reach for my bag and try to tug it out of his grip. But he holds on tight like he doesn't want to let go. Even more confused, I say the only logical thing. "Christian, my bag."

Looking down, he shakes his head. "Sorry," he mumbles before handing it over. His grip on the bag is so tight when he releases it, it swings back, hitting me hard. An "oof" slips from my lips as I try not to fall.

"Sorry," he grumbles again, still not making eye

contact. Then we just stand there, knee-deep in discomfort.

When it's obvious neither of us will talk, I quietly whisper, "Night, Christian," before I walk away and into my building. After I'm safely behind the doors, I glance back and see him still standing in the same spot. His head hung low. I briefly wonder what's going on with him and hope he'll be past it the next time I see him. Then I turn and head for the elevators.

The elevator ride to my floor is slow. As I walk to my apartment, I remember Josiah is visiting. My steps become hurried as I move toward my apartment. I open the door and hear my most favorite sound, a yodeled "Mo." Josiah gave me that nickname when I was born. He's always been a busybody, and apparently shortening my name was a timesaver for a toddler on the go.

"Mo. You're finally home," Josiah shouts before he wraps me up in a tight bear hug and lifts me off my feet.

"Put me down. I'm up too high." Like our other brothers, Josiah is tall. Apparently, the males in my family are like giants. My brothers are all over six feet tall, and I'm five foot nine, making me feel small when I'm around them. Despite that, size didn't matter where I was concerned. Growing up on the farm, I'd always been in the thick of it with my brothers, desperate to keep up in all things. Even though I was younger and smaller, they let me tag along on most days, and I cherished that time with them. We filled our relationship with typical sibling bickering, but we were all extremely close. We leaned on each other in times of trouble, and after what just happened with Christian, I needed my big brother's love.

"Nope," he answers, still holding me high above the floor and swinging me around.

I squirm. "I'm going to be sick," I threaten.

"Oh, geez," he hollers before setting me back down. Once I'm on the ground again, I drop my bag to the floor.

"Awww," I moan as I kick off my Chucks before following Josiah back into my living room/kitchen area. Like he owns the place, he plops down on the couch, waiting for me to join him. I do. Apparently, he's been binge-watching reruns in my absence. Instead of *Friends*, like me, his go-to is *Seinfeld*.

"Missing me, were you?" I motion to the smorgasbord of snacks scattered across my coffee table. I notice they're not all his favorite but mine too.

I love when Josiah visits, but I was surprised when he called last week, telling me he was coming into the city. Time had escaped me. It was already time for his yearly cancer checkup. His doctors wanted to run blood work to make sure his testicular cancer was still in remission.

Josiah looks relaxed sitting next to me. I don't know if I'd be. The fear of his cancer returning is terrifying.

But maybe I just need to harness some of the chill vibes he's embracing. *I could do that, right?*

"Is your scan and blood work tomorrow? How do you feel about it?" My nervousness is evident in my voice. *Yeah, no chilling for me.* I'm scared for my brother.

"Yes. And then my doctor's appointment is on Wednesday." Removing his ball cap, he scratches his head. "It's cool. I'm confident everything's fine. In the meantime, are you cool having a visitor for a few days?"

Smacking his arm, I say, "You know you're welcome anytime. Especially if you bring me Milk Duds and buttered popcorn." Grabbing a handful of popcorn, I kick back. "This is the life."

"Hey, Mo?"

"Yeah?"

"Why are you trying so hard not to look sad?" he questions.

"What do you mean?" I answer.

"You looked like you were going to burst into tears when you came in. That's why I rushed you with a hug."

Shaking my head, I tell him, "It was a hard trip. Samantha's had her heart broken, and I am worried about her." *Well, that's half the truth.* "It will be okay. It'll just take time. I'm okay. I promise."

Tipping his head to me, he asks, "You sure?"

"I am," I answer as I throw popcorn at him. *At least, I hope so.*

Sitting next to my brother, thinking about his cancer diagnosis and recovery, my silly crush on Christian that I still cannot seem to get over is insignificant and unimportant. I frown, knowing it's ridiculous for me to feel sad about my unreciprocated feelings, but I do. After all these years, you'd think I could move on, but I haven't been able to. Now, looking back over the previous week, growing closer to Christian has only made things worse for me. It's stoked the fires of my hope and desire, and the only one who got burned was me.

Maybe this time I need to go about getting over Christian in a new way. Something I haven't tried before. I've heard guys mention, "the best way to get over someone is to get under someone else." Perhaps that would work for both Sam and me. Would she be up for that? Would I be up for that too? Of course, I'll have to wait a few weeks, until the sting of heartbreak isn't as strong before I broach the idea with her. Plus, I'll need a few weeks to convince myself of my plan to move on.

Chapter 18

Christian

Standing frozen in place on the sidewalk in front of Monica's apartment building while it rains is my penance. When we'd pulled up to the curb, I jumped out of my car, resolved to set boundaries between us. I knew I'd spent too much time with her recently, and I'd done a horrible job of maintaining my protective walls. Over the past week, we'd gotten closer. We'd laughed, talked, joked, and flirted freely with each other. Every time she was near, I could feel her desire for me, and just sensing that made me feel powerful. It isn't that I don't reciprocate her feelings, but I know we don't want the same things from each other. I am the epitome of a playboy who is content in moving from casual fling to casual fling. She's looking for her forever.

While growing up, I'd seen what it took to have a committed, lasting, forever relationship, and I know that isn't in the cards for me. In fact, I'm not sure if it will ever be. I can admit I know what my ideal woman looks like. Surprise. It's... Monica. But at this point in life, I can't offer her what she deserves. She's too good for me, so over the years, I kept myself busy with absolutely forgettable women. Ones who were the complete opposite of Monica. Sam liked to call me Peter Pan and tell me I needed to grow up. She was always telling me how good Monica and I would be together and that I was going to be sorry if I missed my opportunity by choosing to be a manwhore.

Truth is, I'm just not ready. Not ready for the feelings, commitment, responsibility, and trust. So, for now, I need to do the right thing and step back once again, no matter how much it hurts. And it hurts a fucking lot.

Standing silent on that sidewalk, I couldn't look at her. Ashamed and conflicted, I couldn't bring myself to say anything to her. After staring quietly at me for a while, Monica rolled her shoulders back, straightened her spine, and reached for her bag. Her hard tug caused the bag to swing back and hit her. She mumbled an "oof" under her breath before she turned and walked away from me and into her building.

Not ready to leave yet, I remain outside, rooted to the sidewalk. I need more time, but I couldn't tell her that or ask for anything more. I don't understand my thoughts and feelings.

The rain turns from drizzle to a downpour in

minutes. Soaked through, a chill ravages my body. Drenched, covered in goose bumps, and shivering, I stand alone next to my SUV, plagued by questions. *How did I get here? Is this a forewarning to my future self? Am I forever going to feel as hollow as I did when Monica walked away?* Years ago, I had walked away from her. Is this how she'd felt? No answers seem to be forthcoming, so I need to get out of the freak rainstorm. Forcing my feet forward, I climb back into my car and drive over to Sam's to drop her off. Returning home, I feel physically and mentally exhausted.

Sitting on my couch, I flip through Lucas's digital file. Gearing up for the coming week and helping to execute Lucas's plan, I'll busier than normal. I need to be on my game. I have to be ready to go in with guns blazing.

Pushing my discomfort aside, I know dealing with my feelings for Monica will have to wait for a more convenient time. Sam is home now, so I don't have any reason to talk to or see Monica anytime soon. That alone affords me a natural break. Problem solved, right? And the distance I created tonight is necessary, even if it goes against everything I want. In no time, we'll both be able to go back to the lives we'd been living weeks ago, without each other. *Why does that sound so lonely and awful?* For me, life needs to resume without Monica consuming my every thought. However, thinking of that bothers me. I don't want to banish Monica from my head. Having her in my thoughts is the only time when I can truly embrace my feelings for her, and removing that from my life feels wrong. A strong ache settles in my chest when I again remind myself that this is how it has to be between us. I'll need time to resurrect the walls I've built to protect myself against her before we cross paths again, because even I know that it's inevitable.

Chapter 19

Monica

After returning from New York, I do everything I can in order to keep myself busy. It's like I'm trying to exhaust myself so I don't feel anything. Christian had again screwed me over, and I'd let him. The incredibly upsetting part is that I knew better. The night we flew back, I naively sat next to him on the plane. My stupid heart filled with so much hope, thinking this time things would be different. Pointing out my mistakes for the thousandth time doesn't change my situation, it just makes me feel worse.

Unfortunately, despite those hurt feelings, my brain refuses to move on. My dreams about Christian wake me, leaving me breathless and wanting. I've always wanted more than friendship from him. But he shut that down time and time again. It's a complete wonder I can't get that through my brain. "He. Doesn't.

Want. You. Hasn't. He. Made. That. Clear?" I ask myself as I look in the bathroom mirror after yet another steamy dream about Christian. My answer should be crystal clear, but it isn't. It more resembles a murky cesspool. No matter what, I refuse to wake up and see all the signs before me.

My anti-Christian, new normal starts off the same way every day. I begin by reminding myself that I mean nothing to him and that I need to move on. I also tell myself I deserve better than what he's giving me. Wrapping my head around those truths hasn't been an easy journey. Thankfully, summer break is coming up soon and I can escape to my family's farm for a while. In all honesty, I want to grieve a loss that I can't share with anyone.

Back in high school, I'd lost my last grandparent. I remember the pastor who'd spoken at the memorial service talking about the five stages of grief. He'd told us the stages were denial, anger, bargaining, depression, and acceptance.

And as I spend weeks at the farm doing chores, working in the kitchen with my mom, horsing around with my brothers, and taking afternoon walks by myself, I realize I've been moving through them. My final stage of grief is acceptance, and it's the most difficult. I find it's easier to hang on and be angry than to deal with what I lost. Being on the farm so that I could work, scream, cry, think, and laugh has been more healing than I'd expected.

One afternoon, Josiah and I head into town. He needs a haircut and I offer to grab a few groceries for our mom. Finishing my shopping quickly, I load the bags into the back of the old, beat-up farm truck we drove in. Sitting on a bench outside the barbershop, minding my own business, a familiar voice calls out, "Monica Fields, that you?"

Looking up, recognition is instant. It's Charlie Young, my high school crush. "Hey, Charlie."

Sauntering over, his boots clomp on the wooden walkway, making me smile. *I love the sounds of country life.* "It's been a minute. Can I join you?"

"Sure can. How have you been?" I ask. Charlie looks similar to what he did in high school. Except now he's definitely all man. Sharp angles cover his jawline and muscles strain beneath his worn t-shirt. His Wranglers are much tighter in certain areas too. From what I see, he's filled out nicely.

"I've been good. Moved home after I finished my social work degree down south. Been interviewing for jobs the past few weeks. How about you? I heard through the grapevine you went to New York and got an elementary education degree."

I watch as his blue eyes hungrily trace up my body. This would have been a dream come true in high school. Now it's not charming as I once assumed it'd be. It's just plain annoying. He's making me feel like a slab of meat. "Yep. I work as a kindergarten teacher in Chicago." Taking a step back, I analyze his whole look. Sure, he's still a handsome cowboy, but I've known him since we were kids, and I know he can be lazy and sloppy. I get it. Things may have changed, but he doesn't hold the same captivating factor he once did.

Charlie slaps his hands together, making me jump. "That's outstanding, Monica. Knew you'd always do something great. I hate to cut this short, but I have to get going. Would you want to go out to dinner with me before you leave? We could catch up more and get reacquainted." I don't miss the waggling eyebrows that made all the girls goo-goo for him in high school.

Smiling at him, I say, "I really appreciate the offer, but I'm trying to spend as much time with my family before I head back to the city. You understand, right?"

"I do." Standing up, he tips his Stetson to me and says, "It was good to see you, Monica. I do hope we can catch up one day."

My nod is all he needs before he gives a wave and walks away. Sitting there, I realize I don't have the same reaction to him I once did. All that runs through my head now is... *He isn't Christian.*

"Oooowee. Mo, was that Charlie Young I just saw you talking to? Wasn't he like your high school crush?" Josiah's teasing tone grates on my nerves.

"Grow up, Josiah. To answer your questions, yes, that is who I was talking to, and yes, he was my crush.

But things change and I'm no longer interested in him," I point out, a little bark in my tone.

Josiah questions, "Not interested in that dude? What's wrong with him?"

Perturbed at my brother's questions, I grate out, "Nothing is wrong with him. He seems like a decent guy, is attractive, and has a college degree in something that will help people. He's great." *He's just not Christian.* "Can we drop it and go home?"

Holding his hands up, she says, "Sure. We can do that." Walking to the truck, Josiah whistles a tune, acting like he's the happiest guy on the planet.

Later that evening, after dinner, I'm tending to the garden when Josiah finds me. "Mo, I didn't mean to tease you about Charlie. I'm just afraid you're lonely in the city by yourself."

I throw a strawberry I just picked at him, and, reacting quickly, he catches it in his mouth. "Hey, thanks. I love snacks."

Rolling my eyes at him, I gesture to the garden and then over to the berry baskets I've left at the end of each row. Picking one up, he squats down, hunting for ripe, red berries. "I really don't mean to push."

"I appreciate the concern, but I'm fine."

He clears his throat, then says, "Then why do you seem sad? All summer long you've been quiet. It's not normal."

"Honestly, I have been sad. I was interested in a guy the last few years and I think I finally realized he's not really interested in me." Tears well in my eyes and I blink them away. *Don't cry in front of your brother.*

Setting his basket down, he walks over to me and wraps me in a warm hug. "I'm sorry, Mo. If a guy doesn't see how great you are, then he doesn't deserve you."

Squeezing him tighter, I whisper, "Thanks, Josiah." After our heart-to-heart, we go back to picking strawberries for Mom. She threatened our strawberry shortcake would be incomplete if someone didn't help. Since Mike and Will are busy with farm chores, I guess that leaves me. Thankfully, Josiah is caught up with his work and he sticks around to help me. I'm really going to miss him when I leave at the end of summer.

A few weeks before the next school year will begin, I head back to the city to get everything ready to welcome kids into my classroom. As always, I have a lot to do before the first day. This year, I came back feeling refreshed and rejuvenated, like a new woman. A Monica 2.0.

During my hiatus, I avoided anything having to do with Christian, which unfortunately included Sam. I needed a clean break from him, and that would have been difficult, seeing that he's her brother and they're really close. It would have been too hard to hear about him. And as if I'm not good enough at torturing myself, my mind reminds me often that Christian isn't dealing with a broken heart, only I am. In fact, he's probably keeping busy with all the women he could ever want.

A few days before classes begin, I finally reach out to Sam. She picks up immediately with boundless excitement.

"Monica?" Sam questions in a happy, high-pitched squeal.

I laugh. Apparently, she missed me as much as I've missed her.

"Hey," I answer.

"Is it really you? Are you still on the farm or back in the city?" she quizzes me.

Before I'd left at the beginning of the summer, I told her I wouldn't be communicating with her until right before the school year began. Sam hadn't been happy about that, but she understood needing to take care of yourself. She didn't know I had a broken heart or that her brother had caused it. I'd explained to her it had been a tough school year and I needed some me time.

"I'm back. School starts next week. I needed to get back to set up my classroom and meet with my principal," I explain.

"How was the farm? Were you ready to come home?"

"It was great to spend time with family and see some old friends. My brothers dragged me out a few nights. I think they were trying to set me up with a guy named Charlie, because he came around often," I admit.

"Wait. Charlie? Wasn't that the older football player you had a crush on in high school? What's he like now? Anything happen?"

I laugh at her excited questions. "Yes, Charlie was my high school crush, who was always too busy pursuing the cheerleading squad to notice me. He went and got his degree in social work from a university in Illinois and then came back to our small town to work. He's good. Still handsome as ever and single too. But..." I don't finish my thought because I can't admit to her that Charlie isn't Christian. Even though I've worked hard to get over him, he's become the measuring stick that I use to compare every other man to. Until I feel sparks with someone like I do with Christian, I don't see the point in pursuing more.

"But, what?" Sam questions pointedly.

I clear my throat, buying time until I can figure out how to answer without disclosing my unrequited feelings for Christian. "We didn't have any sparks," I explain, hoping she'll take that as my final answer.

"I'm sorry. But I totally understand."

Of course she understands, I tell myself. After moving from Mitch the dick to Lucious Lucas, and seeing how intense a connection you could have with someone, why would you ever accept anything else?

Wanting to move the conversation on to some other topic, I ask her how she's been doing. Before leaving for the farm, she still sounded so sad, but today she sounds happy. Something has happened and I'm dying to know what. "Are you up for lunch sometime this week? I can come to you," I offer.

"Yes, let's do that. How about Thursday? We can meet at Fox, and after lunch we can go get pedicures. My treat," she suggests.

"I can't wait," I tell her before we say goodbye. I'm looking forward to catching up with my best friend. I miss her.

The week passes quickly. I'm busy setting up my classroom, meeting with the principal, and conducting kindergarten intakes. I meet all the students slotted to be in my class, and it looks to be a wonderful group of kids. They excite me for the upcoming school year.

Finishing up the early training session at school, I grab an Uber into the city. Fox Sporting's building is intimidating. As I climb out of my ride, I look down at my super casual outfit and grimace. I'm dressed in jean capris, a V-neck tee, and strappy sandals. It's hard not to compare my outfit to all those people flowing in and out of the office building. Instead of caring, I shrug. Sam won't care about the way I'm dressed, so why should I? The new Monica—Monica 2.0—doesn't. I flip my wavy blonde hair over my shoulder and head into the building. Instead of seeing disdain on people's faces for my lack of business attire, I see jealousy from the ladies and desire from the men. What a nice ego boost.

After riding the elevator up to Fox Sporting's floor, I check in with the receptionist, who escorts me back to the executive's offices. In moments, I'm led into an elegant office that screams power and sophistication. Behind a large white desk sits Sam, who's busy on a call. She looks up when the receptionist knocks on her door. My bestie waves me in and, as quiet as a church mouse, I tiptoe into her office, taking in all the luxurious finishes. I step over to the wall of windows directly behind her and gawk at the magnificent view. I bet it looks incredible at night. Lost in thought, I don't hear Sam finish her call.

Stepping up behind me, she wraps me in a tight hug and I laugh. "Miss me, did you?"

She snorts. "Hardly. Barely noticed. I haven't seen you in weeks," she answers with humor in her voice.

"I can tell. I missed you too. Let's go eat. I want to hear all that you've been up to."

Sam grabs a beautiful black quilted clutch sitting on the corner of her desk. Looking closer, I notice the iconic mirrored Cs of Chanel and have to stop myself from drooling. Truthfully, I'm not an accessories girl at heart, but the clutch is amazing.

"New clutch?" I question with a raised eyebrow. She nods and mutters something about retail therapy. I wish I had the finances to afford some luxury retail therapy, but nope, broke teacher here. Sam and I are from two different worlds, but to us, it doesn't matter. We ground each other. Honesty, respect, and love are at the forefront of our friendship and always have been. We head off to the elevator arm-in-arm, ready for some much-needed quality time.

While riding down in the elevator, Sam turns and runs her eyes up and down me and says, "Monica, you look fantastic. Spending time on the farm looks like it agreed with you."

I smile because time on my family's farm was exactly what I needed to get myself back on track. "Thank you. It was good to be home. Healing."

We arrive at the ground floor and the elevator doors part. Looking down to make sure my sandal doesn't snag, I'm not paying attention. *Smack.* I run into a well-defined chest. "S-sorry," I stutter out, knowing if I'd been looking up, I wouldn't have caused the collision. Going to apologize again, my eyes lift to the owner of the muscular chest that I'm still touching. Shit! It's Christian. My hand flies off his chest like he's made of lava and I'm going to get burned. His eyes latch on to me. They're deep, swirling with a mix of desire and surprise.

He huffs out a hearty laugh, and I immediately step back as if he's a threat. My eyes widen as I take in his incredibly handsome appearance. He's dressed in well-fitted navy-blue slacks and a white button-up shirt, which is tucked in around his trim waist. He isn't wearing a tie but has left a few of the top buttons undone. He also has his sleeves rolled up to his elbows, revealing his tanned, corded forearms. *Could he seri-*

ously be any sexier? Stunned and unable to speak, I step to the side and rush over to Sam, who's giving me a confused look.

"Ready?" I shakily ask her. I glance over my shoulder and realize Christian is still standing there, staring at me.

Confusion still covers her face, but instead of pressing me, she takes my arm, says, "yep," and we head for the exit without another word. I'm beyond mortified. All the work I'd put in this summer, building walls to deflect Christian's charm, just about collapsed after one insignificant run in. *That's not good.*

I feel shaken as Samantha and I walk a few blocks down to Say Cheese, a trendy new restaurant specializing in gourmet grilled cheese. Most of the lunch crowd has already been through the eatery, so by the time we arrive, it's relatively empty. The menu's huge, offering everything from the standard grilled cheese to more sophisticated and complex options like the apple, bacon & smoked gouda.

"Everything smells amazing. What are you going to get?" I ask while my eyes hungrily roam over all the delicious items on the menu.

"I'm craving salt, so I think I'm going with the dill pickles and ham. How about you?"

"They all look so good. There are so many options. If these are as good as I think they'll be, we will be back, right?" Samantha nods her agreement. "Then I think I'll get the Caprese grilled cheese."

Once our number is called, I jog up to grab our order.

While eating, we avoid any conversation about men, choosing instead to catch up on our summers.

"How was the farm?" Sam asks me.

Letting out a sigh, I reply, "It was good. I worked in the neighboring town, so I basically just had weekends to enjoy it, and those were crazy busy."

Samantha looks at me confused. "Why were your weekends busy? I mean, I get that it's a farm and the cows probably have to be milked daily, but don't you have workers for that?"

"We have workers for Monday through Friday, but we give them the weekends off so they can be with their families. And the cows are milked twice a day." Samantha's eyes bulge as she mouths *"twice."* I can't help but laugh at her response.

"So, what did you do while I was gone? Let me guess. Work... and more work?"

Taking a bite of her sandwich, she muffles her answer, but I still hear it. "Yes."

Feigning shock, I cover my mouth with my hand. "Okay, what else did you do? Yoga? Visit your parents? Sleep in? Anything remotely interesting and fun?"

Rolling her brown eyes at me, "I'll have you know... I went to yoga weekly and out for Taco Tuesday twice with the ladies from the office."

"Look at you! I'm glad you aren't staying in sad because of he who shall not be named."

"Who?" she replies before giving a pained laugh.

I give her a small smile. "I know it hasn't been easy, but I am so proud of you."

Not wanting to be late to our pedicure appointments, we quickly finish our sandwiches. And guess what? They were amazing!

Following lunch, we head to a nail salon that's a few blocks over to treat ourselves to pedicures. Picking out our nail polish provides entertainment.

"Sam, I found your color." Showing her the deep navy-blue color, she asks, "What's it called?"

"Get Ryd-of-Thym Blues."

"Oh, that's amazing. Can I have it?"

Handing it to her, I ask, "What should I pick?"

"Definitely hot pink. It'll look amazing with your tan and blonde hair." I grab the brightest hot pink I can find, and when I turn it over, the name makes me laugh. Samantha gives me a look.

"It's called La Paz-itively Hot. And it's exactly what I need."

Being pampered feels divine, and it's something we both needed. With brightly painted toes, we walk back toward the Fox offices, stopping to grab an iced latte from a corner coffee joint.

I order an Uber when we reach the building. While waiting for it to arrive, Sam and I make plans to grab brunch in a few weeks. She knows the beginning of the school year's busy and stressful and I'll need an outlet or a mimosa or two.

When my ride shows up, I get an enormous hug from my bestie. As we're hugging, Christian walks out from the building and our eyes lock. He freezes just outside the revolving door and gives me a forced smile. His pained expression does weird things to me, making me feel both nervous and angry. Seeing him again, I realize that he and I haven't had any contact since we brought Sam back from New York months ago. My phone dings, letting me know my Uber is here. Needing to go, I release Sam and back up. "Thanks for today, Sam. Love you," I say as I climb into the car just as Christian approaches.

"Love you too, Monica," she says before stepping away. As I'm pulling away, I watch Christian step up behind her while he's still staring at me. Sam looks at him and notices the direction of his stare. She says something and his face falls, breaking his gaze from me. My Uber turns the corner and they both disappear. Letting out a deep breath, I relax into the seat. Even after today, my plan hasn't changed. I'm still moving on, I remind myself.

Chapter 20

Christian

The past few months dragged by. I've been busy with work, but my personal life remains non-existent, and if I'm honest, I'm the only one to blame. After Monica walked away from me the night we got back from New York and I vowed to put space between us, I tried to move on. Really, I did. In the past, hitting the clubs was always the simple answer. Grabbing drinks with my buddies was a sure-fire way to score. But I soon discovered that even when the offers presented themselves—and they did, often—I didn't want them. Those women no longer were of any interest to me. I mean, in the past, I had only seen them as a good time, but now that didn't even sound appealing.

Something is wrong with me, and I don't know how to fix it. I know I can't talk to my buddies because they'd be completely useless, suggesting my cock is probably broken and I need the little blue pill. *That isn't the issue.* Without a doubt, I am screwed, but not in the good sense.

Putting the pieces together, I suspect my situation has to do with Monica, because everything worked just fine before we'd gone to New York together. Now the only time I get any action is from my right hand when I'm alone and Monica comes to mind. Unfortunately, that is happening far too often. But in my defense, I need release, and it's the only way I get any. Wanting to maintain my persona as a pleasant guy, I've taken matters in to my own hands, literally.

Then today happened, bringing me to my knees. It had already been a long week, where my ass had been bested by another firm. A rival sports agent, who is a major dick, used unscrupulous methods and stole an up-and-coming NBA star out from under me. It wasn't just that I was pissed; the dick made me look bad in front of a potential client. I feel bad for the young star. I know his new agent isn't just a horrible person, but he also does a shitty job representing his athletes. But I guess he'll have to learn. I tried to warn him, but the slick too-good-to-be-true offer was too hard to turn down.

During lunch, I go to the gym to work out some of my stress with a run. I push myself to the max and spend almost the entire hour on the treadmill, burning miles into the belt. Thankfully, the gym I frequent is only a few blocks from my office, so I can get back quickly if I'm running late. Still wound up after my run, I shower and dress quickly. I pocket my tie and leave the top buttons of my shirt undone. I don't have any meetings scheduled, so I don't care that I look more relaxed than professional. Truth be told, there are only a handful of hours left in the day, so no one will care.

Standing at the elevators, waiting for them to open, I look down at my phone. I type out a message to my assistant to see if she'll grab me a sandwich from the café around the corner on her way back. She quickly responds with a thumbs up and I smile. A win for the shit week!

When the doors open, I step forward and halt immediately when a woman slams into my chest. Her tiny hand lands on my pec and it feels like I've been burned by a branding iron. Heat immediately spreads across my body, radiating from the tips of each of her fingers.

"Oof," a tiny voice says. It's adorable and somewhat familiar. Looking down, I see Monica staring back at me. Unable to believe my shitty luck, it figures the girl I've been avoiding is standing in front of me. I laugh nervously. She steps back with a look of alarm on her beautiful face. Of course this would happen to me. The only woman I can't have, but the only one I want, wants to be nowhere near me. I can't really blame her. I haven't seen or talked to her since we got back from New York. I know I needed space, but if I'm being honest, she was never far from my thoughts, dreams, or fantasies.

Saying nothing, she steps to the side, loops arms with my sister, and walks out of the building. Still like a drug to me, I instantly crave more than just the brief contact we exchanged. I already miss her. *Is that possible?* Standing there, I follow her with my eyes, savoring each second until she's out of sight. Just one accidental touch from her lit my entire body on fire and left me wanting so much more. I breathe deep, sucking all of her scent from the surrounding air.

Replaying her exit from the building, it's undeniable she's as stunning as ever. Only dressed in jeans, a tee, and sandals. No one has ever been more beautiful or aroused me more. But now that she's gone again, I find myself questioning whether she was really here. Surely Monica wouldn't have given me the cold shoulder, right? I pinch myself to check and see if maybe I'm dreaming. "Ouch." Guess not. Seeing Monica's reaction to me rips me to shreds. She seemed so distant and withdrawn, not cheerful like she usually is. Would things ever be normal between us again? *Maybe?* The electricity I felt coming off her touch was just enough to give me hope. And wish for more.

Daydreaming about how it would feel to have her hands on me is making things tight down below, and if I don't take care of that soon, I'll embarrass myself. Heading upstairs to my office and my private bathroom is the only way to handle this current situation. Once I deal with my current pre-*dick*-ament, I can face my feelings about seeing her again.

My assistant, Jane, strolls into the elevator just before the doors close and hands me a bag. I thank her. I don't even care what's inside. She knows what I like, and I'm glad to have something to cover my growing situation. Apparently, no matter what I try to distract myself with—thinking about contracts, old wrinkly people—nothing will curb the extreme response my body is having to seeing Monica.

When we get to our floor, I shuffle out as best I can with a boner painfully pushing on my zipper. I escape to my office and shut my door without a word to anyone. Then I hustle into my bathroom like my ass is on fire and lock myself in. The relief I feel once I free myself from my pants is unreal. Pulling down my boxers, I palm my hot, throbbing cock in my hand and squeeze it firmly, willing it to calm. Needing a moment to get my bearings, I remind myself to keep quiet. After all, if I'm going to jerk off in the middle of the day in my office bathroom, I'm going to enjoy every moment— just silently.

As I stroke from root to tip, I close my eyes and recall the delicate touch of her hand on my chest. I imagine her hand is wrapped around my cock, stroking me. My mind calls up the sway of her hips, wrapped tightly in jeans. The V-cut of her shirt had afforded me exquisite views as she stood before me. My mouth waters and I lick my lips, wishing I were using it to trace all over her body. Recalling the scent of vanilla and sugar in the surrounding air sends a shiver up my back and goose bumps across my body. Even the octave of her *oof* makes my fantasy come to life vividly behind my closed eyelids. I can imagine it all. Her hand strokes me perfectly, applying the right amount of pressure and making me harder than steel. With her other hand, she rolls my balls lightly, tugging on them. As I picture her lips, her eyes, her face, my balls grow tight, and I feel the telltale signs of an orgasm ready to explode. Two more strokes are all it takes before I erupt into my sink. The orgasm stealing my breath from me. Using a hand, I steady myself against the sink basin.

When the high has passed, I open my eyes and take in my appearance. Sweat peppers my forehead and my skin is flushed like I just completed a strenuous run. Looking down, I see the mess I made of the sink. My aim was a bit lacking. Turning on the water, I wash away the evidence of my desire, not wanting the janitorial staff to clean up my mess. When my cock is no longer pulsating, I tuck it back into my pants and right my clothes. Splashing cold water on my face helps me to cool down. I wash my hands, tidy up, and return to my desk, where I unwrap the sandwich I tossed on it in my frantic dash for the bathroom.

Starving, I make quick work of the hoagie my assistant grabbed for me. Still hungry, I snag a granola bar from my desk drawer and a bottle of water from my mini fridge.

After spending the next couple of hours answering emails, I decide I'm done for the day. It isn't common practice for me to leave early, but I'm still reeling after my run-in with Monica. What am I going to do about her? Obviously, I'm still incredibly attracted to her. Months apart had done nothing to extinguish what I feel for her. Actually, I think my attraction to her has gotten more intense. How can I ever move on if I'm feeling like this?

Needing to work off some of my pent-up aggression, I make plans to go play nine holes of golf with my friend Jacob. After checking with my assistant, I take off for the day. Nothing needs my urgent attention. I'll be back in the office in the morning, plus I'm always reachable by phone. Just as I'm about to head to the company car I use daily, I glance up and catch the eyes of the most beautiful woman I've ever seen.

Twice in one day, my eyes have locked with Monica's, and both times it felt like she was looking straight into my soul. Feeling incredibly vulnerable, I force an awkward smile. She's hugging my sister tightly, which makes me incredibly jealous. *I want her to hug me like that.* After a moment, she steps back and says something to Sam, even while still locked in a stare down with me. Monica moves backward to an unknown car as I walk up behind my sister. Sam senses me and says something just as my eye contact with Monica breaks and she climbs into the car and drives away.

When Monica is out of sight, I move my eyes back

toward my sister. I'd caught a little of what she'd said, something about fancy grilled cheese and pedicures. Honestly, I don't care. I just want to know about Monica, but I don't know how to ask. Not wanting to be too obvious, I try to think of clever ways to ask so Sam won't suspect and interrogate me. But I'm drawing a blank. Today, of all days, I'm not ready for her questions. Instead of forcing a conversation, I tell her I'm late for a tee time and I have to go. Sam waves me off before she walks to her company car and climbs in. I do the same and ask my driver to take me over to the club so I can meet Jacob. Maybe hitting some balls will make me feel less edgy.

When I get home from golf, I still feel like I'm wound up tight, like a spring. I change into athletic shorts, planning to grab another run before dinner. My building has a decent exercise room, which includes treadmills, bikes, and free weights. As I ride the elevator down to the main floor, I place my dinner order at Olive, a delicious Greek restaurant that makes the best gyros, spanakopita, and baklava in the city.

After thirty minutes on the treadmill, my phone dings, letting me know my food is almost to me. I stop the machine, clean it off, then wipe the sweat from my brow. I grab a refreshing drink of water from the water fountain and head out to the building's lobby to intercept my dinner.

While waiting, my phone rings. It's a New York area code, and it looks slightly familiar. I'm still waiting to hear if what I've been working on for Lucas went through, so I answer it, hoping for the best.

Before I can say anything, a gruff voice calls out, "Christian."

"This is Christian," I answer, unsure of who is calling.

"Hey, man! It's Steve, the GM for the New York Chargers."

I breathe out. This is it. Did I pull off a miracle? "Hey, Steve! It's great to hear from you. What can I do for you?" I ask nervously.

He laughs, making me even more anxious. "No, I think the question is, what can *I* do for *you*?"

We then go into the deal I've been trying to broker for Lucas.

"I've submitted paperwork outlining the details of the offer to ensure this deal goes through. We are just waiting for your approval." I speak confidently, although I'm trembling slightly. *Maybe it's because of the run and not my nerves about the deal?*

Just then, a delivery person walks into my building with an Olive bag. Saying nothing, I walk over to him and show him my order confirmation. He hands over my food and leaves. While riding the elevator back up to my floor, Steve finally responds.

"I'm going to be honest with you, Christian. This offer took us by surprise. Could this have been prevented?" he asks.

Unlocking my penthouse, I address his comments

firmly. "Lucas wanted this deal for personal reasons. It isn't motivated by money or any negative feelings he harbors. He needs this in order to pursue his future dreams. I know my answer is vague, and I'm sorry for that, but I need to protect his confidentiality. If he wishes to share more about what motivated his request, he can do so, but my job is to facilitate making his requests come to fruition. And I do hope I have."

Steve clears his throat and pauses, making me wait for his answer. When he finally speaks, my nerves are completely frayed. I want this deal, not only for Lucas, but for Sam too.

Since our talk when he asked for my help, Lucas has confided in me more and more, admitting all his feelings for my sister. At first, I didn't want to hear it because I was pissed he'd hurt my sister, but the more he persisted, the more I willingly listened to him. His confessions were full of vulnerability, love, and acceptance. I was jealous of him and his ability to do that. Desperately, I wanted to be like that with my feelings for Monica, but I know I'm not even close. Hell, the thought of settling down still makes me flinch. I'm not ready for that, but Lucas is, and he's putting everything behind it to make sure it happens. Honestly, I couldn't pick a better guy for my little sister. But if he hurts her again, I'll have no problem kicking his ass.

"Christian," Steve says. "I have talked to everyone involved to get their thoughts and concerns. We reviewed the offer and have concluded that it's fair. We accept the terms."

I mask the excitement I feel coursing through my body. I want to jump in the air and shout Wahoo! loudly. After I hang up, I'll be calling Lucas to share the news.

"That is fantastic news, Steve. Thank you for calling to tell me. I need to call Lucas and share the news with him. Please let me know if you need anything from us to get this deal inked. Thank you again," I spit out, rapid fire. My excitement is palpable.

Steve laughs, sensing my excitement. "It was great working with you, Christian. I'm sure we will talk again at some later date. Take care." And then he hangs up.

I stand there in my penthouse, staring at my phone. Scents from my dinner permeate the surrounding air, making my stomach rumble. I'm starving, but I need to make this phone call before I can eat. Without wasting a moment, I select Lucas from my contacts and hit dial. The phone rings twice before he picks up.

"Christian?" Lucas says in a questioning tone.

"Hey, man!" I say, wondering how long I can drag this out before I confess why I'm calling.

"Everything okay?" he asks, sounding suspicious.

I laugh. "Yep. Everything is better than okay."

He groans, then asks, "You drunk?"

"Nope. Haven't had a drink in weeks."

"Okay. Then why are you calling me at six o'clock

on a Thursday night?" He sounds genuinely concerned. "Is something wrong? Is it Samantha?"

"Whoa, buddy. Calm down. Nothing is wrong. Sam is fine. I just called to tell you I heard from Steve."

Lucas lets out a breath. Then he timidly asks, "What did they say?"

Not wanting to torture him any longer, I say, "The deal is done."

A loud "Wahoo!" comes across the line, making me pull the phone from my ear. After a few moments, I move it back and Lucas is still cheering. In my career so far, no deal has felt as good as this. Not only is Lucas my client, but he's also one of my closest friends and, who knows, maybe more someday. His victory is mine. So, I celebrate with him.

"Remember, this still has to stay quiet. The deal happened before training camp, so I am assuming you'll get the details of the next steps soon. Are you still planning to surprise Sam at the game?" I ask.

Without hesitation, he replies, "Yes. The plan is still on. Can you help me with a few other things to make sure everything is ready?"

Flipping through my calendar, I see I will be in Chicago the next month, so I am free to help him. "I can do that. Send me what you need from me. Also, let me know what I need to do to help with Sam's surprise."

I hear rustling over the phone and then frantic writing. The line remains quiet for a minute, then

Lucas finally speaks up. "Sorry, I was making a list of what I have to do in the next weeks. Holy shit, is there a lot to do. Do you think it'll be tough to convince Samantha to go to the game, or can you maybe somehow get Monica to attend too?"

Crap. How am I going to get Monica to attend the game? She and I still haven't talked since our New York trip. And today was hella awkward and there was only minimal exchange between us. Unfortunately, I can't admit any of that to Lucas. I didn't tell him how close we'd gotten and how it stirred up a lot of unresolved feelings I have for Monica. I haven't admitted to anyone how I feel about Monica. Knowing my uncertainty about getting Monica to the game would stress out Lucas even more and that wasn't an option, I do the only thing I can. I lie.

"I can totally get Monica and Sam to the game." I'm hoping I sound more confident than I feel. Sam will take some minor convincing; I'll probably tell her it's work related. But Monica? I'm not even sure she'll answer my call. If I can get her to talk to me, my best bet is to tell her the truth about the game and what Lucas had planned. She'll do anything for Sam's happiness, and I know my sister told her all about Lucas. The secrets of it were written all over their faces while we were in New York.

My stomach growls loudly. I'm not sure if it's because I'm famished or if it's nerves from thinking about calling Monica. I only plan to address one of those things right now. Finishing my phone call with Lucas, I take my food to my couch. I flip on ESPN and watch *SportsCenter* while I scarf down my dinner. My phone dings with a text from Lucas, with the contact information for someone he wants me to get in touch with. I'll call her tomorrow, even though I know that would be an easier call than the one I have to make to Monica.

After throwing away all my trash, I pace around my penthouse, pre-planning what I'll say if Monica even answers my call. Terrified, I tell myself, "Just get it over with. Rip the Band-Aid right off." Bouncing on my toes, trying to get myself psyched up, I take a few moments to run through my arguments again before I actually call.

When we'd been talking before New York, Monica hadn't confessed I'd hurt her in the past, but I'd always gotten the impression I had. Sometimes her comments seemed tinged with sadness, anger, and pain. But when I tried to press her on it, she either shut down completely or changed topics. It felt like there was something there, but she wouldn't admit it. Would she ever?

Knowing what I need to do, I grab my phone. Even though I'm tempted to waste more time, I know I'm just avoiding it, and that won't make it any easier later. The entire time, I'm reminding myself that I'm doing this for Sam and Lucas before I hit dial.

The phone rings and rings. She doesn't answer.

My heart sinks, even though it doesn't really surprise me. *Why would she answer my call?* Not leaving her a message is easy because I don't know what to say. Well, fuck me! Guess that is my answer.

Sitting back on my couch, I try to imagine any other scenario in which I can get Sam and Monica to Lucas's game. Maybe Fox Sporting could fake a raffle where they won tickets. Would they buy that? No, probably not. Honestly, it isn't something either of them would even enter. Could I convince Sam to go and just bring her along? Not likely. As far as I can assume from today's interactions, Monica's back to avoiding me, just like the past few years. To be fair, I was avoiding her too. Maybe I could bribe them? Perhaps give them tickets to an upcoming concert, a day at the spa, or a shopping spree for attending the game? They're women... they'd be into that, right?

Just when I'm sure I have a backup plan, a familiar tune, "Farmer's Daughter" by Rodney Atkins, comes from my phone, and my stomach bottoms out. It's the ringtone I set for Monica when we were talking before New York. I know if I don't answer it, I'll look like a major asshole, seeing as I just called her. I swallow hard and swipe to answer the call.

"Hello," I choke out.

"You called?" Monica accuses in a harsh tone. *She obviously doesn't want to talk to me, so why'd she call back?*

Shit. She sounds pissed. Asking for her help is

going to suck. *It's for Sam*, I remind myself over and over. Sucking in a quick breath and harnessing the courage I wish I had, I verify, "I did."

"What do you want, Christian?" she growls.

Shyly, I explain. "Listen, Monica, I know I am the last person you want to hear from, but I need your help." I hear her scoff loudly, and I rush to squeeze in a few more words before she hangs up. "It's for Sam."

Silence fills the line. I nervously shift in my seat, awaiting her response.

"It's really something for Sam?" she quietly asks.

I nod—*not like she can see you, dick*—then answer, "Yes, it's a favor benefitting Sam."

Giving her a few moments to process what I've said is torture. I know she probably wants to say no just to spite me, but she's reevaluating because the help involves my sister.

"What do you need this time, Christian?" Her question pains me. It's like she says that just to hurt me. Is she implying that I only talk to her when I need something? Running that thought through my mind reveals a dark spot I'd rather ignore. The truth of that hits me hard, like a direct strike to my heart. Wait, is it true? Does she feel like that? Does she think I use her? That isn't true. I don't want her to feel like that. The thought of that makes me sick to my stomach. My leg bounces out of control after I break into a hot sweat. Of all people, I would never want Monica to feel used by me. But does she?

"Are you mad at me, Monica?" I nervously ask.

"Nope," she utters far too quickly and in a tone that puts me on edge.

Unsure how to proceed, I remain silent, pondering what to say. This is confusing. I know I need to select my words carefully. Something my mom always said pops into my head. *Be honest.* I tell myself to just do it as I breathe out deeply.

"You sound upset, and I understand that I'm probably the cause of that. When we got back from New York, I was busy and I let our budding friendship fall by the wayside. I'm sorry about that. I didn't handle it well, and I never meant to hurt you." *Well, that was a half-truth.* I'm not sure I'm brave enough to tell her the entire reason we hadn't connected recently.

Monica remains silent on the other end of the line while I sit back and fiddle with my athletic shorts. Not normally an anxious person, this feeling is odd to me. I feel my body tighten, my breathing become labored, and my thoughts race. What's happening to me? Why do I feel dizzy or like I'm going to pass out? Listening for any clues from Monica is debilitating. I want to fix things between us.

Unable to handle the silence on the other end of the line, I beg, "Please talk to me."

"I'm tired, Christian. What do you need from me?" She speaks in a quiet, defeated voice.

She seems unwilling to tell me what's going on, and although I hate to have tension between us, I know I need to respect that and not push. "It's for Sam," I tell her again, hoping that will sweeten the ask.

"I understand that," she firmly replies.

Here goes nothing. My plan is to tell Monica Lucas's plan and hope that she will help me get Sam to his game without Sam knowing it's a special game.

"While we were in New York, I met with Lucas and he asked me to help him with something. He told me what happened between him and Sam and he confessed he was in love with her and miserable without her. He asked me to help him do something that will show Sam how much she means to him," I confess.

"What does he want to do?" she asks.

I give her the details of Lucas's plan.

Monica sighs, and the sweet sound gives me a strange, unfamiliar feeling in my chest. Of course she would see Lucas's request as romantic. What did he call it, a grand gesture or something? I wonder how it'd feel to do something like that for someone I love. In all my life, I haven't ever been in love. Honestly, I'm not sure it's possible for me. If I ever find it, it won't be with the type of women I'd been with over the years. No, if I were ever to make any grand gesture toward a woman, I would aim it directly at Monica. She is the only one I can ever see myself loving. And just the thought of that terrifies me.

"Wow! That is amazing!" Monica gushes, tearing

me from my thoughts. Then she asks in an excited voice, "What do I need to do?"

Glad to hear she's willing to assist with the plan, I launch into the rest of it, filling her in on what I need from her. We talk about Lucas's game and when it is. I tell her I'll need her help to convince Sam to go to that game.

"Wait! How are you keeping this all quiet? How are you managing this monumental news?" she questions.

I laugh, happy that she no longer sounds defeated and dejected. "You're right, it is monumental news, but I took care of keeping it confidential with nondisclosure agreements between all parties involved," I explain.

"Wow. Okay. Do I need to sign one of those now that I know?" she asks.

I lower my voice, trying to sound serious and stern, when I say, "I don't know. Can I can trust you not to tell anyone?" Knowing I'm teasing her, Monica laughs. I smile to myself. It feels good to be talking to her again and to hear her sounding happy. During those few months when I was giving us space, I missed her more than I'm willing to admit. Over the week before we'd gone to New York, I'd called her every night, and we'd talked for hours. I always pretended it was because I was trying to find out who'd hurt Sam, but the truth was, I really enjoyed talking and spending time with her. But no matter what, I can't admit that to her now.

I'm not ready for her to see me so transparently. For her to know the power she holds over me.

"So, I just need to get Sam to the game and you've got everything else covered?"

"Between Lucas and me, we should be good."

"Great! Now just to think of how I'll lure my best friend, who doesn't care about sports, to a hockey game that will only remind her of the guy who broke her heart. Sounds simple enough."

Laughing, I say, "You think? Glad it's your job, not mine."

"I've got this handled." Her confidence is mind-blowing.

As we talk over the ins and outs of how to convince Sam to attend the game, I smile at the relaxed state of our conversation, glad that Monica's words are no longer laced with pain and disdain. Uncertain what that means for us, I shrug off the worry that it won't last or I might fuck it up again. We both avoid talk of New York and what transpired between us afterward. Our conversation lasts longer than I expect, and two hours later, I don't want to hang up, but I have some contracts to review and calls to make before the next day.

Before saying goodbye, we make plans to reconnect the next week. We really don't need to, but I want an excuse to call her. Just talking to her makes me feel energized. It's a feeling I can't explain, no matter how much I try.

* * *

Over the next few weeks, I call Monica often. Even restraining myself so I don't call her every day, despite really wanting to. Even though we discuss our plan ad nauseam, we still find things to talk about for hours. My favorite was when we answered twenty get-to-know-you questions over text one night.

ME

What's your favorite color?

MONICA

Pink. What's yours?

ME

Blue. What's your favorite snack?

MONICA

Chips Ahoy! But you already knew that. How about you?

ME

That's tough. Chips of any kind. What is your favorite type of book to read?

MONICA

I love romance books. How about you?

ME

Romance is not my preference; I like true crime. In your free time, what do you like to do?

MONICA

Spend time with my friends. What do
you do in your free time?

ME

We have the same answer.

Throughout the evening, we gain ground into rekindling our friendship. It feels like we're making strides toward building something more. Just thinking about that more than excites me. She is coming back to me.

At first, she was hesitant, but as time passes, our conversations turn effortless and easy. Every time we talk, it's like coming home. She is becoming so important to me.

Chapter 21

Monica

Christian and I grow closer after he asks me to help him with Lucas's surprise. We talk almost daily about everything and nothing. Rebuilding trust with Christian and rekindling the friendship we'd flirted with before New York starts slowly, but the longer it lasts, the stronger it becomes.

During one of our many conversations, we talk about many things. One day, we end up talking about golf.

"Since you're a sports agent, do you have to love every sport?" I ask.

Christian laughs. "Well, you're a teacher. Do you love every student?"

Smiling, I answer honestly, "Yes, I do."

Though he knows I genuinely do, he ribs me a bit. "Even sneaky Scott or gregarious Gary? How about obnoxious Owen?"

I huff. "Those aren't actual students. I love all my students, warts and everything."

"Yeah, I know you do. Just teasing. And to answer your question, yes, I love all sports, but of course I have my favorites: hockey, football, basketball, and golf."

"Golf? Really? Don't tell me you're secretly eighty, you love wearing plaid, and playing in sand pits."

Christian snickers. "It's called a sand trap, not a pit. I hate plaid, and I am definitely not eighty."

"Well, promise me you'll never take me golfing. I couldn't swing a club to save my life."

"Ever played miniature golf?" he asks.

"Nope."

"You're kidding, right? Everyone's at least played a round of mini golf or putt-putt in their life."

"Not once," I answer.

Christian scoffs. "Then you know what we're going to do? We're going to play a round. Are you game?"

Trying to sound serious, I reply, "I'm ready, coach. Put me in."

"You're ridiculous. But we are so doing this. I'll teach you everything you need to know." His firm voice is so commanding, and it doesn't leave any room to question, only believe.

Driving up to Putter's Haven, my panic sets in. Things are getting real. Swallowing down my nerves, I force a smile.

"Are you ready?" Christian asks with a smirk on his face.

Crossing my arms across my chest and rolling my eyes, I answer, "Sure. It doesn't look too hard."

When we approach the first hole, Christian lines up his ball and squats down. What's he doing? It's confusing. Peering at him, I'm not sure. Maybe he's giving his ball a pep talk? I'd once stumbled across the Masters on TV, and even the professional golfers were doing something similar. Maybe it's a thing. I don't know.

When he stands back up, he aligns himself with his ball and takes a practice swing before he hits it for real. His golf ball travels down the green, avoiding the obstacles, and moves rapidly toward the hole where it disappears inside. "Hole in one!" he shouts as he leaps in the air, performing some kind of ninja jump

He's ridiculous, but he makes me laugh. "Nice job, Tiger." His grin stretches wide across his handsome face. After he retrieves his ball from the hole, he steps aside to give me a turn. Setting my ball in no particular way, I swing my club in the hole's direction—*Thwack!*—hoping my ball will travel where it's supposed to. My hit isn't too powerful because I've never played before. I don't want to over-hit it and send my ball flying across the course.

I'm disappointed when I see my ball only traveled a few inches from me.

"Nice hit!" Christian calls out.

"Yeah, sure," I mumble to myself.

Stepping up behind me, he aligns his body with mine. "Here, let me help." Placing his hands on my hips, he positions me, lining me up with the hole. It's difficult to focus with his front pressed to my back, and I feel the heat between our bodies. I want to snuggle into it. Unintentionally, I wiggle my hips and rub up against something hard. *Oh my!*

Christian growls, "On this next turn, hit it the same as before, just a bit harder." Nodding my head, I line up again and strike the ball, sending it flying right off of the green.

"Oops." I cringe.

Christian pulls me close and laughs. "Wow. Didn't realize I was playing putt-putt with Wonder Woman."

"Har, har," I call to him while I march over to collect my ball. "What now?"

"Want to take a drop?" he asks. What is he talking about? About now, I'd like to drop him.

Scowling, I complain, "A what? I don't speak golf, Christian."

He shakes his head. "Never mind. We'll just start on the next hole. Do you want to go first this time?"

"Sure. Want to help me again?" I suggest.

Again, he steps up behind me and adjusts my hips. His firm touch sends tingles up my spine. To position my grip on the club, he runs his hands up and down my arms, making sure they're straight and squared. His hands are warm and gentle but firm and resolute. And I like it.

That hole goes well enough. I manage to get it in the hole in five hits. Hell, I'm not complaining. At the beginning of each hole, Christian lines me up. The snug feel of his body against mine is driving my libido insane. When he steps away from me so I can swing, I have to repress the urge to moan. The end of eighteen holes can't come fast enough. If it doesn't, I might from all the sexual tension coursing through my body.

Thankfully, the rest of the course goes well. I definitely lost... by a lot, but we had a great time together.

During all this time we are spending together, whether it's over the phone or in person, it's hard not to assume it means anything. I try not to develop butterflies in my stomach every time he invites me out for a meal or something else. Actually, self-pep talks about Christian and his playboy ways are something I've become practiced in the more our relationship progresses. I have to remind myself that we are friends only. To protect myself, I can't allow myself to believe it's anything else. No matter how hard that is. And it borders on impossible.

It's October finally, and the night of Lucas's game has arrived. We get Samantha to the arena without too much convincing. Watching her reaction to everything that'd been planned is magical.

As I sit next to Christian in the arena, our thighs touching and his heat warming me, it's hard not to wish that someday I could have that. Understanding that he'll probably not be that man for me, I know I need to examine all the other possibilities available.

Over the last five years, Christian has remained at the forefront of my romantic interests despite all that we'd gone through. No other man I've met has ever compared to him, but how long am I willing to wait? Watching my best friend find her HEA, I think maybe it's time for me to find my own. More than once, I'd heard Christian say that he was never settling down, so I know continuing to lust after him is just plain stupid.

After the game, we all wait in the players' tunnel for Lucas. Christian introduces Samantha and me to Lucas's mom, and she's amazing. It's tough not to be slightly jealous of my best friend. Here she has an amazingly sexy man who just pulled off a grand gesture to top all grand gestures, and he has an incredible mother who not only seems like she would be the best mother-in-law but a friend too. Samantha has it all, and I'm so happy for her. Someday I hope I'll find mine too.

Exhausted from all the excitement of the surprise and ensuring it happened without hiccups, I lean against the brick wall, trying to hide my incessant yawning. Christian approaches, rubs my back, and quietly asks, "Are you tired?" Another yawn hits and I cover my mouth with my hand and nod my answer. "Thank goodness it's Friday and I can sleep in tomorrow."

Christian nods, whispering, "We can leave as soon as Lucas comes out."

When Lucas enters the tunnel, the love he has for Samantha is palpable. Honestly, I'm ecstatic for my friend. I just want a little piece of romantic happiness for myself. Focusing on my feet rather than the reunited couple makes the sadness I feel for myself a little less overwhelming. *One day you'll have that.* I remind myself. Following official introductions to Lucas, where I lay down my *hurt her and I'll kill you* look. We leave the lovebirds in the hallway and head to Christian's SUV with Momma Bouchard in tow.

We drop her off first, since she's staying in the suburbs and both Christian and I live in the city. While we drive back toward the city limits, I try to stay awake, but the lull of the car rocks me to sleep. When we pull up to my apartment building, Christian gently wakes me up. Leaning over, I give him a hug, as it has become customary for us as we've grown closer. Christian hugs me extra tight, which is not his norm, and it strikes me as odd. It feels like one you'd give someone you don't plan on seeing for an extended period. Feeling that is silly, right? I mean, we haven't planned anything, and now that Lucas's surprise is over, we probably won't talk all the time. But we aren't saying goodbye, are we?

Confused, I pull back and lock eyes with him. His gaze is clouded, and I wonder why. Not big about sharing feelings, I don't know how to ask him what's going on. Do I come out and just say how I feel? Will I sound crazy? Unsure, I do nothing. We've gotten so close lately. He wouldn't walk away from that, would he?

Yes. Yes, he would. And just like before, he does it again with no explanation. For several months, I allow myself to be hurt by his actions. Angry with myself for trusting him yet again, I funnel my energy into my job, setting up an after-school tutoring program that is getting rave reviews in our district. No longer am I happy sitting by the sidelines; I'm making things happen now.

After I successfully dissolve my ill-placed crush on Christian, I go after what I want. With some friends I made at yoga, I visit clubs in the city and spend many of my weekends dancing the night away. Before long, I meet a fun group of twenty-somethings who are single and ready to mingle. Just like me.

The weekend before spring break, I go out with some of my clubbing friends to a newly renovated club that is supposed to be packed with athletes and A-listers. Not thinking about the clientele, I wonder if I'll get a chance to rub elbows with someone famous. Maybe share a dance or score an invitation to the VIP section.

About an hour after arriving, and spending most of that time on the dance floor, I am beyond hot and tired. Sneaking off to the bathroom to splash cold water on my face sounds exquisite. When I emerge from the bathroom, as I'm straightening my necklace, I walk right into an incredibly well-defined chest.

"Sorry," I say, while stepping back. A large hand attached to a very tattooed, well-muscled forearm reaches out and grabs my wrist, halting me.

"It's no problem," an extremely handsome man says as he steps closer, eating up the space between us. Right away, a crisp but not overly obnoxious, pine-tinged scent surrounds me. I feel like I'm standing in the middle of the forest. Sucking in a deep breath, I force myself to relax.

Looking up, I notice the man is considerably taller than me, even in my heels. He is thick, but not fat. More solid and sturdy. Seeing that, I assume he is either a professional athlete or in the special ops of the military. He has a strong jawline and piercing blue eyes that captivate me. His chin-length dirty blond hair isn't scraggily or unkept, making me settle on his athlete status. Clothed in tailored black suit pants and a luxurious short-sleeved button-up, I assume he's wealthy too. Understanding my place, I again apologize and search for an easy exit. However, Tarzan—that's what I decide to call him—has other plans.

"Why don't you join me and some friends in the VIP section? Or do you have a boyfriend to get back to?" he says.

Dumbfounded, I can't imagine why I'm being invited to the VIP section. Sure, I'd been there before when my friend Chelsea had been invited and she'd drug me along, but tonight she is nowhere to be found and the invitation is solely mine.

With my wrist still in his grasp, I pull myself closer to him and seductively answer, "Sounds fun. And no boyfriend for me."

Tarzan's eyes go wide, and he licks his lips before he drops his voice and says, "Lucky me."

His large hand remains wrapped around my wrist as he leads me to the VIP section. As we pass the two large bouncers, both nod to me and I smile. I can't believe where I am. My friends are likely still gyrating on the dance floor, none the wiser about my current situation.

Tarzan leads me over to a rounded couch in the room's corner, and I note the hungry eyes of many skimpily dressed women following his movements and glaring at me. Letting me go, we settle next to each other and he tugs me close. A waitress approaches and takes our drink orders; a scotch for him and a seltzer with lemon for me.

Leaning into him, I can't fight the magnetism I feel. "What's your name, beautiful?" he murmurs seductively, and I laugh nervously. *Is that his standard line?*

"It's Monica. What's yours?" He gives me a smile that screams, *you should know*. Only, I don't, so I shrug.

His eyes show his shock. "Really? You don't know who I am?" he questions in a surprised tone.

Embarrassed, I shake my head. "Truth? I don't. I just thought you were incredibly handsome." A deep-throated laugh falls from his sexy lips, bringing the room's attention to us. His warm hand patting my thigh sends tingles rushing to my core.

He leans in closer and whispers against my ear, "Luuckyy mee." Dragging out each letter is beyond sexy and gives me shivers. Relaxing back, he crosses his heel over his knee and grins. I'm confused and rather curious, as he still hasn't given me his name. The waitress returns with our drinks, and while she drops them off, I glance around the section. Some patrons look familiar, but I honestly couldn't name them. I'm confident I've seen them on the television or in magazines.

Looking back at Tarzan, I ask, "Well?"

"Well, what?" he answers with a smirk on his face.

Sliding closer so our bodies are against each other, I place my hand on his muscular forearm, squeeze, and lean in. "Are you going to tell me who you are? The suspense is killing me."

A megawatt smile appears across his lips, reaching

toward his high cheekbones, and he suggests, "How about we play a game instead?"

Intrigued, I let my eyes peruse his entire body, noting how fit he is. He's definitely an athlete. Feeling bold, I reply in a sultry voice as I lay my hand high on his thigh, "What type of game? What are we playing for?"

Shifting in his seat to turn more fully toward me, my hand moves and brushes against his lap. His lap that contains a very large, firm cock. *Had I done that to him?*

Tarzan takes my hand, which is dwarfed by his, and places it back on his thigh, higher than it was, and leaves his hand resting on top. Heat radiates between us, and it feels like everyone around us has disappeared. My body pulses with excitement and I want things that normally would make me blush.

During those crazy few weeks of my freshman year at NYU, I'd done some things that were completely out of character for me. Most of them because I was too tipsy to make good choices, and I'd suddenly found myself free from adult supervision. Right now, though, I am completely sober and wanting to walk on the wild side with this complete stranger. Fantasies of hot, heady hookups flash through my mind, making my panties wet with desire. *Can he sense that?*

Looking up into his emerald green eyes, I see they are full of lust. Testing that, I slide my hand farther up his thigh and a low growl comes from him as he tightens his hand around mine. Goose bumps cover my feverish skin.

"Want to get out of here?" he mumbles.

I can only nod my head in response. He keeps hold of my hand and stands up, swiping it past his hard, throbbing cock, and I suck in a breath while trying to steady myself on my strappy heels. His other hand comes up to my shoulder to steady me, and I melt into his touch. Just as we're heading out of the VIP section, someone steps in front of me.

But I don't register who it is because my body buzzes with anticipation for what fun Tarzan and I are going to do. I can't wait to see him naked or to trace his incredible muscles. With. My. Tongue. An angry-looking Christian blocks my way as I try to leave the club with Tarzan. Lost in the thought of doing scandalous things, I barely hear the growl directed at me. "Where do you think you're going?"

My head whips up. *Excuse me?* "Christia...." His name dies on my lips. Why is he here?

Tarzan's grip on my hand falters. "Is Christian your boyfriend or something?" he asks.

Dumbfounded, I stare at him, then squeak out, "You know Christian?"

Tarzan nods. "He's my agent. How do you know him? Is he your boyfriend?"

Again, I look at him, then at Christian, who has a busty blonde suctioned to him, and then back to Tarzan. Motioning to Christian and his plus one, I growl, "Obviously, I'm not his girlfriend, or why would he be here with her?"

Tarzan looks to Christian, gives him a chin lift, mouths *"She's hot,"* then turns back to me and says, "Okay. Ready to get out of here, babe?" *Pig. I am standing right here.*

Before I can even react, Christian responds by touching my elbow and issuing a warning growl that is thick with a threat. "Monica, don't."

Tarzan reaches out for me, again asking me to join him.

Appalled, I step back from both men. Apparently, they both want to claim me; one for the night and the other... who the fuck knows what Christian is thinking?

Just wanting a night of fun, not the bullshit it has quickly turned into, I move toward the exit, alone, anger dripping from me. When I'm steps away, I hear Tarzan mutter, "What a waste. Bet she would've been a good lay." Then I hear a scuffle, and I move even more quickly away from the VIP section.

Finding the friends I came with is easier than I expected. They're still dancing in the same spot I'd left them in earlier. Whispering to Dakota that I'm leaving, she gives me a hug and makes me promise I'll show for yoga on Tuesday night. "That's the plan," I shout, trying to speak over the booming dance music.

Within minutes, I reach the front doors, and I can finally escape the drama of this night. *Where does he get off? What is his problem? Whatever it is, he needs to get the fuck over it.* Christian had no right to react that way. What an asshole. I don't know why it surprises me. Repeatedly, he shows me just who he is: an egotistical asshat. It doesn't make sense. He doesn't want me with anyone else and he doesn't want me for himself. I lose either way and he gets control over me. No, thank you. "No more," I tell myself.

A large, warm hand wraps around my bicep, effectively stopping me.

"Get your hands off me," I shout to whoever grabbed me. Spinning around to remove their hand, I see it's Christian.

"What do you want, Christian?" I growl at him, already tired of the bullshit that went down in the VIP section.

The tight grip on my arm loosens, and I lock eyes with the man who ghosted me twice after I'd assumed something was happening between us.

Focused on his shoes as if they are the hottest thing out there, he mutters, "I'm sorry, Monica. I couldn't let you go home with Aaron. He's a playboy. Has a new girl every night. I want better for you, so I had to step in and say something."

His confession is convenient, and I'm not sure it's all the truth. It feels like he's hiding something. After all, when he described Aaron, didn't he recognize the similarities to himself? It doesn't matter. Christian has no say in what I do with my life or my body. His opinion isn't of any concern any longer.

Pulling my arm free from his light hold, I step away from him. "Go back to your own hookup and don't worry about mine," I spit out, then stomp off into the night.

It's still warm as I wait outside the club for my Lyft to arrive. Christian's behavior was inexcusable and makes my blood boil. Where does he get off? He isn't my protector. I don't see why it matters to him anyway. He had me. For years. I'd given him all my attention, and he walked away and ghosted me. Not once, but twice. The third time would not be the charm. The saying of fool me once, shame on you, fool me twice, shame on me, holds true. I am the epitome of a fool.

Driving back to my apartment with Lincoln, the Lyft driver, I feel like I'm suffocating. The city is closing in around me and I need to get out. Pulling up a group chat with my brothers, I type a simple message.

ME

Coming home tomorrow for spring break. Don't tell Mom and Dad. I want to surprise them.

JOSIAH

Are you really coming home? What happened?

MIKE

Leave her alone. While you're home,
can you watch the kids so I can take
Maddy out on a date?

JOSIAH

Mike, I just watched them last week
so you could have a date. Greedy
SOB. Let our sister have a break.

MIKE

Josiah, shut up. If she doesn't want
to watch her incredibly cute and
sweet nieces for one night so I can
wine and dine my exhausted and
stressed wife, she doesn't have to.

ME

Yes, Mike, I'll watch Addie and Hazel
so you and Maddy can have a
night out.

JOSIAH

Don't let him bully you, Mo.

ME

It's fine, Josiah. It'll be an excellent
distraction.

JOSIAH

Distraction? What do you need a
distraction from?

WILL

Am I too late to ask for babysitting
help too?

ME

Nope. I got you. How's Trevor feeling?
Kayla told me he's been teething.

WILL

He's teething alright. Those molars
are no joke. Doctor said at his
checkup, he's cutting them early, but
maybe that'll be a good thing. Get
them out of the way.

ME

Yes, definitely.

WILL

Hey, Mo. Thanks for watching him. I
appreciate it.

ME

No worries. You know I love kids,
especially my nieces and nephew.

JOSIAH

Mo. Answer my question.

ME

See you tomorrow. Remember, don't
tell Mom or Dad.

I can't answer Josiah's question right now, but I suspect he'll make me once I see him in person. I'll just pretend I didn't see it.

Once in my apartment, I set my alarm for the butt crack of dawn, strip off the dress I wore to the club, kick off my heels, and brush my teeth before climbing into bed.

Six a.m. comes way too early after staying out until two, but it isn't anything an extra-large cup of bold coffee won't fix. Tossing some clothes into a tote, I text

Sam to tell her I'll be at the farm for the next week, then I pull on some clothes and my favorite Chucks.

While waiting in the drive-thru line of the coffee shop, I flip through the radio, trying to find something to listen to for the drive. US Country 99.5 catches my attention with Tyler Hubbard's song "5 foot 9." There is something about country music that makes me feel grounded. It reflects real life and lets me know I'm not alone in my mistakes.

It's tough not to groan when the barista hands me the steaming hot cup of heavenly nectar. Running it under my nose so I can inhale the rich scent of roasted beans is the instant pick-me-up my weary body needs.

Hours later, and after a few bathroom breaks, I pull into the driveway of my family's farm. Field Farms is proudly on display, with a hand-painted wooden sign that instantly brings a smile to my face. So many of my favorite memories are from this land. Land that has been in my family for generations. Pulling past the metal gates I'd spent hours swinging on as a child makes me grateful I hadn't gone too far from home when I moved to Chicago.

Three honks on my horn announce my arrival. It's how my family always says hello or goodbye. The front door to the house flies open as I'm parking my car. My mom drops the kitchen towel she'd been holding and rushes down the stairs with our family's aged Labrador, Ollie, at her heels. Before I can even get the door open, my dad is there, smiling wide, proud that he got to me before my mom.

Shutting off the car, I hear a loud whistle. My dad's called my brothers. Before long, Mike, Will, and Josiah saunter out of the barn. My family is the best. They literally dropped everything for me.

After many hugs where I am lifted off the ground, my mom shoos everyone away before she pulls me in for a hug of her own. No matter what ails me, her hugs always give me just what I need. Maybe that's why I ran to the farm after my exchange with Christian last night. I needed the chance to recenter myself, and this is the only place I feel truly comfortable doing that.

"Hi, Mom," I whisper. "Is it okay I'm here?"

"Heaven's, child. Of course it is. You are always welcome." Mom pulls back and looks me over as if she's expecting to identify what's wrong, why I came back to the farm unexpectedly. She's like a bloodhound. Kathy Fields could sniff out the truth, no matter how well you camouflaged it. More than once when I was growing up, she'd caught me in a white lie and the consequences had been stiff. But this is different. I'm not lying about something I'd done. I'm home tending to my broken heart, that no matter what, refuses to heal properly.

I'd been working on it over the summer, too, and when I'd returned to the city in the fall, I'd sworn I'd built up sturdy walls around my heart. But Christian breached my carefully constructed barriers with little effort. And I was stupid enough to let him. *Will I ever learn?*

Grabbing my bag from the back seat, we make small talk while walking arm in arm toward the house. Ollie nudges me with his nose, scooting me along. The smell of freshly baked bread wafts through the ragged screen door, and my stomach growls.

"Hungry, sugar?" Mom asks while pulling the door open.

Ollie pushes past me and curls up on his dog bed with his favorite toy—a stuffed elephant we named Ellie. Before I can set my tote by the stairs, he's already snoring. It's adorable.

The oven timer dings and Mom pulls two loaves of white bread from the oven. The loaves are golden brown and make soft crackling sounds when they come into contact with the air in the room.

"Is that for lunch?" I ask, licking my lips.

"It is. The boys wanted stew and homemade bread for lunch, so that's what they're getting."

Laughing, I reply, "They don't know how good they have it, Mom. You spoil them."

She smiles at me and matter-of-factly says, "I'd spoil you, too, if you were here." I nod my head, knowing what she says is true. But I didn't want to live on the farm like my brothers did. I want to do my own thing, spread my wings beyond this little plot of land.

"Want any coffee, tea, or lemonade? Did you eat any breakfast before you got on the road?" Mom asks.

"I grabbed coffee on my way out of the city, but I'd love some lemonade."

Grabbing a glass and filling it full of the tart beverage, she brings it over to the table with a blueberry muffin she pulled from a Tupperware container. My stomach growls again as I unwrap the muffin and take a healthy bite. "Delicious. Thank you."

As she wipes counters, cleans dishes, and stirs lunch in the crock pot, she asks simple questions about teaching and tutoring, Samantha, and what else I've been busy with since we last talked a few weeks ago. Once we exhaust all her questions and she catches me up on farm life and the trouble my brothers have been cooking up, she pours another cup of coffee for herself and joins me at the table.

"Honey, tell me why you really came home." See. Bloodhound, like I said.

Shifting in my chair, my body suddenly feels overheated, so I pull my sweatshirt off, hoping that'll cool me down. No luck. Unable to make eye contact, I lower my gaze to my glass and stare at the perspiration that covers it. "I just needed to get out of the city." There. A half-truth is better than a full lie, right?

"Why? Are you in some kind of trouble?"

I laugh because, honestly, the thought of me in trouble is definitely amusing. I shake my head no. "I just needed some space from someone." Mom's eyes go from stern inquisitor to compassionate friend in a moment. She understands without all the details.

"Is this the same person you were trying to get over this summer?"

Shocked she knows so much, I scramble to come up with an answer that serves dual purposes. That's telling, but not too telling. "Yes, but I'm not ready to talk about it. Can I ask a question, though?"

"Sure, sweetie. You can ask me anything." Then she reaches out and grabs my hand, giving it a squeeze.

Taking a moment, I slowly ask, "Last summer… How did you know I was trying to get over someone?"

Mom squeezes my hand again and then looks at me as if she's hiding something.

"Mom, tell me."

"I overheard you talking to Josiah one night after you'd both assumed I'd gone to bed. You sounded heartbroken, and it killed me listening to you, but I knew I needed to stay out of it. So, I did."

Pulling her into a hug, I let it all go. All my hurt, anger, rejection, disappointment, grief, and regret. *This is painful. Love isn't supposed to be this hard. It is if it's with the wrong person or at the wrong time, though.*

Still not wanting to give up on Christian, I set my feelings for him on hold. They're too messy to sort through in one morning over a cup of coffee with my mom. Most likely I'll sift through them by myself while decimating a package of Chips Ahoy!. Plus, I still need to calm down after the events of last night. Having another man's attention feels amazing, and that's something I longed for, but it wouldn't be fair to another person to pursue something with them while I'm still harboring unresolved feelings for Christian. My dream that Christian is going to wake up one morning after realizing he's been in love with me for years will never happen. If he ever admits to having feelings for me, it will be a struggle on his part, one that I'll either have to accept and endure or reject and walk away from, for good. I'm not sure which sounds less painful.

Just as I dry the tears from my cheeks, the screen door slams, telling us the lunch crowd is on the way. On weekends, my family does all the farm chores while our staff is off. Sure, it makes for long days, but we appreciate all our employees, and we want to keep them around instead of overworking them and driving them away. So, on Saturday and Sunday, Mom cooks extra-hearty meals.

Saturday on the farm keeps me busy and distracted. Early in the day, I help my mom make rolls for dinner. By late afternoon, I'm pulling on my Xtratuf's and heading outside to help.

Will and I bottle feed the calves while Mike works on feeding all the others. Dad does maintenance and repair in the milking parlor. We're all so busy that we only know it's dinner time when Mom rings a cowbell from the front porch. Probably sounds cliché, but that's what we've always done.

Dropping our muddy boots at the door, we wash up before heading to the dinner table. My sisters-in-law and my nieces and nephew are there, so it's great to catch up. Once we finish dinner, we head back out to milk the cows again.

By ten o'clock, I'm exhausted and barely able to brush my teeth before falling asleep. The next day goes much the same, and it feels great to be back home with my family. Here, I don't have to worry about anything. I can busy myself with chores and farm duties.

Following dinner that night while Mike, Will, and Dad go out to milk the ladies again, Josiah and I take a walk. Seeing that it's March, it's still pretty bland and desolate, no wildflowers for me to pick. When we're far enough from the house, he turns to me and asks, "Mo, why did you really come home?"

Feeling ashamed and confused, I answer, "It's difficult to explain." He reaches over and stops me, forcing me to look at him. "What's difficult? Is this about a guy? That one you've loved for years but he remains clueless?"

When I was home this summer, Josiah and I spent a lot of time together. Neither one of us was responsible for daily farm chores, so we often snuck off together in the evenings to walk and talk. It was during these talks that he confessed how scared he'd been with his cancer diagnosis and everything that came after it. He confided in me and I did the same, telling him all about Christian without giving him his name. Even though I'd told him what happened, I didn't want him to have that one detail. My family knows Christian. Over the years, they've seen him and spent some time with the entire Fox family. It felt like my sharing my hurt feelings might cloud his—my entire family's—good impression of him, and I didn't want that.

"Yeah. It's about him again." Kicking rocks on the dirt path, I blow out a frustrated breath. I don't understand why I feel such a potent attraction to Christian and why I simply can't get over him. To the outsider looking at it, I probably seem pathetic, which is exactly how I'm feeling.

"Want to talk about it?" Josiah offers in his deep, smooth voice.

I really don't, so I shake my head, ending the discussion. The newest hurt is so recent and I'm not sure I can handle rehashing it yet.

We walk in silence, both lost in our own thoughts, neither of us wanting to share. When we arrive back at the house, it's quiet and we both slip inside silently.

At the top of the stairs, before pulling me into a hug, Josiah says, "You know, Mo, I'm here for you, whenever or whatever you need." Feeling emotional and about to cry, I just nod against his chest. Pushing me down the hallway toward my childhood bedroom is his answer for the heavy moment.

The next morning, I wake up feeling a little lighter. The weight of my feelings for Christian is still there, but the stranglehold they had on me when I arrived has lifted some. Needing to move my body, I decide to start my day with yoga.

Chapter 22

Christian

Watching Monica storm out of the club the other night shredded me, but there was no way I was going to let her leave with Aaron. Sure, he's a nice enough guy and an excellent client, but he made my status as a playboy laughable. He'd been drafted to the Chicago Falcons, the city's professional football team, two years ago, and he's living the life of a celebrity in every imaginable way. Fast cars, booze, women. Thank fuck he's avoided bad press so far, but I'm sure that won't last forever, especially if he continues down the same path. It's always the same with these guys. They get their million-dollar contracts, and with it, the ability to make good decisions disappears.

* * *

Considering Monica is pissed at me, my arrival at her family's farm to beg her forgiveness probably borders on insane. But here I am. Last night as I sat in my condo for the second night in a row, considering Monica and my feelings for her, I realized I couldn't deny any longer that she means something to me. Defining us and what I want isn't anything I'm ready for, though.

After the past few months, where I'd purposefully avoided her—again—her absence from my life has been painfully noticeable. However, I still can't define why that is. I'm afraid. Like putting it into words makes it real. The only thing I know for sure is that I want her in my life. Ignoring my unresolved feelings for her has become unmanageable, as is evidenced by the way I behaved at the club. Ashamed, I offered to take Veronika, my blind date for the evening, home. But she opted to stay at the club while I tucked my tail between my legs and ran home.

At about nine on Sunday morning, I couldn't handle the uneasy feelings coursing through my body anymore. I needed to apologize to Monica for what happened. Only problem was, I didn't have a plan. In conversation with Samantha on Saturday afternoon, she'd mentioned that Monica had gone to the farm unexpectedly. I knew it was because of me and what happened Friday night. I'd embarrassed her unnecessarily. And for what? To save her or me?

I could admit to only myself that as long as I've known Monica, I've never handled our relationship correctly. In fact, if I give it too much thought, I find my behavior deplorable. Monica is worthy of so much more, and because I can't figure out what she means to me, I instead act like an asshole. Repeatedly.

My penance has come due, and as I drive up the driveway to the Fields Farm, I hope I haven't lost her forever. If I did, it's my own damn fault and something I'll have to deal with for the rest of my life. Even if I can't define what she means to me, I know it's important and critical to my future.

Until now, I've never been to a farm, and there is so much to see. To my left are acres of land dotted with cows as far as the eye can see. A stereotypical red barn sits on one side of the property and a house sits on the other. There is an oak tree with a tire swing out front of the house and a large empty garden space situated to the side of it.

Spotting Monica's car, I pull mine in behind. After all, I don't want to block anyone. I packed a few outfits and made reservations at the nearby Motel 6, in case my apology goes better than I expect.

Looking next to the house, I see a woman doing yoga. She must have headphones in because she doesn't know I'm only a few feet from her. She stands up in the only yoga pose I know, the tree pose, and I realize it's Monica. As I sit in my car, gathering my courage, my eyes hungrily roam over every curve she has on full display in her magenta yoga pants. Willing my body to control itself, I push open my door and am greeted by three large men. Each is over six feet tall and covered in muscles. Two are dressed in dirty jeans and t-shirts that say Fields Farm. The other guy, who looks vaguely familiar, is slightly less bulky, wears clean clothes and a backward ball cap as he stares at me. Each of them wears a matching scowl that would make me shit myself if I wasn't so fucking terrified. *Should I get back in my car and forget Monica?* It might be smart if I have to go through these three to get to her.

Intimidated and scared, I swipe my sweaty hands on my designer jeans and then step forward with my hand extended. *Am I about to get my ass kicked?* Probably so, but I deserve it. The way I've treated Monica is horrible, and I need to rectify that. So if this is how it has to be done, so be it.

Before our standoff can end with me broken and bloody, a high-pitched whistle draws our attention. My eyes track over to where it came from and there she stands. The woman of my dreams, arms crossed, the same scowl of the giants standing in front of me gracing her lips. *Wait. Are these her brothers?* Oh shit, I am totally getting my ass kicked.

"Guys, leave him alone," Monica hollers across the drive.

"You know him?" the biggest one asks in a gruff tone.

Monica nods, grabs her phone from the grass, pulls her earphones out, and slowly saunters over, prolonging my fear.

"You do too. It's Christian Fox. Remember, you met him a few times while I was at NYU. He's Samantha's brother?"

When she reaches us, she glares at me and then points to her brothers. "Christian, this is Mike, Will, and Josiah, my older brothers. Welcome to our farm. Now, why are you here? Is Sam okay?" She flips her phone open to see if she missed any messages.

Nervous, I answer, "Sam's fine. I talked to her yesterday. I'm here for you." She sucks in a breath and her eyes go comically wide. Her brothers all growl, and immediately I want to hurl myself into my car and speed out of their drive like I'm channeling Dale Earnhardt, Jr.

Continuing to look at Monica while keeping her brothers and their fists in my peripheral view, I mouth, *"Can we talk in private?"*

Nodding at my request, she turns to her brothers and says, "Don't you guys have things to do? We have officially welcomed Christian to the farm. I'm going to show him around. You might see him later. Maybe next time, try to be less growly. Okay?"

Then she grabs my arm and pulls me away,

muttering under her breath. Her brothers return to their duties just as Monica leads me toward the front of the house.

"This is where you grew up?" I ask, looking around.

She nods, and I can't believe how beautiful she is. A natural beauty. No one I've ever met comes close in comparison, so why can't I just admit that aloud? What would it hurt?

Despite doing yoga daily, it surprises me that Monica still looks like a tightly coiled spring.

"Christian, why are you here?"

Kicking my feet at the ground, I run through the verbal argument I've had on repeat since learning she ran off to the farm. Looking up, I cringe when I see disdain staring back at me. A quick check-in with myself reminds me that my need to make a genuine apology and plead for Monica's forgiveness outweighs my fear of her, and so I spoke. "I came here to apologize in person."

She waves her hand at me. "It's fine, Christian. You really didn't need to drive out here for that. For me." She turns her body away from me, as if she doesn't want me to hear that last part.

Grabbing her hip, I turn her back to me, lift her chin so we make eye contact, and continue on with my apology. "Yes. I did. From the first time we met, I've screwed this up, and I've hurt you again and again."

I finally realize what I've done. Problem is, I don't

know why I did it. Or did I and I'm just afraid to admit it? But why now? Am I scared? Samantha always threatened me, saying that I'd find no one better for me than Monica and I needed to wake up and do something about it before she got fed up with me and walked away. Is that what's happening? Is that why she came to the farm? Fear sits heavy in my gut. Shifting nervously, I release her hip from my palm and step back, giving her space. Today isn't about formalizing anything, it's about apologizing, forgiving, and moving forward. That's if she is willing to do that.

"I'm so sorry, Monica. It's taken me too long to see all the ways I've hurt you, and I feel terrible about that. And because of it, you've kept your distance and probably hate me."

Monica looks at me with tear-filled eyes that crush me. "I never hated you," she admits, and I breathe a sigh of relief. Until she adds on, "That would have been easier and was the opposite of what I'd been feeling." The words, *I'd been*, strike me like a well-wielded weapon, sharp and precise. Past tense. Does that mean she doesn't have feelings for me anymore? Did I miss my opportunity? My head falls as the realization of her statement registers. Should I walk away, leave her alone, do my best to move on? Not that it would be possible. Every time I spend any time with her, it hits me all over again just how incredible she is. There isn't anyone else like her and there never will be.

"Okay," is all I can say as I turn back toward my

car, feeling destroyed. When I'm a few steps away, overwhelmed with my chaotic thoughts and emotions, something occurs to me. I'll be a coward if I don't make it right and tell her the truth. Determined to fix it, I whip back around, hopeful. "Monica," I start.

She steps closer, interrupting me and asks, "Why did you really come out here?"

Making eye contact, I whisper, "Truth?" She just nods.

God, she has incredible eyes. I could stare into them for hours. Shaking my head clear, I tear down the last remaining wall. "The truth is, I'm afraid of losing you. What happens when you decide it's too much—*I'm* too much—and you walk away? Until now, I've always known you were there, and I took that for granted, treating you poorly instead of cherishing you, and I'm sorry for that. I can't tell you all that I'm feeling because, honestly, I don't know. But I know you are my favorite person, and the thought of you not being around anymore slays me." There. I've poured out my heart to her. Now I just have to wait for her response. And waiting is terrifying.

Stunned by my confession, Monica's lips move but no sound escapes, confusing me. Pulling her closer, I wrap my arms around her, tentatively at first, gauging her reaction. When I feel her arms circle around me, I squeeze tighter. It's anyone's guess how long we stand like that. Finally having her in my arms feels amazing.

I've wanted to touch her since meeting her six years ago. Her hand moves up my chest and taps me. Pulling back, I gaze into her eyes and they aren't full of tears anymore. They're bright and sparkly. "What now?" she asks.

Chapter 23

Monica

When I started my day, Christian was the last person I expected to see, but here he is. *For me.* Apologizing.

Words I never imagined hearing from Christian suddenly fill the air as he confesses his feelings for me. Sure, they're scattered and somewhat unidentifiable, but they're more than he's ever given me before.

My heart is exploding. *What does it all mean?* Christian doesn't do relationships. Which is a shame, because I have a feeling it isn't just chemistry between us. There's something more. I just don't know if he knows that.

Just as I ask him what happens now, Mom rings the bell for lunch, not allowing time for him to answer.

Sighing at her poor timing, I look at Christian and ask, "Would you like to stay for lunch?"

"I'd love to," he replies with a grin.

Leading him into the house, I call out to Mom to let her know we have a guest. Mom adores the Fox family, so it thrills her that Christian dropped by.

Lunch is beyond uncomfortable, as my brothers continue to scowl at Christian. Their protective nature is appreciated, but I'm not a little girl anymore, so it isn't necessary.

That afternoon I show Christian around the farm, introducing him to the new babies we have and exploring our hundred acres. More than once, I cringe as he declines my offer of muck boots. On his feet are a pair of stark white, uncreased, Air Jordan Air Force 1s. I know they'll be filthy in no time, but he doesn't seem bothered by that.

As we move through the farm, with me showing him all the different areas of operations, he seems genuinely interested, asking pointed questions of me. Doing my best to answer him, I explain what I know. Then I get a great idea.

"Are you headed back to the city tonight?" I ask him, hopeful his answer is no.

Shaking his head, he replies, "No, I took the rest of this week off in case my visit went well. Is that okay? I have a reservation at the Motel 6 in the nearby town."

"You can stay here. We have empty bedrooms in the house because my two oldest brothers are married," I offer.

He scratches his head as if he's weighing the

options. He looks at me and hesitantly asks, "Your parents wouldn't mind?"

I give him a bright smile. "They'd definitely be okay with it. But they'll ask you to help with some farm chores. Are you up for that?"

Looking down at his outfit, he laughs. "Have any clothes I could borrow? I didn't quite pack for farm work."

"I bet Josiah has some clothes you could use. I could show you what he does on the farm. It's much cleaner and something you might better relate to."

Leading him up to the dairy's office, we walk close, our hands brushing, sending tingles coursing through my body. My fingers long to wrap around his, to feel the warmth and comfort he'd offer.

In mere steps, we reach Josiah's office. Knocking on his door, Christian stands a step behind me, placing his hand on my back. Heat travels from his touch and sets my body on fire with desire. Goose bumps appear and my nipples harden. Looking down, I pray my thick black sports bra covers them.

"You busy?" I ask Josiah.

Pushing back from his computer, Josiah smiles at me and then looks at Christian with curiosity. If I have to worry about anyone discovering Christian is the guy I've been trying to move on from for years, it will be Josiah. *Play it cool, Monica.*

"Christian is going to stay a few days at the farm and see how we run things. He has more familiarity with business than milking cows, so I thought maybe you could tell him what you've done for the farm. Also, we wanted to ask if you have any clothes he could borrow because he's going to help with farm chores too."

Josiah smirks and grumbles under his breath, "You sure that's smart, Mo?"

Nodding, then looking at Christian, I answer, "He'll be fine. Won't you?"

Christian swallows hard and hesitantly answers, "I hope so."

"That's fair," Josiah says as he claps his hands together and then motions for Christian to come closer.

Leaving them in the office as they rapidly start talking about tracking, production, and utilizing technology, I head back to the house to let Mom know Christian will be staying for a few nights and helping with chores.

"Mom, you in here?" I ask while crossing into the kitchen.

"Laundry room. I'm just switching loads," she answers. In minutes, she's back in the kitchen. "Where's Christian? Did your brothers scare him off already?"

"No, they didn't. Actually, he's planning to stay in town for a few days, and I told him he can stay here."

"That shouldn't be a problem," Mom agrees.

"Great. Thanks. Heads-up, I told him that because he's staying here, he has to help with farm chores."

Smiling widely, Mom smirks and shakes her head. It's not a clause they would have given Christian, but I think it's fair payment.

"Where is Christian? You didn't leave him with your brothers, did you?" Laughing, I answer, "He's with Josiah, and they were fine when I left. I'm heading back now. I just wanted you to know he was staying."

Mom gives me a hug before I leave. "Love that smile, my sweet girl."

As I walk out of the house, I trace my smile with my finger. It's wider than it has been in months, and I can't deny it. Christian is responsible for it.

Strolling through the barn, I say hello to some cows. Of course, Claribel, my favorite lady, is included in my rounds. Surrounded by moos, I laugh. When I get back to the office, Josiah and Christian are laughing and not talking about farming. They're getting along, and I'm glad at least one of my brothers is giving him a chance. After all, if things progress between us, I want my family to like him.

"Ready?" I ask when there's a break in their conversation.

"What's next?" Christian asks as he rises out of the chair. Josiah shakes his hand and tells him that after dinner he'll get some clothes Christian can use over the next few days.

Leading him outside, Christian again places his hand on my back. "Want to go for a walk around the property?" I suggest. He smiles, and I take that as a yes.

Looking down at his shoes again, I notice they aren't perfect and pristine anymore. "This way." I motion with my arm. We walk in silence until we're about one hundred yards from the barn, past cows that are out in the pasture. Knowing that we are tromping through the same land our cows do, I'm watchful of cow patties. But I hadn't thought to caution Christian.

"Oomph." He grunts as his body goes down. Horrified, I watch as if he's in slow motion. Slamming into the ground, he nearly misses his face, landing directly in a pile of cow poop. Trying hard to muffle my laughter is no use. *At least it wasn't still steaming.* He glares at me, unamused, as I sputter and snort.

When I've gathered myself, I pull Christian to his feet. Surprisingly, the only causality of his tumble is the bottom of one of his shoes. Striding over to a fence, he wipes his shoe on the grass, trying to transfer the remnants of cow patty from it. Using the fence as a prop, Christian pulls the shoe from his foot and frowns at it. His fall embedded poop into the intricate pattern on the bottom of the shoe, and I hear him mumble, "Fucking gross."

Again, I laugh, and his attention shoots to me. Putting my hands up, I mumble, "Sorry." Then I add, "We can head back to the house and use the hose to clean off your shoe." Looking back at the house, I hope he wants to continue on our walk and deal with the shoe later.

"I'm good. Let's keep going. I'll do a better job watching where I step."

My heart flutters. He wants to spend time with me alone. We meander through the fields until Mom rings her dinner bell, which Christian finds hysterical.

Walking back hand in hand, I'm on cloud nine. Christian took my hand shortly after the cow patty incident. My nerves grow the closer we get to the house, as I'm not sure how to explain Christian to my family. They know he's Samantha's brother, but they don't know I've been lusting after him for years. Oh, and that we have a rocky past.

My brothers approach us as we're trying to clean his shoe off. I found a sturdy stick near the house and we're using it to push the poop out of his tread.

"Is that cow shit I smell? What happened to you, Christian?" Josiah asks while laughing.

"Bad run-in with a cow patty in the field," Christian answers, his smile proudly displayed on his face.

Mike and Will look at each other and laugh. "That sucks," Mike says.

"Done that a few times," Will adds.

Christian flashes me a smile. It seems like my brothers might accept him. We'll see how chores go in the morning and how the rest of the week plays out before I draw conclusions.

The rest of the evening goes well, and the next

morning, Christian is up bright and early with my brothers, milking the cows. Not wanting to interfere, I sleep until breakfast, figuring I'll see him then.

Over breakfast, my brothers and Christian seem chummy. Even Josiah got up early and helped milk the ladies. I plan to have Christian help me bottle feed the babies the rest of the morning and then have him help my dad with fence repairs and pen cleaning.

By dinnertime, Christian is dead on his feet. Taking pity on him, my brothers wave off his offer to help with the second milking, but insist he help them in the morning.

Christian and I sit close together on the couch and watch an older movie. So far, we've hugged and held hands occasionally, but being this near to him and doing nothing else is pure torture. Almost wishing we were back in the city so we could have some privacy, I remind myself that we haven't talked about what will happen when we return.

Concentrating on the movie after that thought enters my consciousness is impossible. Nerves and worry gather in my belly, making it hurt and cramp. The gentle touch of his finger tracing up and down my arm calms me. I glance down to watch as he moves it, noticing the feel of the calluses he already developed in the past day. A shiver rocks through my body as I sense eyes on me. Flicking my eyes up, I see Christian is staring at me with a lust-filled gaze that whispers hints of what he wants to do to me.

Remaining the gentlemen, when the movie is done, he walks me to my bedroom, gives me a hug, and kisses me on the cheek.

"Really?" I question myself after shutting my bedroom door. He's a playboy. He has a very well-known reputation. And all I got was a hug and a chaste kiss on my cheek?

The next two days pass by just like the first two. Again, physical contact between Christian and me is limited to hugs, hand holding, and cheek kisses. Like a teapot, I'm getting all sorts of steamed up and am about to shout.

Then Thursday comes around and I agree to watch Mike's girls so he and Maddy can go on a date. Watching Addie and Hazel is easy. Christian tags along and he does relatively well. Seeing that the girls are four and two, we have limited things we can do. After feeding them dinner, we take them outside, where we blow countless bubbles that the girls pop excitedly. Covered in bubble juice, we head inside, wash off, and get them ready for bed. I told Mike not to rush home, to enjoy his time with his wife.

"This is the life," Christian says while he relaxes on the couch.

Poking his side, I ask, "Has farm life been tough on you, city boy?"

He nods seriously. "I didn't realize all it took to run a farm. I have mad respect for your family and all the farmers out there. I don't think I could do it."

Smirking at him, I say, "No, you like your luxury items far too much to give them up for a pair of boots and Wranglers. No matter how good they look on you." My cheeks heat at my confession and Christian just smiles.

My heart beats a crazy rhythm inside my chest. Anticipation and anxiety course through my body. We're all alone. The kids are asleep. Now's his chance. I stare at him, willing him to finally make his move. I need to feel his touch, or I'm going to explode. Having him this close, in my personal space, forming relationships with my family, is messing with me. Until we define us, I don't want to get any more attached, but I'm horny as hell, and touching myself after slipping into bed after his cheek peck each night has left me feeling unresolved and needy.

Knowing that Mike and Maddy will be out until late, I throw caution to the wind. We've always had an intense chemistry between us, and now I'm beyond ready to test where that might take us.

Ever since he arrived on Monday, we've exchanged looks and subtle touches that scream at something amazing lying just below the surface of our restraint. As we sit on the couch talking, our bodies mirror each other: faced in and intimate. The heat between us is insane. Reaching forward, I place my palm on his chest. Christian's eyes widen, and he leans into my touch. He reaches up and tucks a strand of hair behind my ear, then grazes his knuckles down my cheek. Reactively, I close my eyes, savoring the touch. When he continues down my throat, I shudder.

Reaching for his shirt, I fist it, barely hanging on. Opening my eyes moments later, I notice he's inched closer and our lips are only centimeters apart. If I lean forward, I could just take what I want, but I'm still unsure if he'll kiss me back. If anything is going to happen between us, he'll have to initiate it. My fear of rejection hangs heavy in my chest as my heart thumps rapidly.

He closes the gap between us, and all the air is sucked out of the room. The moment his lips touch mine, I swear I see stars. My eyes flutter closed, and he moves against me. Nudging his tongue forward, asking for more. Opening my mouth, I accept him in, and our tongues tentatively stroke at each other. Christian angles my head so he can deepen our kiss, and we go at it like horny teens playing seven minutes in heaven. His hands travel down my sides and over my hips. He pulls me forward, having me straddle his lap. *This is unreal. I'm making out with Christian Fox. Am I dreaming?* When I feel his cock flinch underneath me, I gasp.

He's huge, and I'm a little intimidated. The few guys I'd been with freshman year of college had been lacking in size. Just the thought of Christian below me and the fact it's been five years since I've been with anyone, I'm legitimately worried. Despite those worries, I still rub against him, wondering how big he'll get. A delicious friction builds up within me and I chase the high it offers with frantic, sloppy kisses and aggressive thrusting against his crotch. Christian's hands wrap around my hips and he pulls me closer, aligning our centers perfectly, encouraging more direct contact. It doesn't take long before my orgasm spikes. A rush of heat travels through my body, relaxing everything in its path. Divine is the only word I can use to describe it.

Chapter 24

Christian

Since coming to the farm, I've had to physically control my urge to touch Monica. I read a study one time that said the average man thinks of sex nineteen times a day. I'm not sure that's right, as I'm confident I logged at least that number by lunchtime on the first day here.

Everything I see Monica do is incredibly sexy. The way she walks through the barn, talking to their cows. When she bottle-feeds the calves. It's all new to my image of who she is. Add to that her outfit of worn, tight jeans, faded farm logo t-shirt, and her Xtratuf boots, and she's a walking wet dream.

The days here run smoothly. At five, I get up and join Monica's brothers in the barn to milk their herd. At the halfway mark, we grab a hot breakfast Kathy prepares for us. Cleaning pens fills the rest of our mornings until lunchtime. Following that, I help

Monica bottle feed the calves. Usually after that, we'll sneak off for a walk through the fields, only coming back when we hear the dinner bell. Milking the cows again is the evening task before heading to bed by ten. Of course, that's always the plan, as the morning comes too early, but Monica and I often talk, flirt, and resist temptation until midnight when I finally walk her to her room, hug her, and give her a kiss on the cheek. It's tough to restrain myself because I want so much more.

Tonight, I tag along while Monica babysits her nieces. Being that they're so young, we don't have too much to do with them before putting them to bed. Monica told her brother to stay out as late as he and Maddy wanted.

Looking at the clock, it's only eight o'clock, and I plan to take advantage of the privacy we have. Sitting on the couch, our last resistance fades, and before we know it, Monica is on my lap, rubbing against my swollen cock as we dry hump like horny teenagers, not even a little sorry that we're on her brother's couch. I cherish every kiss she gifts me. It's absolute heaven on earth.

Because acting on our intense chemistry is new for us, I don't know where her boundaries are and I want to be respectful. If I could have my way, I'd flip her over on the couch and make her come on my fingers, tongue, and cock before her brother arrives home. But I don't want to make the choice for her. I know we need to have a conversation about it. About us. However, thoughts of that drift away as she continues to rub against me.

My want for her is nothing I have ever experienced before. It's immeasurable. Anchoring her hips to me so I can thrust harder into her is both painful and pleasurable. I'm giving myself the worst case of blue balls I've ever had, but the possibility of seeing Monica come is worth it.

"Oh, Christian... feels so good. Right there." Needy words for a desperate man. Thrusting my hips harder, I make sure I hit the same spot, giving her what she needs. After a moment, a moan falls from her plump lips. Her back arches, pushing her amazing breasts into my face. Looking up through heavenly cleavage, I see her eyes are closed, and a look of happy contentment spreads across her gorgeous face. Seeing it is better than any high I've ever had, better than any contract deal I've ever negotiated. Monica is radiant. Just as she comes down from the high, the garage door opens and we both freeze.

Monica hustles off my lap and tries to tidy up the living room, picking up the pillows we knocked on the floor during our heated hump session. Shifting so I can adjust my angry, throbbing cock is torture, but I'd rather deal with that than her brother if he notices something happened between us.

Mike and Maddy come into the house, whispering to each other. Apparently, they had a great night out. Happy for them, I glance at Monica, who has pinkish cheeks and looks more frazzled than normal. Did I push her into doing something she wasn't ready for or didn't want? Mentally kicking myself, I move to the side of the room to let Monica, Mike, and Maddy have a moment to rehash the evening.

Once she's given her full report on the night's events, she turns to me and nods to the front door. I wave to Mike and Maddy on my way out and wonder if they felt the sudden coldness of the room. After they arrived home, the air went from stifling to frigid, making my mind spin aimlessly.

The drive back to the farm is eerily quiet. Not knowing what to say kills me. Just having a taste of Monica, I want more, and she's giving off strange vibes. *Am I the only one feeling something between us?* Does she regret what happened?

Parking in front of the darkened farmhouse, we both step out from Mr. Fields's truck and silently walk toward the house. Before we go inside, I need to know we're okay. Our relationship over the years has been bumpy, and now we've crossed a boundary that can't be ignored. Grabbing her hand, I pull her into me. Unshed tears sit heavy in her eyes and she wipes at them.

"Hey. What's going on in that beautiful head of yours?"

Shaking her head softly, she whispers, "Nothing. I'm just tired. It's been a long day." Not buying her answer, but knowing that I shouldn't push her, I force myself back.

Kissing her on the head, I say, "I'm not tired. I think I'm still wound up. Would it be okay with your folks if I just sit here on the porch for a bit?"

Monica looks at me with confusion coloring her face and nods. "They won't mind. Good night, Christian." In a few steps, she's inside the house and I'm all alone.

Sitting on the porch, I ponder what happened. Everything between Monica and me was going great and then it all changed. I can pinpoint the exact time, but I can't for the life of me figure out the why. What am I supposed to do now? Go back to the way things were, where we avoided each other while it was so obvious we wanted to be together? Knowing I can't even define what being together looks like, or even if it has a timeline, I wonder if it's even fair to pursue her. Even if she gets past whatever just happened, can she handle the fact that I don't think about long terms or forevers?

For hours, I wrestle with that. When the darkness fades into light and I hear the coffee pot click on at four, I know I've made my decision. Even though it pains me more than I care to admit, I'm going to step away. Let Monica work out her thoughts and feelings, and when, or if, she's ever ready, I'll be here waiting for her. I'm not going anywhere. For the first time, I have felt confident in what I feel. I'm at peace. I don't know where that road will lead us in the end, but I'm all in. No matter what.

Rising off the aged wooden porch, my joints ache from lack of movement. Limping into the house, up the stairs, and to the bathroom, I shower and dress. When I come downstairs a half an hour later, Mrs. Fields is up and already starting on breakfast.

Setting my duffle bag by the front door, I step into the kitchen. When she turns toward me, her smile fades. "Morning, Christian. How'd you sleep?"

Scratching my head, I focus on my dirty Nikes, which were brand new and never worn when I drove up here days ago. Now they're far from in perfect condition and in much need of some TLC to regain their status. Funny, it's similar to how I'm feeling.

"Didn't sleep last night. Too much on my mind." My answer comes out sounding as sullen as I feel.

She approaches me, a look of worry across her face. Extending her hand to my arm to provide comfort, she says, "I'm sorry to hear that. Is everything okay?"

Unsure how to answer, I just shrug. She's a mom. She'll get the gesture without needing to hear the words. "It's been really nice to visit, but I think I need to head back to the city. I just wanted to thank you and Mr. Fields for all the hospitality and fantastic food. It's been an experience I will never forget."

"Oh. Well, if that's what you think is best. Let me get you a to-go mug of coffee and a muffin. I baked them last night." Mrs. Fields can't hide the surprise and shock in her voice. I ignore the disappointment I hear too. She didn't expect me to leave, and it probably seems strange, as I was originally planning to stay all week.

"I do, and thank you again," I say. My heart feels heavy as I take the coffee and muffin from her before heading out the door. Kathy follows me out.

When I get to the steps, I stop, turn toward her, and ask, "Could you give this to Monica? I didn't want to wake her up since we got home late last night." She nods, takes the folded paper from me, and watches as I climb into my car.

Starting it and driving away feels like I'm tearing myself in two. It's agonizing. When I get to the main road, it's fairly empty, seeing as it's still early. I pass both Mike and Will on my way out and give a quick wave to them. They both look confused, but so am I. Swimming in a sea of unknown feelings and thoughts that I don't know how to explain, I made sure I left Fields Farm before they arrived.

The drive back to Chicago isn't bad. My mind wanders a lot, mostly to what Monica's reaction will be to me leaving. And then what she'll think when she reads the letter I left for her.

Chapter 25

Monica

After tossing and turning for hours after we got home, I finally passed out at three thirty and slept like a log until nine. Stretching in my childhood bed while I wake up, I decide I'm no closer to an understanding of what happened last night between Christian and me. In all honesty, it was amazing, but no matter how much I tried, I couldn't come up with an understanding of what's next. We never talked about us. In fact, the idea of anything happening has always been a wish and not likely to occur.

However, last night, we acted like horny teens. Having my brother walk into his house right after I'd dry humped Christian to an orgasm was mortifying. Ashamed of my behavior, I pulled away, dissociating myself from Christian. He doesn't do complicated or relationships, and that's all I can offer. There is no way I could be a hookup and nothing more. He knows that I only want a relationship, and because my best friend is his little sister, drama would undoubtedly follow.

Coming down to breakfast late means I can avoid all the noise of my loud brothers. Seated quietly at the table is my mom, cradling a coffee mug. She must have been sitting there a while, because the mug is nearly empty and steam isn't rising from it. She looks troubled, and I wonder why.

"Morning, Mom."

Letting out an audible sigh, Mom looks at me with sad eyes, and I question what I missed. "What's wrong, Mom?" As I walk to the table, she makes eye contact and then focuses on something in front of her. It looks like a folded piece of paper with my name scribbled on it. *What is it?* "What do you have there?" I ask, pointing at the paper.

"Christian left it for you." Her words hit me, and I look around as if expecting to see him.

"Okay," I mumble. My mind is racing. *What does that mean?*

Seeing I'm confused, she explains, "He left early this morning. Before your dad was up and your brothers were here. He thanked me for the hospitality and said he needed to get back to the city."

"Okay," I say again, taking the letter from her. In a daze, I trudge to the front door, pull on my boots, and leave with my heart full of worry. Heading away from the house, far from the barn, I take quick steps, reaching the small pond on our property. It's my safe place. No one comes here, so I know I'll be undisturbed.

Collapsing on the bench put out here when I was a child, I feel the heaviness of my unease. Reaching down, I grab a pebble from the pile I'd left over the summer. I'd visited the bench often to think. The first pebble I throw makes a hollow *plunk* sound as it hits the water. It quickly sinks. The ripples it leaves in its wake are smooth and soothing. Throwing a few more feels cathartic to my weary heart. The letter sitting next to me fills me with dread and I don't want to read it. Honestly, I don't know if I'm strong enough to handle another brush-off from Christian.

This past week has been amazing. It's hard to believe how different it was between us. Then last night happened, and I'd freaked out. All my insecurities floated to the surface, making me question his intentions.

"Just read it," I tell myself as I reach for the white paper, my name across the top. I trace it with my finger before I open it, my heart feeling like it's going to burst.

Monica,

Please tell your family thank you for me. Welcoming me into your home, your lives, is something I will cherish forever. I'm sorry I didn't say goodbye in person, but I knew it'd be too hard, and honestly, I'm a coward. This week, with you, has been one that I'll never forget. Our walks and talks meant more to me than I can ever say. It feels like I finally could show you the real me and you revealed the true you. You completely blow me away!

We can probably both agree that last night was intense. It felt like we crossed over into uncharted land. I wanted to apologize if you felt like I forced that, because that was not my intention. All week, hell, the entire time we've known each other, I've been drawn to you, and last night I allowed myself to surrender. My hope is I haven't hurt you.

For years I've clung to the excuse that I was unsure of my feelings for you, and that's not entirely true. I've always had powerful feelings for you. You are radiant, bringing light to all those around you. You embody love and kindness, and I feel unworthy of that. After all the things to keep us apart, I feel like I'm not good enough for you. I cannot deny our intense connection that I admit has kept me running scared since I first felt it. To say it simply, I think you are incredible. Anything else between us will be under your direction. Out of respect for you, I'm stepping back and giving you the time and space to figure out what you want. Please know that I am not going anywhere. I respect and care for you deeply and will support whatever decision you make.

Yours,
Christian

Fat, ugly tears fall from my eyes, rolling down my cheeks and splashing on the letter I have clutched in my hands. It feels like my heart is again breaking into a million pieces and I don't know what to do. My sobbing becomes uncontrollable and my body shakes. Strong, warm hands wrap around me and pull me into a hard chest that smells familiar. Pine and musk swirl around me, letting me know I'm wrapped in Josiah's arms, and I cry harder. Until now, I haven't let anyone see me upset over Christian. But I can't hold in this reaction. It's seeping from every pore of my body.

"Mo, what's wrong? Who do the boys and I have to kill?" Josiah grinds out.

Instead of words, I shake my head against his chest, using him as a human Kleenex. *He'll need a fresh shirt, for sure.*

Sitting there by the pond, squeezed on a tiny bench, I cry and cry while my brother holds me. Just like Mom when we were sick, he circles his hand on my back, patting occasionally, letting me know it's okay. A few years ago, I did the same for him shortly after he disclosed his cancer diagnosis. Now the roles are reversed. When the crying and tears slow down, Josiah nudges my forehead back and looks me in the eye. "Does this have anything to do with Christian and why he left at the ass crack of dawn this morning?"

Looking up at him with swollen, puffy, sore eyes, I only nod, and he brings me in for a tighter hug. "Mike and Will each owe me twenty. I called it." Annoyed, I huff and push back off his chest, enraged. "Whoa, Mo. Slow down. You're looking a little crazed right now. How about we rewind it for a moment?"

Poking him in the chest, I growl, "You guys were betting on me?" He nods guiltily, looking a lot like a little boy who's been caught with his hand in the cookie jar.

"What the hell, Josiah! Really?"

He grimaces and tries explaining, but I'm not listening. I've already jumped from the bench and started stomping over to the barn where my other idiot brothers are mucking cow pens.

When I get to the barn, Josiah runs ahead of me, hands cupped around his mouth, yelling, "She knows!"

Glaring as I stomp by him, I move over to the pen and remove the pin holding it shut. Knowing that sound, the cows move, and before I know it, a full-on stampede's happening in front of my eyes.

The heifers trap my two eldest brothers in the chaotic fray. It's hilarious to watch as they're bounced between our bovines, every so often falling. By the time all the cows have escaped into the pasture, I feel somewhat vindicated. Looking at them all, I say, "You should be ashamed of yourselves," then turn and stalk away. Leaving them in the middle of the pen covered in mud and manure feels right. Passing Josiah, I warn, "You better watch your back." I leave the barn and return to the house to figure out what to do.

Sitting in my room, I open the letter again. Evidence of my tears is apparent in all the smeared ink. Christian finally admitted he has feelings for me, even if he couldn't name them. He promised to be there for me, but in what capacity? Being just friends isn't something I'm interested in. So, what does that leave us? For years I've wanted a relationship with him, but being a self-professed bachelor, he'd gouged a hole in that possibility. Being physical is something I desired, especially after last night, when I'd finally gotten a taste of the chemistry we have. Can I convince him he wants more with me? I don't know. Plus, I don't think I could handle that type of relationship. *But what if it's the only way you can have him?* "Stupid brain, shut up. You aren't helping," I chastise myself.

The remainder of the week goes by in a haze. On Sunday, I head back to the city early enough to make sure I have everything set for the upcoming week because spring break is officially over. Looking at my school calendar, I see we don't have any more days off until summer. It's going to be a long few months, especially while nursing a wounded heart.

Rereading Christian's letter several times, I still haven't decided what I want to do. Yes, I want more. But would it be enough? If not, will I settle or walk away broken? Feeling stuck and having no one to talk to about it, I drown my muddled feelings in my familiar friend, Chips Ahoy!. By the time I head to bed, the only thing I'm feeling is sick to my stomach because I stuffed myself full of cookies.

Christian

Once I'm back within the city limits after leaving Monica and the farm, I notice everything seems excessively loud and over-crowded, bothering me and making me edgy.

Growing up and living in New York City, I'm more

than used to noise and crowds, but after a few days on the farm, I'm desperate for a tranquil space. Unfortunately, returning to the farm isn't possible, so the only place offering peaceful silence is my penthouse. It's definitely not as spacious, but I can guarantee it's plenty quiet.

For the next few days, I remain a hermit, ordering delivery and staying in, avoiding everyone. My phone, as usual, rings non-stop, but I let everything go to voicemail and listen to the messages periodically, making sure nothing is urgent. Everything can wait until Monday.

When Monday arrives and I still haven't heard from Monica, I question whether I did the right thing. There is no one to ask. Maybe I could call Josiah. He seems like a good dude. Would he give me details about his sister? Probably not. In fact, all three of her brothers would probably come into the city and pummel me, especially if they knew how I'd treated her all these years. How the week ended is just another example of me not being good enough for her. Her not calling tells me she came to the same conclusion, which sours my mood immensely.

Chapter 26

Monica

Weeks pass, and as I get back into the groove of school, I realize I haven't heard from Christian at all. He really is intent on giving me space. Although I appreciate that, I miss him desperately. But until I know my answer, I refuse to reach out. Otherwise, it won't be fair to either of us.

After a crazy week at school, one of my work friends, Camille, who I also do yoga with, suggests we go out dancing and burn off some steam.

Samantha and I had gone out to brunch the previous weekend, and she told me she and Lucas were headed to New York. She invited me along, but I couldn't afford it, so I told her I already had plans.

On Saturday night, Camille and I meet at a hip whiskey bar called Barrel, and after we toast the evening, we walk to a nearby dance club, Move. We've been here before and soon run into other friends of ours who are celebrating a night out.

Needing to sweat out some aggression, I hit the dance floor right away. With music pumping and lights pulsating, I close my eyes and let go. My eyes don't need to be open to know that others surrounding me are shaking, gyrating, and thrusting to what the DJ is spinning.

After a dozen songs, I'm hot and parched. Nodding to Camille, I mouth *"water"* to her, and she gives me a thumbs up and keeps dancing with a very attractive man. Like a dork, I wait until he's turned away and flash her a smile with an excited thumbs up. She just laughs and moves closer to him.

As I approach the bar, I hear a high-pitched squeal and turn toward it. To my left is something I wish I could unsee. Christian, looking more than delicious, surrounded by a horde of ladies dressed in short, tight dresses that leave little to the imagination. My stomach heaves and cramps, and I fight the urge to bend over and empty my stomach. Emotions lodge in my throat, making it difficult to swallow. Panic sets in and my breathing becomes faster. Feeling like I'm going to suffocate, I need to get some air.

Looking back toward Christian, tears form in my eyes, and I try to blink them away. This is it. I had taken too much time thinking about what I want and what I would accept, and he moved on. I feel so stupid and naïve.

My heart flinches, ripping open the old wound he left there months earlier. The room spins, and the dots I see appear in my vision go in and out. Am I going to pass out? Taking a step toward what I think is the exit, I feel myself stumble. This is just my luck. I'm going to pass out and make a scene in front of Christian and all the ladies vying for his attention.

Just as I'm blacking out, muscular arms sweep me up into the air. Coming to quickly, I notice I'm cradled into a hard chest; the man carries me like I'm the most precious thing he's ever held. With the world spinning, I keep my eyes closed so I don't throw up. The stranger carries me through the crowded nightclub as if I weigh nothing, not stopping until we're outside and away from the crowds.

"Monica, are you alright?" the stranger's voice asks in a strong, sexy tone. Delirious, I think the man sounds, and even smells, like Christian, but that doesn't make sense. Why would he have rushed to my aid? Plenty of attractive women were occupying his attention. I hadn't even assumed he'd seen me in the crowded club.

Ripping my eyes open, fighting back the nausea I'm still experiencing, I discover it is Christian who holds me tight in his arms, placing chaste kisses along my hairline.

"Christian, is it really you?" My voice strains and cracks as I squint at him.

"Babe. Are you okay? You have me worried."

My body freezes. "Sorry. I'm fine. You probably need to get back to your date... uh... dates?" I mumble.

Shaking his head, he growls, "I don't have a date or dates in there. I came with a client, and when he didn't show any interest in them, those women flocked to me and I was just trying to figure out how to get away."

Disbelief weighs heavy. "Really?"

Again, he kisses my head and says, "I've been waiting for you."

My eyes get teary and my throat tightens as I stare at him. "Really?"

Christian sets me down, makes sure I'm stable, pulls me into him, and rests his forehead against mine. "Really," he answers.

On the sidewalk, completely absorbed in each other, our breaths sync and Christian pulls back, asking quietly, "Do you want to get out of here?"

I'm nodding before I can even think about it.

Christian

As we head out, I remind myself that there are no expectations. I haven't designed some master plan to seduce her. Although, I wouldn't say no if that's where the night leads. Monica has been irresistible and off-limits to me for over six years. Can you blame me for wanting and hoping for more?

After taking a Lyft to my penthouse, I show her my meagerly decorated home. Even though I've lived here for almost two years, there isn't much life to it. It's not sterile, per se, but other than a few pieces of sports memorabilia and some furniture, I can admit it's sparse, lacking warmth, if you will.

"Love what you've done with the place," Monica pokes in a playful tone.

Being the smartass that I am, I ask, "Oh yeah? What's your favorite part?" Then I give her my million-dollar smile that turns into a smirk. *Gotcha. Two can play this game, beautiful.*

Looking around, she taps her finger to her chin as she considers the space, then laughs. "The color. Yes, definitely the color. The palette you've chosen makes a bold statement. It's very monochrome, don't you think? Kind of reminds me of a hospital ward. Wouldn't you agree?" The smirk painted across her pink lips and her dancing crystal blue eyes are impossible to resist.

Striding over, I use my body to back her up against the nearest wall. When she hits it, she lets out a breathy gasp. Her eyelids flutter and I lean in until my lips are an inch from her neck, then whisper, "Monica, if you tell me no, I'll back off. But right now, I need to touch you. Can I?" My voice is strained, like it's paining me to admit that I want her. My need is intense and feels like nothing I've experienced before. Waiting for her permission, I nuzzle my nose against her soft skin, inhaling her memorable citrus and vanilla scent, calming me immediately.

Monica nods, and I waste no time responding. Slowly, I kiss up her neck, relishing each time I'm allowed to touch her after our time apart. Time I'd forced upon us. But now she's here and I don't plan to let her go. Once my brain settles, I move from her neck to her earlobes, where I suck and nibble. "You are beautiful," I whisper before I softly blow into her ear, making her body shiver and squirm against me. I know she likes what I've done because her hold on me becomes aggressively needy, pulling me in tighter.

Wanting to see her, I pull back to watch as she unravels before me. Her cheeks turn rosy and her eyes flutter closed. Her back and neck slightly arch toward me, creating an incredibly sexy profile. My hands ache to touch her even more than I am. Tracing my hand up and down the s-curve of her side, she lets out a throaty "Mmmmm," directly registering in my cock.

He, my greedy man down below, has turned hard and heavy, only willing to accept Monica in exchange for his promise to behave. Only thing is, I know once this progresses further, I can't promise jack shit. Don't misunderstand me, I wouldn't force her to do anything. I just know my desire for her is driving me fucking crazy and I am so ready to take things to the next level. And that level might not last as long as I want the first time, if you get what I'm saying.

When I reach her hip bone, I circle it roughly,

providing more delicious pressure. Soon, her hips are circling in time with my ministrations and it almost makes me come in my pants. I want her to be doing this with my cock buried deep inside of her as she rides me. The image of that has been one of my favorites since she straddled me while we were at her brother's house. Yes, she remained clothed that night, but my imagination is expansive and detailed. However, I know that when I get to see the real thing, it will be so much better than what I've imagined.

Monica's eyes peek open, and in a throaty voice, she begs, "Christian. Please. Kiss me." Not needing a second request, I lower my mouth to hers and place a tender kiss against her lips. Her hands slide up around my neck, pulling me closer. Opening my mouth, I push my tongue into hers, demanding more. And she gives it to me, making what we're doing messy and chaotic. Eventually needing air, I force myself back from her. We both pant while we exchange heated, needy eye contact. Smirking, I study her, wondering if she's thinking the same as me. Because, fuck, that was the hottest kiss I've ever had.

"Intense?" I question.

Wide-eyed, Monica just nods.

Concerned about her, I ask, "Are you okay?"

Again, she just nods.

Leaning into her, I set my forehead against hers and nuzzle our noses together. "Words, babe. I need your words before I take things anything further."

Monica moves my head, forcing me to look into her eyes. She replies, "Yes, Christian. I'm good. This is what I want. I want you." Her voice hitches on the last sentence, and I wonder if she meant to say it. Looking deeply into her eyes, I nod and kiss her again with matched passion. Moving closer, I feel her body melt into mine.

While still kissing, I dip slightly and pick her up so she can wrap her legs around my waist. Monica does so and I walk to my bedroom. Pushing the door open, I hope it's clean. Earlier tonight, I didn't have any plans to bring anyone back to my place, so it didn't matter how I'd left it. Now, I'm hoping for the best.

Chapter 27

Monica

Having myself wrapped around Christian feels so natural, so right. When he walks us to his bedroom, my body gyrates with excitement. *Finally.* My brain and body are completely overwhelmed and spinning out of control. Christian notices and sets me gently on the edge of the bed. Softly. He nudges my legs apart and steps between them. With our centers lined up, it's difficult to not get lost in the heat radiating between us. I always expected we'd be nuclear together, and I'm excited to find out.

"Monica," Christian whispers, drawing my eyes to his. Staring into his blue eyes is like staring into the pictures of ocean water in the Bahamas. Clear, deep, and majestic. It's tough not to get lost in them, but when he says my name again, I focus and concentrate my gaze on his soft, pink lips. A deliciously devilish grin comes across them, and I know I'm in trouble.

"Babe, what do you want?" Suddenly nervous, I look down at my lap. I'm not that experienced or confident in the bedroom. I don't know how to ask for what I want. Hell, I don't even know what I want because I haven't done much.

Christian uses a finger to tip my chin, tilting my face up to him. He stares into my eyes as I do my best to hide my embarrassment.

"Monica, do you want this?" he asks hesitantly.

I nod. "Yes, I want you. I always have." *Shit. I shouldn't have confessed that last bit.*

A million-dollar smile stretches across his handsome face. It's like he won the Mega Millions jackpot. His reaction makes no sense to me. After all, I'm just me. Monica Fields, kindergarten teacher, dairy farm girl, plain Jane.

Christian removes his shirt slowly, toying with the buttons the entire time. He seeks approval with his eyes, checking to see that I'm okay with what he's doing. I most definitely am. Once the shirt is removed, he takes my hands and places one on his well-defined pectoral muscles and one on his rigid abs. Holy hell. This man's body is unreal. Over the years I'd read hundreds of romance novels, but I'd imagined nothing this amazing. *Shit. Am I drooling?* Licking my lips, I trace my eyes over his incredible midsection and know the rest of his body will be equally impressive. And I can't wait to find out.

Unsure what to do next, I relinquish my control to

Christian, and he willingly takes charge. His hands running up and down my thighs feels incredible. Each time he gets closer to my center, a warm buzz travels through the lower half of my body. When he reaches the hem of my short dress, he tugs at the stretchy material. My body hums with anticipation and I want to rush him forward with his exploration, but when I reach down for the hem of the dress, hoping to pull it off, he stills me, restraining my hands. Looking into his eyes for an explanation, I see they've gone dark and mysterious. *What does he have planned for me?* Goose bumps cover my body, and a tantalizing shiver runs down my back. My nipples pebble and my center becomes moist.

Christian leans into me and kisses me with an intensity that is both wild and possessive, stealing my breath from me. When I pull back to suck in some much-needed air, he lifts my dress over my head, leaving me in my matching black lace bra and panties. A deep-throated, growling groan falls from Christian's mouth. We haven't done anything yet, and I'm already on edge. It won't take much to tip me over. I've wanted him for too long.

Suddenly realizing I'm in only my underwear, I cross my arms over my waist. It isn't that I think I'm fat, I'm just well aware of the women Christian has been with, and I'm easily a few sizes bigger. Trying to distract him, I reach for his face to kiss him, but he refuses and remains still as he stares at my body. The longer he stares, the more self-conscience and uncomfortable I become.

I dip my head so I can't see the disappointment I'm sure is evident in his eyes. A single tear falls on my thigh. Christian wipes it away and then tips my head up. My eyes are heavy with fear. *Will he not want me anymore?* Worry consumes me. Is it too late? Could I still leave now and avoid any more embarrassment? Would I ever recover from this?

Christian must sense my unease because he anchors my legs to the bed, preventing me from leaving. My eyes flick up to his perfectly sculpted face, and once our eyes are locked, he says one word to me. "Beautiful." Shaking my head in disbelief, he leans in closer so our foreheads are touching and growls, "Monica. You. Are. Fucking. Beautiful." When his words and the way he says them registers, my heart rejoices, and I relax for the first time in months.

Scooting myself back on the bed, I pull Christian with me. Before crawling above me, he removes his dress slacks, leaving him in his black Calvin Klein boxer briefs that stretch over his muscular thighs and enormous protruding cock. Sexy doesn't accurately describe him.

Spreading my legs, I welcome him between them. Feeling all of him pushed against my center makes me desperate. Thrusting my hips up, our bodies rub up against each other, creating a deliciously hot friction that lights my body up. Wanting more, I wrap my legs around his waist and pull him closer. As our bodies work together, creating a natural rhythm and building pleasure, Christian lifts, resting in a push-up position. At first it seems odd, but once I realize the movement has dropped his hips, creating more pressure and friction for me, I feel like I've been elevated to another plane of existence.

It doesn't take long for my body to succumb to the combustive sexual energy we're creating between us. A hot, needy tension builds up within me, and the longer we grind against one another, the faster my body responds. Starting at my clit, a rapidly throbbing pulse begs for more. And I deliver. Rubbing, grinding, and thrusting against Christian, I have no shame acting like a sex-crazed maniac.

Once my orgasm has traveled through me, my body relaxes on the bed below Christian. Panting because of our frantic pace, he pushes my wild hair away from my face before he lowers and gives me a sweet kiss on the lips. My heart soars. I have never been this happy before. Sure, the hormones from the orgasm definitely improved my mood, but being here wrapped up with Christian, I couldn't imagine anything better.

Chapter 28

Christian

Finally having Monica in my bed is an honest-to-God dream come true. Since we met, it's all I've ever wanted. But I honestly never thought I'd get to experience it.

It had only taken six-plus years and me pushing her away for most of it, believing that the only lifestyle I could be happy living was that of a bachelor. Over the years, as my buddies settled down and started families, that belief had been tested, and now I question it completely, especially with the way I feel with Monica curled into my side. No other woman has ever been in my bed. This is a first for me, and I don't know how to tell her that. I don't want to sound like I'm bragging when I emphasize just how special it is that she's in my bed. However, I want her to know the significance of it. Until Monica, no one had ever been good enough to even consider bringing into my personal space. *What does that mean?*

Confused feelings swirl around my head as she quietly dozes next to me. Watching her unravel before me had almost been my undoing. It was beautiful to watch her body chasing and succumbing to the pleasure we'd created. I wanted that feeling more than I could say, but for once, I will not be greedy. For years, I stood in the way of us, allowing our insane chemistry to simmer, unresolved. As penance, I figure I owe her a few orgasms, to say thanks for sticking with me and my stupid self.

Tucked protectively into my side, I trace my gaze all over her body, memorizing it. When I get to her black lacy underwear, a lump forms in my throat. Monica went out tonight wearing sexy undergarments, and from what I'd heard from eavesdropping on too many female conversations, women only did that when they were planning to have sex. *Who was she going to sleep with?* Had my appearance at the club tonight been fate's way of getting Monica and me together? I don't know, but I won't question it.

Finally ready to take this further, I lean over Monica and kiss her eyelids, nose, and lips. Pulling back, I see her eyes open slowly.

"Christian." Her voice is dreamy and makes me smile. Monica in my bed is the most beautiful thing I've ever seen.

Hungry for more of her, I maintain eye contact as I

tug at her panties. She lifts her hips, giving me permission. Dragging the lace down her legs, I can see how damp they are, and my heart thumps in my chest. Prideful. *I did that to her.* I kiss each ankle, then each knee and hip bone as I move back up her incredible body. Monica sucks in a breath each time I get near her middle. Using my finger, I trace the small patch of hair over her mound before I place open-mouthed kisses above it. Her hips rise to meet me, welcoming me in. Climbing in between her legs again, I help her open wide for me. Her legs shake with uncertainty.

"Monica, is this your first time?" I question. It doesn't matter to me. I'm just happy to share it with her.

Shaking her head, she replies, "No, I've had sex before. Why?"

I just assumed she knew I meant oral. "Babe, I'm asking if you've ever had oral sex."

"I've given a blowjob before, if that's what you're are asking. Although, I don't understand because your head is between my legs, not the other way around." Her snarky tone makes me smile.

"I don't mean to embarrass you. Have you ever had a guy perform oral on you?"

Her hand flies up and rests between her breasts, as if she's appalled at my question. Then she drops eye contact and shakes her head no. It must be my lucky day, because I'm going to be showing her what she's been missing.

Pulling her hips into me, I place the flat of my tongue against her clit and flick it rapidly a few times. Monica moans, and it's the best sound I've ever heard. Licking through her warm, moist folds, a heady excitement travels through my body and I have to remind my cock to chill. I tease her clit, providing just enough pressure to make her hips move. "Ahhh," she whimpers, and I insert my tongue into her hole. A deep moan bounces off the walls as Monica's head moves back and forth.

I take one hand and massage her breast, pinching and plucking the nipple. Monica arches her back, following the pull of her flesh. Her moaning becomes breathy as I replace my tongue with my fingers. After a few thrusts inside, the tips of my fingers graze back and forth over her G-spot. Her hips wiggle, pulling my mouth off her. Taking my other hand, I trace over her breast, travel down to her center, and firmly grab her thigh, setting her in place. While thrusting my fingers inside her, I lower my mouth to her folds once again. Sucking her clit into my mouth scores a hip roll as she gasps, "Oh, Christian."

I'm on cloud nine right now. I am the orgasm king of the world. Monica's legs begin to shake and her muscles squeeze at my still thrusting fingers. Sensing she's close, I lick her from ass to clit and then bite her swollen nub. Her body arches off the bed and I lap at the juices flowing from her core.

Panting and wearing a sated smile, Monica's the

happiest I've ever seen. I want to keep her this way forever. Not knowing how will pose a problem, but I'm committed to trying. This woman is special, and I know I don't deserve her, but I'm going to do everything I can to keep her.

Chapter 29

Monica

Christian climbs up my body, kissing my nipples as he goes. When he reaches my lips, he places a gentle kiss on them. Wrapping my arms around his neck, I pull him to me, forcing the kiss to deepen. When his tongue dips into my mouth, I taste myself for the first time, and it doesn't repulse me like I assumed it would. Instead, it fuels my desire for him. Grabbing his bottom lip between my teeth, I whisper across his lips, "Christian, I want you. Now." Even though his lip is caught by me, I can still feel his smile.

Pulling back, he looks in my eyes, asking, "Are you sure?" Without hesitation, I smile widely and nod.

Leaning down, he places another kiss on my lips before he rolls off me. Reaching into the nightstand, he grabs a few condoms, and I smirk. "Ambitious?" I question.

Christian looks at me with all the smolder he can manage and replies with one word. "Realistic."

His confidence is beyond sexy, and I can't wait to see what happens next. I know he is very experienced, and I plan to reap the rewards from that. Sure, it could have bothered me that since I'd met him—while I lusted after him for years—he'd built himself a hefty sexual resume. But, here and now, he is with me, saying and doing all the things that matter. And despite how jealous I want to be because I'd been missing out for years, I have him now, and that makes me happy. Fully aware of Christian's past, I don't know how long I'll have him, but I'll take what I can get and see where it leads us, heart be damned.

While still on his side, he tugs his boxer briefs off, unveiling his enormous cock. My eyes bulge as I try to swallow. My panic must show clear as day across my face because he says, "Don't worry, I'll go slow. Tell me if it hurts, okay?"

I'm nervous, but I believe him. He doesn't want to hurt me. He doesn't know it's been five years since I've been with anyone.

Crawling back over me after putting on the condom, he settles between my legs. Our centers line up perfectly and his gentle movement nudges my still sensitive clit. Zings shoot through my core and it tightens, still wet from his mouth and from the pleasure he delivered.

He places the head of his cock at my opening and

inches himself slowly inside. Widening my legs, I give him more room to thrust. When he's almost all the way in, my muscles flinch and tighten around him. "So tight," he says on a groan before lowering his hand to my clit and making languid circles on it. Between that and his deep thrusts rubbing up against my G-spot, I feel myself climbing higher and higher. When I'm teetering on the edge, my muscles squeeze around him and his thrusts become frantic as he moans my name.

But he isn't done. Still thrusting, the orgasm I felt coming hurls into me like a bullet train, knocking the wind out of me. My whole body tightens down and Christian roars out above me. It's the most empowering thing I've ever experienced. I did that to him. I'm sure it's because of our insane, natural chemistry, but we'd have to test that theory again and again. And we do just that.

Getting up the next morning is difficult. Christian unwinding himself from me to answer his phone reminds me of the commitment we made weeks ago to Lucas. Originally, we hadn't planned to go together, as we weren't really talking. But when Lucas mentioned calling me, Christian interrupted and said he'd do it because he had to ask me something anyway.

After taking the world's quickest shower, I dress in a shirt and an excessively large pair of Christian's shorts before we head out. Exhausted from lack of sleep, we do our best to help Lucas pull off an epic surprise for Sam. Guess what? She said yes!

Later that day, after a much-needed nap, Christian drops me off at my apartment so I can get ready for the Stanley Cup game we're going to watch. If the Steel win it, they'll win the entire series, and it will be the first win for the organization.

Chapter 30

Christian

This last year that we'd been dating flew past. Monica's in her fourth year of teaching and almost daily makes me laugh with the crazy shenanigans her kindergarteners get into. I'm still incredibly busy at Fox Sporting, trying to bring new talent into the fold and ensuring they have the best representation with their contracts and endorsement deals. Representing the clientele that I do, going out to a club or bar is almost necessary. And let me tell you, it is so much better now that I know I can talk business and after that's done, I'm going home to the woman of my dreams. If I'm going out on the weekends, I can usually convince Monica to come with me, which is amazing because after I've got my client settled, I can sneak off with my woman to dance. The best thing about those nights is going home together at the end. I didn't realize how unfulfilling hookups were until I had Monica in my life. She's my home.

After a night out clubbing with an NBA star I represent, Monica and I Uber back to my place around midnight. Having her in my arms and grinding up against my body all night about killed me. I'm more than ready to strip her down and show her what she's doing to me. When we enter my penthouse, Monica steps out of her sky-high heels and tiptoes into the kitchen. Lazily, I saunter behind her, curious to see what she's doing. Grabbing herself a glass for water, her mini dress rises, giving me a tantalizing peek of her creamy white thighs. *Goddess.* Desperate to touch her, I stride forward and press my front into her back. "Ahhh." She gasps when she feels how much I want her.

Drawing back a few strands of her blonde hair that have fallen, I whisper in her ear, "Are you ready for me?"

Pushing her butt out, she grinds against me and I anchor her hips, not allowing her to move. "So thirsty," she moans. Turning her around, her hip rubs up against my steel-like cock and a zing runs up my spine. When she's all the way around, I use my hips to pin her against the counter. Grabbing the glass from her, I reach for the faucet and fill the cup with cold, refreshing water. "Ahhh." Falls from my lips after I take a large drink. Monica licks her parched lips and my cock flinches. "Mmmm. Please, Christian?" she moans.

"Darling, do you want the water or me?" I ask, my voice filled with gravel.

Monica flutters her eyelids and mouths *"both."* Not being able to wait anymore, I hand her the glass and then pick her up and set her on the granite counters. While she sips the water, I push her skirt up to her waist and my eyes are met with wet satin panties. "Fuck. Monica. Fuck." She giggles and then hiccups.

Lowering my head to her, I push the drenched fabric to the side and nuzzle my nose in the small landing patch of hair that covers her mound. "You smell amazing. You smell like mine." I lick from back to her clit. "Hicc-uh-Christian-ahh." Her hiccup turns into a throaty moan that sets my body on fire. I need to get her to our bed now. Lifting my head, I see she has a death grip on the glass. Removing it from her hands, I ask, "You done?" She nods. Setting it on the counter, I pick her up and place her over my should before I carry her to the bedroom.

The next few hours are a blur, but I know they are steamy and leave us both completely sated. After a quick shower, I pull fresh boxers out of my dresser. Opening a lower drawer, I pull out a baby-soft chemise I purchased the other day for Monica. It was a conversation starter. Handing it to her, she looks confused. "Thank you, Christian. You didn't need to buy me anything. I have pajamas in my bag over there." She points to the bag she brings back and forth a few times a month when she stays over.

"I know I didn't need to buy you anything, but I wanted to show you what I've done," I confidently tell her.

Still looking confused, she says, "Okay. What did you do?"

Pointing to the drawer that once held the chemise, it's now empty. I wait a second to see if she's understanding. Unable to control my excitement, I grab her hand and say, "I cleaned out space in my dresser, closet, and bathroom for you to keep some of your stuff here." Monica's eyes go wide and I immediately panic. "If you want, that is."

"Christian, that's huge for you. Are you sure?" she questions. *Man, does this woman know me?*

Nodding, I confess, "I'm sick of you looking like you're a guest here."

Stuttering, she asks, "W-what are you saying?"

"I want you here with me," I tell her.

"Are you suggesting we move in together?" she asks with uncertainty, and again I panic. *Am I?*

"No, I'm not there yet. But I know we'll get there, eventually. Just not yet."

Monica lets out a shaky breath. "Okay, that's good. I mean, yes, eventually I'd like to live with you too, but for now, I'm just not ready to do that. I mean, you know, I still have time left on my lease."

I wasn't expecting her hesitation. Scratching my

head, I agree. "Okay, but just so we're clear, I do consider us exclusive and you are mine."

Monica laughs. "I understand. Maybe one day soon, I'll be ready for that next step. But for now, as long as we are on the same page with our commitment to each other, I'm happy. We're okay, right?"

Pulling her in for a hug, I caress her still naked skin. "Yes, babe. We're good."

Chapter 31

Christian

Since my late teens, I'd believed that bachelorhood was the only way to live a worthwhile life. Sex with the same person, night after night, seemed boring and dull. And definitely not for me. Sure, I'd grown up with parents who'd been married forever and had remained faithful and in love. But it seemed like what they had was an oddity rather than a norm. Basically, I was sure it didn't happen to many, and I knew I wouldn't be so lucky, so why hope for something that was completely out of reach?

But now, at almost twenty-seven, I've concluded that I was so fucking wrong. It isn't out of reach. You just have to find the right person. And I have. Monica is amazing. She is the woman of my dreams in every sense of the word. Not only is she an incredible person, but the chemistry we share is insane. And, bonus, she's put up with my previous inability to label my feelings and our status. Things have changed for me, and I'm ready to admit how I feel.

Every day, I try to show her how much I love her. At least I've finally gotten up the nerve to say those three little words. Maybe it was recent, but those words, even though they're little, are fucking terrifying. They carry some massive weight with them, and I refused to use them unless I was absolutely positive I felt them.

The night I tell Monica is just a typical night. She stays at my penthouse most nights, unless Josiah is in town, and she's waiting for me when I bring dinner home. Having her in my space is a dream come true. Ever since we got together months ago, she's turned my penthouse into a home. Now, instead of hospital white, the walls are a soft gray. My black leather couch, which seemed so masculine when I bought it, is now covered in throw pillows, and a basket of mismatched gray blankets sits next to it. We even selected a few pieces of art for the walls. But the best feature by far is the beautiful woman snuggled in my oversized chair, totally lost in a book.

After I kick off my shoes at the door, I stroll into the kitchen and set dinner on the counter before moving over to her. So absorbed in her book, she doesn't register my approach. Sneaking up behind her, I peer over her shoulder to see what she's reading. Of course it's a romance novel; they're her favorite.

My girlfriend is a dichotomy. A pure kindergarten

teacher by day, guiding and directing little minds as they grow and develop. In the evening, she becomes a filthy smut reader who drools over things like dirty talk, nipple piercings, tattoos, and light bondage.

Occasionally, when a particular section of a book, um... stimulates her, she uses her teacher's voice to read the passage to me, always making herself sound extra sultry and seductive. It's hot as hell and always leads to exciting, sleep-depriving, orgasmic evenings for us. Her love of books is something I will always encourage. In fact, a few months ago, I snuck onto her Kindle, added money to her Amazon account, and uploaded several books from the bestsellers list. So far, she's mentioned something about duct tape and blow pops. I'm not sure what either of those mean, but I'm down to try anything her heart desires.

Tonight, as she reads someone else's words, I lean over, kiss the small dip in her neck below her ear, and whisper something I've never said before. To her or anyone. "I love you, Monica."

She gasps, and I hear her Kindle drop. I stand up, and when her eyes meet mine, I shrug and smile. Tears appear instantly in her eyes and she jumps at me. Catching her in my arms, she nuzzles into me, saying, "I love you too, Christian." Our lips seek each other and we kiss until we're both breathless.

Setting her back in the chair, I motion toward the kitchen. "I brought home dinner from Mateo's." Monica squeals as she runs into the kitchen. Following behind, I laugh. My girl has spunk. And I love that and everything else about her.

Hours later, once we've had our fill of delicious Italian food and taken our time reenacting a scene from her latest book, we snuggle together in bed. Monica nudges my side and says, "You love me, do you?"

Chuckling, I tip her head to me so she's looking at me. "I do. So much." Monica's blue eyes glisten and she nods. It feels like she wants to say something but won't. "What is it?"

Breaking eye contact, she nuzzles into my chest. "When did you know?"

Seeing she's uncomfortable, I squeeze her tightly before answering, without hesitation, "Thanksgiving 2014."

"What?" she gasps as her head flies up. Her eyes trace back and forth over my face, looking to assess whether what I've said is true.

Shrugging my shoulders and nodding my head, I whisper, "It's true. I've just been fighting it for so long. You had me running scared since that night in the movie room."

Suddenly, tears appear in the corners of her eyes and my stomach clenches. I know what she's going to say is going to be painful to hear. "Is that why you treated me so badly?" Yep. That fucking sucked. But she's right. And so far, we haven't really talked about it. Guess there's no time like the present.

"There's no easy way to say this other than yes.

Having feelings for you scared the shit out of me. At first, I was scared because they were unfamiliar and uncomfortable. Then I was scared you didn't feel the same. Next, I was scared because I wanted you so badly, but it went against everything I had ever thought for myself. Then I was scared I wasn't good enough for you. And finally, when I was scared you were moving on, I got serious and did something about it." Shock covers Monica's face and I know I've just released an emotional bomb on her.

"Oh. Ummm," Monica babbles. *Shit, did I break her with my confession?*

"I know that's a lot to take in. And I know dragging you through that was painful and wrong, but I was a coward when it came to admitting I cared for you. I am so sorry for the way I treated you. You deserved better than that. I only hope that you'll forgive me and we'll move forward together. Because I do love you."

Snuggling deeper into my side, Monica is tracing her pointer finger over my abs. Her touch always feels amazing, and I am kicking myself when I realize how many years I wasted being stupid and stubborn.

"I think I understand why you behaved the way you did. And I won't deny that what you did... hurt. But it wasn't all bad. Through the years there have been some memories I absolutely cherish, and those are what made it impossible to wash my hands of you and walk away."

I kiss her head. "I am so sorry, Monica. Please

forgive me for being an idiot." Her giggles warm my heart, and I know we will move past this. "I love you, Monica Fields."

"I love you too, Christian Fox. Now that that's settled, can we do something more energizing and exciting?"

Rubbing my chin, I ask, "What do you propose?"

Sitting up, she pulls back the sheets and says, "I want to try what the couple is doing on page one hundred forty-five."

Flipping to that page, my eyes go wide. We haven't ever tried this before. Dropping the Kindle off the side of the bed, I smile and say, "I'm game if you are."

"Yee-haw," is all Monica hollers as she climbs on top of me, facing the opposite direction. *Yee-haw is right.*

Chapter 32

Christian

Things between Monica and me have been amazing. Almost too good that I'm afraid of what's coming. This week we've decorated my penthouse for Christmas, and I've seen nothing so festive. Monica loves everything Christmas, and it now covers every surface of my home. Even the toilet is decorated. If I didn't love her so much, I'd probably find it annoying and bothersome. But it makes her happy, so in turn, it makes me happy. Shit, I'm sounding like a sap. WTF is happening to me? I need to get together with my boys and find my man card, stat.

We are ridiculously perfect together, and our relationship is rock solid. We've had enough run-ins with ex-hookups of mine to prove it. Every time, I worry it'll be the final nail in my coffin. But Monica has definitely surprised me. She tells me that yes, it bothers her, but she's confident in our relationship. Even if I still struggle to define it. Yes, I am well aware of how stupidly stubborn I am.

With Christmas approaching, that also means Lucas and Samantha's destination wedding is too. The tickets are booked. We made room reservations. We are all set. I'm beyond ready to leave cold, windy Chicago for hot, breezy Maui. My girl is the maid of honor and I'm the best man. This isn't the first wedding I've been to, but it is the first I'm attending with a girlfriend. And not just a girlfriend, but a serious one who believes in happily ever after. I suspect this wedding is going to stir up a lot of different emotions for both of us.

Tonight, Samantha is coming over to watch Lucas's game with Monica and me. Basically, I'll be watching the game while they review last minute wedding details. Because they've mentioned fitting into their dresses a million times over the past months, I'm having organic salads with grilled chicken delivered for them while I plan to devour a supremely meaty pizza by myself.

The game tonight feels different from most. When I talked to Lucas earlier, he said the New Yorkers weren't happy he was back in the city and playing for a different team. Mika, another client of mine, even said the vibe in the arena for morning skate felt strange.

By the second period of the game, the hostility is taken up a notch when one of the New York players deliberately takes out Ace, by slamming him into the boards, headfirst. After the dirty hit, Ace remains on the ice, motionless. When the referees stop the game, the entire Steel team leaves the bench, forming a protective barrier around Ace while the team doctors assess him. Finally, Ace is loaded onto a backboard, taken off the ice, and readied to be transported to the local hospital for evaluation. Coach Tristan calls his team together to give them a brief pep talk before play is resumed. I can only imagine how tough that would have been. Knowing the team, they are more like brothers than teammates. And I'm sure they are all angry and want to get even.

Over the last year, I have gotten to know Coach Tristan better, and I can just imagine he told the guys to finish the game by playing good clean hockey. The guys do just that. They win the game despite all that happened. They have another game versus New York tomorrow, and I'm not sure it will go much better.

When I text the guys the next morning, they assure me that Ace is bruised up and missing some teeth, but he's okay. Nothing major appeared on his scans, so after taking some time to heal, he'll be back at it. While reading the news on my iPad after checking in with the guys, I come across something that makes me sick to my stomach.

A salacious article referencing Mika is front and center. The headline and accompanying photos are horrendous. Over the years managing athletes, I've learned to be discreet about what I see. Choosing to keep pertinent information close until I can verify its authenticity. However, this news is about one of my closest friends and will affect one of Monica's best friends, Shiloh. I'm at a crossroads. What do I do? Unsure, I do nothing.

Later that night, while I sit in our bed, I'm reviewing a contract while Monica reads another steamy novel, when my phone rings. It's Mika. Slipping from bed, I head out into the living room to find out what's going on. He sounds horrible as he explains what happened. Once I hear the article is a lie, I feel better. I caution him about needing to tell Shiloh before she hears it from someone else, and he agrees. We come up with a game plan and I promise him I'll reach out to our PR department for their advice on how to handle this situation.

The next morning, when I finally pry my eyes open, I see Monica frantically pacing. When she realizes I'm awake, she stops. "Did you know?" she asks, her voice heavy with emotion.

"Know what?" I ask.

She whips her iPad around and there, in bold print, is the headline from yesterday's article.

"Mika's in the City Looking to SCORE!"

My stomach drops.

"You knew," Monica says in a scary, calm voice. She's disappointed.

Putting my hands up in surrender, I answer, "I saw it yesterday. But I wanted to talk with Mika before I rushed to any conclusions."

Monica crosses her arms in front of her, scaring me a little. When she cocks her head to the side, I feel shivers spread across my body.

"It's all lies," I rush out. "Mika told me last night what happened, and it is a lie. Shortly after those awful pictures were taken, he and Connor left the bar alone."

Monica acknowledges my words, but worry for Shiloh is evident across her face. I understand fully. I'm worried about Mika too. Monica grabs her phone. "What are you doing?" I tentatively ask.

"I have to warn her, Christian," Monica says tearfully. When she finally gets Shiloh on the phone, it doesn't sound good. Shit! What am I supposed to do? I call Mika.

When he picks up, he sounds odd. It's a combination of adrenaline, exhaustion, and sadness.

"Monica saw the article this morning, and she's been calling Shiloh every fifteen minutes until she finally answered. And... their conversation... it's... it's not going well," I tell him.

"It fucking figures," he grumbles at me, then tells me it was my responsibility to keep Monica from telling Shiloh. *Fuck that, I'm not a babysitter.* If he wasn't man enough to handle telling Shiloh what happened, that's on him. "I got to go," He grumbles before hanging up.

A few hours later, I call to check on him and colorful language fills the other end of the phone. "Mika, slow down. What's happened?"

"She ended things with me, and through a text too. What the fuck am I going to do?"

Shocked, I say, "Shit, man. I don't know. I don't do relationships. And this is a big reason why!"

"You? You don't do relationships? Excuse me? What is it called that you're doing with Monica?" he snaps at me, his voice full of spite and anger.

"What I'm doing with Monica is different. We are not in a relationship. We are more like friends with benefits," I tell him, because what we are is tricky to explain. I want to scream at Mika that it's Monica who won't label us. That I finally figured out what I want —*her*—and now that she knows that, she's gun shy. But really, it's no one's business but ours, and I won't throw her under the bus just to make myself look or feel better. If Mika needs to vent, I'll be a target for him as long as he doesn't cross the line.

Still pissed, Mika prods, "Would she be cool with that title? If I asked her if you were just her friend with benefits, would she agree?"

Defensively, I lob back, "You will not be asking her that. She knows the deal with us, and I don't want you messing it up!" This is bullshit. He's taunting me because he has no fucking clue what Monica and I have.

He laughs humorlessly. "Oh, I see. I would mess it

up? Is that right? Huh? It would have nothing to do with you and your inability to commit to someone who is fucking perfect for you? Whatever you say, man."

What the fuck! He's really pissing me off. "What do you mean, Mika? I thought you called about your woman problems not to psychoanalyze mine."

Mika growls out, "So, you're admitting you have women problems? It's about damn time. Christian, even though I don't really like your woman right now, considering the shit storm my life has become in the last forty-eight hours, even I know Monica deserves better than being temporary. She is the one, and you'd be the stupidest man alive to keep calling her your fuck buddy and not make her permanent before she gets sick of the shit you're selling and walks away *forever!*" Then the fucker hangs up on me.

Angry, I stalk around my living room. This is on him. It was his responsibility to tell Shiloh, no one else's. Even I agree it's complete shit, but his attack on me and Monica, that's unnecessary. He doesn't know what we have, only we do. And I'm certainly not going to throw her under the bus and tell everyone she's the one in limbo right now. After all I've put her through, I can continue to shoulder the blame.

Mika's words cut deep, and I'm trying to remember he's dealing with a lot. For now, I think our friendship needs some space. Maybe by the time we're all in Maui in a few weeks for Lucas and Samantha's wedding, things will be back to normal.

Chapter 33

Monica

My bestie is getting married to a certifiable god. Okay, not really, but Lucas Bouchard is the real deal. Not only is he a gifted hockey player, he's a great guy, and he loves my best friend more than anything in the world. After watching her with Mitch the dick all those years, I'm so glad she finally found her HEA.

This week we are all in Maui doing all things wedding to help them celebrate this next step in their lives. Because Christian and I are only semi-official in front of our close friends, we have to lie low this week. We won't be sharing a hotel room or escaping for romantic getaways. To tell you the truth, this stay is my fault. For the longest time, Christian wouldn't admit that we were anything and then suddenly he did. And instead of being excited about that, I grew worried. It was frustrating. For so long, he had kept me as the secret and I'd been content with that. Hopeful that one day he'd realize he wanted more, but then he did and I panicked. Everything that I wanted was being handed to me, but I wasn't sure I wanted to accept it. Because if I lost it, I knew it would hurt so much worse than anything I'd been through before. So, we headed to Maui, still keeping our relationship from two people, George and Susan Fox. And every time I saw them, I felt guilty. This time, Christian hadn't asked me to keep us quiet. I'd asked him. And the shame of that was killing me.

After a full day of sun where the guys go golfing and the ladies spend the morning at the spa and the afternoon poolside, we all meet up for dinner. During this week, Samantha and Lucas want everyone to spend dinners together, so tonight we are all heading to a Japanese restaurant on the resort's property. Not feeling too adventurous, I order Yakisoba noodles with chicken, and it's amazing.

Following dinner, I decide to go for a walk on the beach by myself. Being here, watching my best friend have her dream wedding, has hit harder than I thought it would. It's not that I'm not happy for them. I am, really. I just wish I knew I'd have the same ending.

Being with Christian is perfect. Well, almost. We we're still in limbo.

Tears stand at the ready and thoughts plague my mind as I sit down on the beach to watch the sunset. It's easy to get lost in the masterpiece painting the sky.

Red, orange, yellow, and magenta all break out in a brilliant display before me. It's spectacular.

Just as the sun sets, I feel someone step up behind me and I freeze. Goose bumps pebble my skin, even though the temperature must still be in the eighties. The sound of waves crashing in front of me battles with my recognition of how close the mysterious person behind me is.

"Monica, is that you?" a deep masculine voice calls out. Turning my head, I see it's Mika, and he's heading toward me.

"Yep, it's me," I answer as I lift my hand up to wave at him. Things have been a little tense between us since the dreaded New York incident and the carryover to my friend Shiloh.

"Can I join you? Or were you out here thinking like me?" He smiles painfully, as if his admission hurts him.

Nodding, I point to the sand. "Just thinking like you, I suppose."

Mika drops down next to me and we sit there in silence, listening to the waves crash up against the shore. I'm not sure how long we're there, but I'm getting tired. Pushing up from the sand, I tell him I'm heading back if he wants to come too. He just shakes his head no, and my heart hurts for him.

"Night, Mika," I whisper before I walk away.

As I'm walking back to my room, my phone rings. Answering it, I say, "Hey, Christian."

"Babe. Where are you?" he asks in a sultry tone that makes my stomach flip.

"Heading to my room. I just went for a walk on the beach and watched the sunset. Why?"

Christian switches the call to FaceTime. "I'm outside your room, waiting to see if you'd like to go for an evening swim with me. One of the hotel employees told me about a private spot where we could swim in the ocean, stare at the stars, be alone with each other. I even packed a picnic. What do you say?"

Smiling like an idiot, I nod and tell him I'll be there soon.

Moments later, in my room, after grabbing my string bikini and throwing it on, I'm barely able to get my cover-up on before Christian mauls me.

"I've missed you so much this week," he growls, while placing kisses on my neck.

"I've missed you too. Especially at night. Sleeping without you beside me isn't the same. I wish things were different." I hang my head with that last confession.

Christian lifts my chin up and stares at me with tender eyes. "I know we'll get there." His admission is filled with confidence.

"It's just your parents, Christian. And they love me. Why can't I bring myself to tell them? I know they'd be happy."

He smiles at me. "Yes, they do, and yes, they would. But you are what matters. We don't need to tell them until we're both ready. Okay? I'm not going anywhere. Nothing has to change between us. I'm still yours. Can't that be enough, right now?" Hearing the emotion in Christian's voice calms me. He knows I love him and I'll figure this out. Getting over my fears is just going to take a little time. And since I waited for him, he's doing the same for me.

His brilliant blue eyes shine as he sweeps me off my feet and hugs me tight, like he never wants to let me go. When he sets me back on the ground, he kisses me with such passion. There's no doubt. This man has my heart completely. I just need to fully trust him.

Chapter 34

Christian

Months pass, and the more time I spend with Monica, the more I realize she's perfect for me. We do everything together, acting just like an actual couple, without the official label. When we're with our friends and they joke about our status as a couple, things always get awkward. After all this time, things have changed. I'm no longer dragging my heels. Monica has put the brakes on, only allowing me so close before she withdraws. Not sure what to do, I remain quiet, giving her the space she needs to help decide what she wants. The longer this goes on, the more uncomfortable the issue gets between Monica and me, and now we both avoid it.

* * *

The rest of the school year speeds by and before I know it, Monica is making plans to head up to the farm to help during the summer break. Normally, she goes up for only part of the break, but a farm employee gave their notice and she decided to help out for the entire summer. We haven't spent too much time apart since we became an item over two years ago.

"Two years already? That doesn't seem right," I tell myself while using my fingers to count the months. Realization sets in. It's been over two years. In that time, the only person I've been with or wanted is Monica. *Holy shit.* Now all our friends' harassing finally makes sense. But if commitment is what she wants... why, now that I'm offering it, does she push back? *Because of you, you dumb fuck. You took too long.*

I'd always said I was a forever bachelor and would never settle down. But I discovered that dude's an egotistical asshole. He didn't know what I wanted or what could be possible. With her. Now that I've figured out I want only her, thoughts of her not being there are physically painful. Three months without her. How will I survive? She'll know, so I'll ask her.

ME

Hey, babe.

MONICA

Hey. What's up?

ME

Are you home tonight?

MONICA

Yes, I leave in the morning. Why? Are
you going to miss me?

ME

Really? After all this time, I'm
surprised you have to ask.

MONICA

So, that'd be a no?

ME

You aren't funny. Yes, I'm going to
miss you so much, babe. Do you
really have to be gone for three
months? I'm not sure I'll survive.

MONICA

You will. Or you could come with me.
Help around the farm. I'm sure my
brothers would love the extra worker
to boss around. Plus, we could
always have sex in the barn. I've
always wanted to do that.

ME

Sign me up. Wait, that's for sex in the
barn. Not the work. You are the only
Fields I let boss me around. Do you
think your parents would let me come
for a visit or two? Three months is a
long time without seeing you. I don't
want you to forget about me.

MONICA

> I won't forget about you. And you can definitely visit. But remember, rules still apply like in Maui. We aren't married. Hell, we aren't officially official. There's no way my parents would allow a sleepover.

ME

I can be really quiet.

MONICA

> Keep dreaming, cowboy. We both know you can't. If you come for a visit, you'll stay in one of my brothers' rooms, just like before. Any hanky-panky will depend on our ability to be creative.

ME

Okay, but I'm pretty sad about you being gone so long, I might need extra-long consoling tonight.

MONICA

> I can do that. I'll miss you too. Meet you at your place in a few. I need to finish packing.

ME

See you later, babe. I love you. I'm grabbing dinner on my way home.

Home? I know it's a turn of phrase people throw around and it has so many meanings, but the idea of home and Monica go hand in hand. It feels right. It's where I want her. Always. But Monica has to decide when it's right for her. *I hope it's soon.* If I hadn't been so stubborn and dragged my feet for so long, I wouldn't be feeling this way.

***

The first two weeks Monica is gone aren't so bad because I'm distracted by work. When we can, we talk and text. But then the summer solstice rolls around and, even though Lucas and Samantha are throwing a barbeque, Monica plans to stay at the farm. Their town has some festivities she wants to attend. She invites me, but she sounds different. It feels like she's not sure she wants me there, so instead I stay in the city and head to Lucas and Samantha's house. At least there, I'll feel welcome.

"Hey, Christian, what's got you so down?" Lucas asks when I arrive late to the party.

Frowning, I grumble, "I'm fine."

"Geez. Well, you know where everything is. Samantha left something on the table over there to help with the s'mores this year." He laughs and walks away.

I nod at some of the guys as I head over to the table. I reach for the box. It's a DIY backyard s'mores kit. Perturbed, I grumble under my breath, "Who am I supposed to do this stupid shit with?"

"Whoa, man. What did the almighty s'more ever do to you? Last year, you were cooking up quite the batch on the grill with Monica, right? Speaking of your other half, where is she?" Mika asks with a dopey grin on his face.

Ignoring his cheery demeanor, I snarl, "Not here, obviously."

Taking a step back as if I've hit him, he focuses his eyes on me and scratches his head. "Is that why you're acting like an asshole?"

"Fuck off, Mika. Recently, you were doing the same, so get off my back."

Mika moves closer with concern on his face. "Whoa, Christian, what is going on? Where's Monica?"

Hanging my head, I mumble, "She went to the farm for the entire summer, and now things are weird between us."

"What do you mean, weird?" he asks.

I shrug my shoulders. "I don't know, it's just a feeling."

Mika places his hand on my shoulder. "Have you asked her about it?"

"No. I'm embarrassed. What if it's nothing and I'm reading into it, or what if it's something and she doesn't want to tell me about it? What if she met someone? We haven't made our relationship official. We haven't labeled us. Basically, she's a free agent and I have no one to blame but me. I should have locked her down years ago. Man, I've been so fucking stupid. And now things are tense and the guy she had a crush on throughout high school is single and lives there." I confess all the fears I've been wrestling with since she's been gone. My thoughts are jumbled and they make me sound crazy. I haven't threatened anyone's life, but I'm not opposed to driving down there and stomping around until she realizes I'm not going anywhere.

"Christian, the worst thing you can do is make assumptions right now. You don't know what she's thinking or doing and you won't until you talk to her, right?"

I nod to Mika, acknowledging the correctness of his words. But I'm scared to go to the farm. Last time I was there, I left early with my tail between my legs, and although things between us have changed dramatically, I'm still intimidated by her father and brothers.

"You're right. Just like you said months ago, I need to do something before it's too late and she decides she's done with me. I couldn't handle it if she walked away. This summer is already killing me."

Mika punches me in the arm. "There's the spirit. And, Christian, I'm sorry about how I said that months ago. The message is still the same, but I didn't have to be such an asshole in my delivery."

Slugging him back, I reply, "It's okay. You were in an awful place, and you were right. I need to grow some balls and get my girl."

Grabbing the s'mores kit, I head back through my sister and Lucas's house on my way out.

"Dude, where are you going? Didn't you just get here?" Lucas hollers at me from across the kitchen.

Samantha pops up from behind the fridge door to see who he's talking to.

Nodding, I call out, "I did, but I have to go take care of something that's long overdue. Thanks for the s'mores kit. It'll come in handy."

Lucas scratches his head in confusion as he waves me off, and Samantha, always quick, replies, "It's about damn time. Go get her."

Taking a quick detour to my penthouse, I throw together a weekend bag before I'm on the road again.

The drive out to the farm goes quickly, as my mind races with all the things I want to say and do. Texting Josiah, I tell him I'm heading there as a surprise.

For the past year, every time Josiah has come into town, he's stayed at Monica's. And although he's said nothing, I know he knows we're together.

Josiah tells me he'll meet me in town because that's where the whole family is for the night. Anxiety courses through my body. Turning onto the main street in town, I tell myself, *it's now or never. Get your girl.*

My hands shake as I pull into an empty spot near the tractor supply store. Before I know it, Josiah, Will, and Mike are standing in front of my SUV with their arms crossed and matching glares. *Shit. Maybe I didn't think this through fully.* Should I forgo my plan and leave? Should I get out and pray they don't kill me? Not really sure what to do, I see Josiah's glare morph into a smirk, and I know I'm okay to leave my vehicle. Letting out a deep breath, I climb out.

"Hey, guys," I say as I wave at Monica's large brothers.

Will continues to glare while Mike spits on the sidewalk. *Are they going to kill me?* Panicked, I look at Josiah, who has a huge shit-eating grin stretched across his face.

"You should see your face, Christian. You look like you're going to either shit your pants, cry, or have a stroke," Josiah says, then laughs like a fucking hyena, setting off Mike and Will. Before I know it, we're all laughing; them in enjoyment, me in terror.

Before I even gather myself, the voice of the woman I've been missing comes from behind me. "Christian, is that you?"

Whipping around, I see the entire rest of the Fields family. *Now or never.* Rushing over to her, I pick her up, spin her around, and hug her like never before. Monica giggles and all is right in my world again. Setting her back down, I take her hand before doing anything else. Then I look at her parents.

"Mr. and Mrs. Fields, it's so good to see you," I say to them.

Her mom steps forward, pulling me into a hug. "It's good to see you too, Christian. Are you here for the weekend?"

Still holding Monica's hand, I squeeze it for support. Wasting no time, she squeezes it back, letting me know she's there.

"I am, if you wouldn't mind a guest," I hesitantly answer.

This time, her dad steps up to me. At six foot two, I'm not small, but her dad has a few inches on me and he uses that to convey his message. "Sure, we could use an extra set of hands with farm chores. That's if you're up for it?" He smirks at his sons and they snicker like a bunch of schoolgirls.

Monica squeezes my hand again, reminding me she's got me. "Good thing I packed for it," I answer him.

He shoots me a grin that reminds me he's watching me and then he takes his wife's hand and asks, "Who wants to go see the pie-eating contest?" Everyone but Monica and I head down the street.

As soon as they're a few feet away, I pull her into my arms and hug her tightly. With her nuzzled into my chest, I inhale her vanilla citrus scent, and my body relaxes. Well, everything but my cock, who's been pissed off lately because he's had to survive on the attention he gets from my right hand while Monica's been away.

"I've missed you, babe. So much," I whisper to the top of her head.

She shimmies her hips, giggles, and says, "I can feel that. It must've been so hard for you."

"Monica," I growl. "Keep it up and I'll show you how hard it can be."

She pushes back, looks into my eyes, rises on her

toes, then kisses me. Hands down, it's the best kiss I've ever received. Loud whooping, whistling, and catcalls travel down the street toward us, letting us know her family just got their visual proof that we're something. "It's about time!" Josiah hollers as her mom clutches her dad, wearing a bright smile.

"Guess that makes us official," Monica says.

"Fuck yeah," I murmur against her lips before kissing her senseless.

Officially, she's mine and I'm hers. Does that mean I have all my shit worked out? Hell no. It's day by day. For right now, I'm just enjoying the feel of my first official girlfriend in my arms. There's no other place I'd rather be. That's a lie. I'd rather be between her legs, but the town square is probably not ready for that show.

Chapter 35

Monica

Christmas time on the farm is my absolute favorite. There's something in the air that makes it magical. Since Christian and I are official now, he's here with me. As soon as school was out for break, I headed here to help, and Christian arrived yesterday after he finished with his last client before taking a much-needed break from work. This is his third trip out to the farm, and he knows well that this holiday vacation is not really a vacation. Vacations don't really exist when your family owns a dairy farm. After all, people need milk, especially to enjoy with holiday treats.

We even enjoy some of the holiday festivities. A few days before Christmas, my entire family, and Christian, of course, head over to our friend's Christmas tree lot and take a non-traditional sleigh ride down the snowy back roads.

"This is amazing!" Christian notes as we snuggle together in plaid blankets, sharing a hay bale on the back of a trailer that is being pulled by a tractor.

"Doesn't get more country than this." I laugh while pulling out a thermos of hot apple cider mom and I made earlier in the day for everyone. "Want some?" I ask. Christian's eyes brighten as he nods.

Sipping our cider, I can't help but be drawn into the spirit of the season. "It's breathtaking," I mumble.

Christian looks at me. "No, Monica, my love. You are." His warm lips place a gentle kiss on the tip of my cold, probably red-tinted, nose and I sigh. *I love this man.*

Later that night, he surprises me with an early Christmas gift. He's taking me away for the new year. I don't know much, other than he rented a lakefront cabin, and I'm excited to get to spend some uninterrupted time together.

While Christian is helping feed and milk the ladies the next morning, I keep busy making Christmas cookies with my mom. Maddy and Kayla will be over later today to have their kids help decorate the sugar cookies we made last night.

This fall was busy with school activities and then there were holidays thrown in there, and before I knew it, I was planning winter holiday crafts for my class. Christian was just as busy at work with sponsorship deals for many of his clients. He also had to attend scouting trips to visit some college football players who will probably attend the NFL Scouting Combine in February. Although he can't sign them yet, he can show up and express his interest.

* * *

The drive up to the lakefront cabin Christian rented doesn't take too long, and thankfully, the owners live nearby and promised they'd be by to clear the new snow before our arrival.

Pulling up in front of the cabin, the structure looks more like a cottage. A beautiful wood deck wraps all the way around it. To the side of the cabin is a stone fire pit surrounded by Adirondack chairs. At the edge of the property is a lake, and the owners used the same beautiful wood from the deck to build a walkway and dock. The lake is frozen over and it looks like people have been skating and skiing across it. Just like when I was a child, I have the sudden desire to make a snow angel, so as soon as Christian stops the SUV, I hop out.

Dropping into the fresh powder, I spread my legs out first and then swing my arms up and down. When I'm sure I've done a decent job, I sit up and carefully extricate myself from my snow art. Meanwhile, Christian has remained nearby, quietly watching, his mouth slightly opened in shock.

"Tada," I say and bow proudly after I inspect my finished work—a perfect snow angel.

Christian just laughs. "Come on, let's go warm you

up. This place has a fireplace and a hot tub. What do you want to do first?" He throws in a saucy wink. Grabbing his hand, I drag him inside and toward a room that I hope has a bed. To my luck, it does, and as I walk toward it, I remove my clothes. Christian spins me around and questions, "What do you think you're doing, beautiful?"

"Getting comfortable," I answer with a wink, then add, "I need these wet clothes off." Within seconds, Christian is on me, lifting my tank top and sweatshirt over my head with a simple tug. My blonde hair comes loose from its messy bun and settles over my lacy, hot-pink balconette bra. Christian's eyes go wide and he licks his lips. As he traces his finger over my lips, I suck it into my mouth, showing him what I'd like to do to another part of him. He tugs it loose, and a pop echoes through the room, displaying the acoustics we will enjoy later. Running his soaked finger down my chest, past my heaving breasts, toward my pants, I suck in a breath when I feel him toying with the button. Excited energy runs rampant through my body as I anticipate what's coming next.

Slowly, Christian lowers the zipper of my jeans. He slides them over my hips, grazing my hip bones with his delicate touch. Goose bumps chase his trail, leaving me soaked and wanting. He lowers to a squat, taking my pants with him. When they get to my feet, he supports my leg as he slides them off. Then he takes his finger and runs it from my ankle toward the juncture of my thighs, stopping at my knee to lick and kiss the soft skin behind them.

His touch becomes heavier as he travels the remaining way up my leg. When he reaches my matching hot-pink underwear, he traces the lines over my hips and discovers it's a G-string. With his large hands, he palms both of my ass cheeks and squeezes while simultaneously shoving his nose into my center and nuzzling.

"Fuck, woman. You smell amazing." He grunts against my lace panties.

"Christian." His name falls from my lips in a throaty moan.

Kissing above my panty line, he flicks his eyes up to me and says, "Yes, babe? What do you need?"

"I need you," I breathe out.

He rises, lifts my limp arms up and hooks them around his neck before he dips to lift me into his arms. My legs wrap around his waist as he walks us to the bed. Lowering me, he gently sets me on the down comforter. He unhooks my legs and arms and lays me back. Bending over, he kisses me senseless before he backs away.

While I'm left in a panting mess, he straightens, strips his black long-sleeve Henley over his head and drops it to the floor. It's hard not to admire his incredible body as he stands before me. Knowing I'm enjoying the view, he teases me by running his hand down his abs slowly. And when he reaches the button of his jeans, he releases it, displaying more of his treasure trail. Licking my lips, I watch as he slowly lowers the zipper, revealing his black boxer briefs and all that they contain. His firm cock is playing peek-a-boo with the top of his boxers, and all I want to do is run my tongue over it and collect the drop of pre-cum I see glistening at the tip.

Flicking my eyes to his, Christian sees the hunger in them and he wraps his hand around his cock, squeezing it.

"You want this, Monica?" His already deep voice drops even lower, his question reverberating in my bones. All I can do is nod. In fact, I probably look like a stupid bobble head, but I don't care. It's insane how much I want him.

Using my feet, I try to drag him to me, but he just smiles. Lowering himself to his knees, he drags me to him. The expectation of what's coming has me ready to climb the walls. Something needs to happen before I combust. Sensing my need, Christian gathers my G-string and drags it down my legs, tossing it haphazardly over his shoulder. Then he dips his head, and I think he's coming for me and I raise my hips, showing him I'm ready. He takes my knees and spreads my legs wide open, as if I'm doing a butterfly stretch. Lowering his mouth to my center, he again tugs my hips toward him and blows on my most sensitive area.

Reflexively, my hips give a little shimmy and he kisses each of my thighs, running the stubble he's recently started growing against me, providing me with even more delicious stimulation. As if he isn't driving my libido insane enough, he takes the flat of his tongue and runs it from my knee to the fold of my leg. His hands anchor my thighs, putting me just where he wants me. This newer dominant side I'm seeing is beyond sexy. *Yes, sir.*

Just as he gets me where he wants me, he pulls back and reaches for something. Lifting my head up to see what it is, I'm surprised to see Christian's holding a black satin blindfold. Standing up, his entire body is on display, and I can't help but gawk. He is perfection.

Wanting to touch him, I reach out my hand. He grabs my wrist, reaches for the other, and moves them above my head. My back arches, presenting my breasts to him. Christian's tongue darts out and circles the already pebbled nipples, making them even more pronounced. Firmly, he nudges my wrists. "Stay," he cautions in a deep, seductive voice that makes me want to listen and disobey simultaneously. The blindfold he's been holding is slid over my eyes and my other senses are heightened instantly. Feeling the heat radiating off Christian's body lures me closer to him, my hands lifting off the bed. He growls, "Monica, what did I say?"

"Stay," I quietly answer as I lower my hands back to the bed.

"Good girl," he whispers against my lips, and a shiver passes down my spine. Christian kisses my lips softly, then traces his finger down my body, stopping to give each breast a nip and squeeze before settling back between my thighs. He strokes up and down them with his hands, heating my skin. When I'm feeling desperate for more, he leans in and blows across my center and my hips raise. He places a palm on my abdomen, forcing them down and holding them in place. Again, he blows across my most private area and it continues to drive me wild. Groaning in protest, I drag out his name, letting him know I'm feeling needy. "Chrissstiannn." Hearing myself, I sound like a petulant child, but in my defense, he's driving me wild on purpose. *Who does that?* Apparently, my man.

He snickers and I panic. Did I do something embarrassing? Why the hell is he laughing? Just as I'm about to break the rules and remove my blindfold, Christian clues me in on what he finds funny. "Tsk, tsk, tsk. You aren't very patient, Monica."

Even though he's cute, the truth remains: with three brothers, I couldn't be patient. If I was, I lost out. And here and now, I'm losing out. "Christian, please," I whimper.

Christian licks through my folds, and when he hits my clit, he flicks it and a buzz shoots through my body. A throaty moan falls from my lips.

"Because you were so polite, I've decided to reward you." Christian continues to lick and tease my folds with his very talented tongue, pushing me closer and closer to the edge of my release. I cannot stand the heat and anticipation in my body. My orgasm builds inside me, and it's never been this intense before. My skin feels tight, like it's a cocoon about to split open to reveal a new creation. Maybe that's symbolic of how I feel. Ever since Christian and I made our relationship official, I've felt different, more confident, steady, and centered.

Sexually intuitive,. Christian recognizes when my brain switches tracks from seeking orgasm to seeking understanding. "Monica," he mumbles against my mons before he inserts two fingers. The additional pressure beckons the lust-soaked section of my brain to get back on track, and it does. It's chasing desire. Pulling his fingers out and then sliding them back in to curl forward like he's telling me to come hither, he rubs against my G-spot, and an explosion travels throughout my body.

While coming down from the high, Christian scoots my sated body farther up the bed, and I can feel him above me. Still wearing the blindfold, I'm at the mercy of the man I love. He kisses me softly as he rests above me. The feeling of his skin against mine is enough to make me desperate for him again. His light scattering of chest hair tickles my erect nipples. Lifting his hips, I feel his cock nudge my entrance, and I pull up my legs, welcoming him in. He thrusts forward slowly and I wrap my legs around him, locking my ankles and pulling him in tight. Within seconds, he's buried to the hilt, and I feel so full.

Christian moves his head to the side of mine and lines up next to my ear. "You were made for me, Monica. I love you so much. I always have. I just wasn't man enough to admit that you were it for me. You always have been." He thrusts through his entire confession, driving each point home and pushing me closer and closer toward another climax. When he confesses his love, we both fall into the abyss.

Christian removes the blindfold and I blink away the darkness I've known for the past hour. Looking at him, I replay his words, and tears gather in my eyes. *He loves me. He really loves me.* Overjoyed, I reach up and grab his face, forcing it to my lips. I kiss my love with all the strength I have. "I love you too," I tell him.

Even though we've been saying it for a few months, this feels different; significant and meaningful. When I first told Christian I loved him, he looked scared. But the more time passed, he openly shared his feelings, and that was good enough for me. All of this; dating, having a girlfriend, and being in love, is new for him, and I can imagine it might be scary or intimidating.

Exhausted and sated, we both fall asleep intertwined with each other. When I wake up later in the afternoon, the bed's empty. Did Christian's confession scare him and send him running? It's not like he'd leave me in the woods at a remote cabin all alone, right? Nervous, I scamper off the bed, pull on a tank top and my panties from the floor where we tossed them, and go in search of my man. *That feels so good to say.*

It doesn't take long to find him; he's sitting in front of the fireplace with wood and matches. There's no fire going, so I tiptoe over to see why he's staring so hard at his cell phone. Over his shoulder, I see him reading an article with instructions on how to start a fire. A giggle slips from my lips and I freeze. He spins around with a smirk on his face.

Pointing over to the fireplace, I ask innocently, "Need any help?"

Placing his hands on his trim waist, he puffs out his defined chest and answers confidently, "I was about to start a fire. Do you want to give it a shot?" Christian doesn't know that I've been starting fires since I was seven, with supervision from my brothers. Actually, if I'm being honest, I was only five when I got the first one going by myself, but don't tell my parents.

Stepping closer to the fireplace, I lean over, sticking my butt out, showing him my G-string, and look over my shoulder. "If I have any trouble, do you think you can help me?" I almost laugh at the seductive naivety in my voice. Christian doesn't answer me, as his attention is locked on my ass. Seeing that, I wiggle it, and he grins, then licks his lips. "Christian," I admonish. His head snaps up, and he meets my eyes. *Gotcha!*

Walking up behind me, he lazily trails his hands over my naked ass cheeks, giving them each a squeeze. "Need some help, babe?" he offers with a chuckle that has my lady bits tingling.

"Can I just try?" I ask while still feigning inexperience.

Rubbing his hands together, he smiles. "Sure, I'll just sit here and take in the gorgeous view," he says while he sits on the couch directly behind me.

Two can play at this. Turning my body sideways so he can see my entire silhouette, I pick up the log in front of me and stare at it, pretending I don't know what to do. Shrugging my shoulders to give extra effect, I set it in the fireplace and then add another. Looking around, I see there is a fire box next to the fireplace that has newspaper and kindling. Crumpling up a few sheets of newspaper, I place them between the logs. After that, I add kindling and a few more logs. It's impossible to not feel Christian's heated gaze behind me. If I already had this fire started, I'd be roasting.

Once I've built up the logs, I grab another sheet of newspaper and roll it to make it look like a torch. Lighting the end, I use it to light my kindling. In no time, I've built a beautiful fire, adding warmth to the cabin. With a look of satisfaction, I turn around and beam at Christian. He looks flabbergasted. His jaw is open and his eyes are wide.

"Holy shit, Monica. Were you a Girl Scout or something? Where did you learn how to start a fire like a pro?"

Joining him on the couch, I tuck my legs up under me, snuggling close to him. Pushing his gaping mouth closed, I answer him. "You know I was raised on a farm, right? I've known how to start fires, mucks pens, and milk cows by hand since I was seven. My first live birth, Mom says I was about three and I named the calf Minnie."

He chuckles. "Why does that not surprise me?" Pulling me tighter to his chest, he tips my chin up and gives me a tender kiss. "You are amazing. Why did it take me so long to admit what I already knew?" Knowing he's asking himself rather than me, I should probably hold my tongue, but that's not me.

"Because you are as stubborn as a heifer who doesn't want to get milked." We both laugh and snuggle closer, enjoying the heat of the fire. Looking around the cabin, I notice it's sparsely decorated. No TV is visible and, on the way up here, I heard we're supposed to get another few inches of snow. Curious, I ask, "What's on the agenda while we're here?"

"Well, there's plenty of snow to enjoy, a plethora of board games, a hot tub, a fire pit, and a bed. Take your pick." Since we just started the fire, we need to do something in the cabin. Games it is.

"What games do they have?"

"They're over there in the hutch. You pick one and I'll pop some popcorn."

After a few rousing hands of Skip-Bo, I crown myself the champion. I'm not sure what that entails, but I still feel victorious. Christian thought of everything, even bringing pre-made meals, so all we have to do is turn on the oven. Over chicken parmesan, we enjoy the fire and talk about our New Year's resolutions. Christian wants to bring in and train another agent, and I want to teach a yoga class as an afterschool activity at my school. *My biggest New Year's hope, which I'm not sharing, is that one day I'll become his wife.*

Chapter 36

Christian

Since Monica is an expert fire builder, I clean up the dishes while she heads out to the fire pit to get it going. Just like years before, it has become a tradition for us to celebrate holidays with s'mores. Usually, it was only the patriotic summer holidays, but I figured it would be symbolic tonight. Watching her from the kitchen window, I can't believe how lucky I am. Monica is the epitome of everything I could ever want in a partner. I'm just glad she didn't give up all those times I pushed her away. She is as stubborn as I am, and I will gladly go toe-to-toe on anything and everything, except this anymore. I'm done letting my fears control me. If I was going to let anything clip me, take me to my knees, it would be the woman who's held my heart for six years.

Grabbing the s'mores ingredients, and something extra, I head out to the firepit to make more memories.

Would they be called s'more memories? Damn, I'm funny.

The fire light dances off Monica's black knit hat, and the glow makes her look angelic. She is an angel, that's for certain. She rescued me.

Now or never. I tell myself.

"Great fire!" I holler as I approach. Monica rocks on her heels and smiles wide, evidently proud of herself. She's adorable. Handing her a roasting stick, I set down all the ingredients so I can dig out a marsh-mallow for her. She told me earlier when I mentioned the fire pit that she was an expert marshmallow roaster. I sure hope so, because I have limited experience. Actu-ally, I've gotten pretty good heating all the ingredients in a disposable cooking pan on the grill.

After loading her up with two marshmallows, I get to work assembling the graham crackers and chocolate bars. Turning away from her, I make sure that the surprise topping I'd gotten for her is unwrapped and in my pocket. Once the marshmallows are golden brown, Monica steps away from the flames to help assemble our desserts. With precision, she delicately sets the marshmallow on the chocolate piece and we both rush to squish our graham cracker covers on the s'mores. While she takes the first bite, I slide the sparkly surprise into my marshmallow so it peeks out.

"Aren't you going to take a bite?" Monica asks as she pulls her sticky mess away from her lovely lips, licking them clean. *Bet her lips taste delicious.*

Looking at my s'more, I smile. *Now or never.* "This s'more looks perfect. You're an expert roaster. It's picture worthy. Want to see?" She nods as she scoots closer. When she's close enough, I hand it to her. Instantly, shock covers her face, and I drop to one knee. Taking the other s'more out of her hand, I pull her attention to me. For a moment, her eyes flick from me to the proposal s'more and then back. She sniffles, and a tear falls down her cheek. All before I've even said anything.

"Monica, babe. When I was thinking about doing this, I tried really hard to come up with something well-written, luxurious, and over-the-top, but the more I thought about it, the more I realized that would be wrong. It wouldn't be perfect for you, and that's what I want to give you. Instead, I thought long and hard about what would mean the most to you, and this is what I came up with.

"For years, I've stubbornly fought my attraction to you, convincing myself what I felt for you wasn't possible or lasting. But you proved me wrong. You never gave up on me. On us. Thank you. Thank you for being the ooey, gooey thing that holds us together. You are the marshmallow to my s'more and I want to make you mine forever. Will you marry me?"

Wiping away tears, she gazes down at me with tender eyes and answers, "Yes, Christian. I'll marry you."

An enormous smile spreads across my face as I stand up and wrap her in a tight hug.

"Need to breathe," she chokes out, and I loosen my hold, laughing. Her eyes dance wildly like the flames of the fire. Pulling her to me for a kiss, I taste chocolate on her lips. I lick into her mouth, asking for more, and I am enveloped by warmth and goodness. Until now, I wasn't aware it had a taste, but what I'm tasting feels like coming home, and right now, there is no place I'd rather be.

Monica's sticky hands go up to my ears. She likes to tug on them when we're kissing. She's told me it lets her feel closer and more connected to me. I don't understand that, but I know it seems possessive and turns me on, so I'm more than willing to endure it. The stickiness of her fingers reminds me she's still holding the s'more with the ring in it. Pulling out of the kiss, I gasp, "Your ring."

Holding up the s'more that's still clutched in her hand, I pull the ring out of the marshmallow. The stunning solitaire is covered in gooey marshmallow cream, and I'm thinking I didn't consider it would be a messy proposal.

Tossing the ring into my mouth, I clean off all the mess and, after using my shirt to dry my saliva, I take her left hand and slide it on her ring finger. We both stare at it for a moment, letting it sink in. Monica lets out the cutest squeal and I can't help but laugh. Needing fresh s'mores to celebrate our engagement, she gets to roasting two marshmallows while I assemble the remaining pieces. Once we have our new s'mores in hand, we toast to the next chapter in our lives and dig in.

Snuggled by the fire after we've had our fill of dessert, we talk about how everyone is going to react to us getting engaged. I confess I hadn't told any of our friends what I was planning, but I asked her parents a few weeks before Christmas and they both gave their blessing. Hearing that makes her smile. I knew that would be important for Monica, so getting their approval became necessary for me to do things right.

"What do you think everyone will say?" I ask.

"Samantha is going to squeal and yell 'told you so,'" she confidently replies. "She's been going on and on about us since freshman year of college."

I nod my agreement. "She's going to be the worst."

An adorable burst of laughter fills the air and then Monica asks, "What do you think the guys will say?"

Leaning back in the Adirondack chair we're snuggled up in, I let out a throaty groan. "I'm changing my answer. Samantha will not be the worst. Mika will."

She gives me a confused look and asks, "Why?"

Until a year ago, I always thought everything we had was temporary. Monica never did. Looking back now, how do I explain that without hurting her feelings? It's not like we haven't talked about all we've been through together, but tonight of all nights, I don't want to rehash old wounds. I know I was an egotistical, immature asshole who took advantage of her feelings for me.

In truth, I've always cared deeply for Monica, but for years I ran from that, not wanting to admit the power she had over me. Until I watched what Mika and Shiloh went through. Some words he and I exchanged during a couple of heated conversations made me recognize how everyone saw my relationship with Monica. Apparently, everyone thought I was using her. The realization of that, and the unfortunate truth of it, disgusted me. Fear of losing her for the way I'd treated her, plagued me. Knowing that if she walked away for good, I would have been the only one to blame.

After some deep reflection, I knew that the conversation I'd had with Mika right after Shiloh had broken up with him was what had made everything clear. His pain and poignant words forced me to reevaluate my feelings for Monica. *Now or never.*

Smirking, I know exactly what Mika will say when he hears I proposed. "Mika will say 'it's about damn time.'"

Smiling, Monica notes, "That's hilarious. Apparently, everyone thought we should be together."

Nodding, I mutter, "Everyone."

Then, as if struck with lightning, she turns to me with big, unblinking eyes. "What are your parents going to say?"

Smiling widely, I reply, "That's easy. They'll be

thrilled. They always considered you part of the family. This way will make it official. We can tell them together."

Monica's response is perfect. "Can we? Maybe we can FaceTime them tomorrow while Samantha and Lucas are still there and tell them all?"

The next day we call the parents and share our exciting news. We haven't set a date yet, but seeing that I've dragged my feet on this whole dating thing, I want Monica to set the timeline for this. Now that I've done the hard part, I'm more than ready to say "I do" to the woman of my dreams.

Chapter 37

Monica

Another summer has arrived, and just like the past ones, Christian and I are attending Samantha and Lucas's Fourth of July party later today. The last year has been full of changes for the Steel family. Yes, I consider myself a part of that family even though I'm not married or engaged to one of its players. On New Year's Eve, though, I snagged the agent to several of their players. We aren't married yet, but it'll happen when it's meant to.

Speaking of weddings, not too long ago we attended Mika and Shiloh's. Because Christian and I had been at my family's farm for Christmas and the cabin for New Year's, we missed the engagement news. And, boy, were they surprised when we shared our own. When we swapped stories later, Shiloh told me that Mika proposed on Christmas morning and both

Sam and Lian helped. According to her, it was absolutely adorable.

Late last night, I returned from my latest visit to the farm. I'd been busy with my mom, getting everything ready for a special event they will hold toward the end of July. In fact, Christian and I are co-hosting it and are inviting our Steel family: Lucas and Sam; Mika, Shiloh, and the kids; Coach Tristan; Ace; Rocco; and Josh. We're hopeful everyone can make it, seeing that it's before the season starts.

I've moved into Christian's penthouse since we got engaged, only keeping my apartment until my lease runs out in a month. For now, when Josiah comes into town to watch baseball games, he has a place to crash for free. Lucky me, since it's the summer, I can hang out with him while he's visiting. I've definitely attended more baseball games this year than I have in the past five, but my brother is one of my best friends, and I don't want things to get weird between us when I get married.

I've noticed he's been a bit more withdrawn since he went back to visit some friends from Penn State. He'd been excited about the trip, but ended up coming home early, saying things hadn't gone as expected and he just needed to get back to the farm. He hadn't even wanted to stay in the city and catch a Cub's game with me. It was strange and something I want to ask about after I let him stew a bit. If he's still grumbling by fall, we'll have a good come-to-Jesus talk and see whose ass I need to kick. Hell, I have an arsenal of fit hockey players who'd have my back any day of the week.

Hopping out of bed, I make my way to the kitchen to grab a cup of coffee from the Keurig. As it brews, I scroll through my phone and see the thread from my two besties already lit up. Looks like between party planning and having young kids, neither one of my best friends could sleep past eight. Lame.

Wrapping my hands around the steaming mug, I sip at the light-roast vanilla goodness and enjoy the tranquility of my morning. The penthouse is quiet, so Christian must be working out in the building's gym, otherwise the sounds of sports media would be traveling through the large space.

Taking my coffee with me, I walk back into the bedroom to shower and get ready for the day. I want to be at Samantha and Lucas's house early to help set up since Samantha is expecting. Even though she's still in her first trimester, her morning sickness has been terrible and often leaves her feeling drained.

Just as I'm stepping out of the shower, Christian saunters into the bathroom with a smirk on his face.

"Just about to shower?" he asks.

Looking at him as if he's crazy, I shake my head. Does he not see my sopping wet hair or the puddle at my feet?

"That's a shame," he states confidently as he peels off his sweaty clothes. When he's naked, he runs his hand down his abs to his erect cock. He strokes himself a few times, and I reach out to him. "Want to join me?" he asks, adding extra sauce to his request. My knees wobble as I drop the towel I'd been using to dry my hair. Like a newborn deer learning to walk, I stumble over to him, following him into the outlandishly large shower.

Taking my hand, he leads me to the right wall. He turns me around so I face it, and uses his body to push me into it. Pressed up against the wall, I feel my body become slick with desire. It's no use denying it. My body wants him, my brain wants him. And soon, he'll be mine.

Taking the coconut body wash, he puts some in his hand and washes all of me. After he's cleaned every square inch of me, I turn back to face him, drop to my knees, and smile.

Christian shakes his head no. But I want to. Taking his hard cock in my hand, I kiss the tip before I pull it into my mouth, sucking him deep. Taking one hand, I wrap it around the base of him and squeeze. In the other hand, I roll his balls while he runs his fingers through my hair. Pulling back to scrape my teeth along the shaft, I treat the head like a lollipop, licking and sucking at it.

When I feel his balls tighten, I pull all of him into my mouth again and suck hard, hollowing out my cheeks. "M-monnn-ica. Baaabe," Christian stutters on a moan, and I know he's about to come.

Stepping back so he slips from my mouth, he wraps

his hand around his strained, engorged cocked and pumps it while maintaining eye contact with me. Within seconds, his cum is spurting out of the tip of his cock in thick ropes. Christian knows I'm not into swallowing, and he does his best to pull out in time. A few times were unprepared and, instead of swallowing, I'd just spat out the warm, salty substance.

Following the shower blowjob, Christian pulls me up to my feet and kisses me passionately. Knowing we don't have much time before we have to leave, I end the kiss and move to the door to step out of the shower. Christian's eyes trace me the entire time as I towel off.

"Just so you know, we aren't finished. When we get home tonight, I'm going to make sure you see fireworks." My cheeks redden and my belly flips at his promise. I can't wait. But first we have to get through the barbeque and inviting all our friends to a surprise event at the farm. We aren't going to tell them anything about it other than we're having it at my family's farm and it involves a barn dance. Or maybe it will be at the barn and there will be some dancing.

Telling our friends about the event goes better than I expected. No one digs too deeply into our lack of details. Some find it hard to believe that after all the years I've know them, I'd invited no one to the farm. Only Christian has been out there, each time making the visit meaningful. The farm holds a special place in my life, and with things changing on the team and individually, I want to pay tribute to its steadfast presence. It was on the visits to the farm that Christian finally confessed his feelings for me. It's symbolic for us and we want to share that with our friends. And in a few weeks, we'll do just that.

Chapter 38

Christian

In a few brief hours, life will change as I know it. Well, maybe. Monica and I invited our friends to the farm, telling them it was for a farm event that we were co-hosting, but we didn't tell them the full truth. Yes, we are hosting it, but so are our parents.

We set everything up and friends are arriving. I'm sure they're wondering what's going on. As far as I know, none of them have been to the farm, so they stay plenty busy with a tour, visiting the new calves, and a sample tasting of some products that are made from Field Farms milk. Once they're done, they'll be escorted to an area close to the house that we've set up just for the special event. I know once the ladies see the chair assembly, they'll figure out what we're up to, but until then, mum's the word.

Monica's family has been amazing about helping us with preparations and setting everything up.

They've cleaned out their old barn and turned it into a dream. Last weekend, Monica, her mom, and her sisters-in-law decorated it all with twinkle lights and ribbon. Earlier today they added flowers, and it looks magical. I snuck a peek while they were finishing up, when I was supposed to be writing my speech. I couldn't help it. Even though it shocks the hell out of me, I'm giddy like a schoolgirl. Never thought that would ever happen, but I'm so ready for this day. To make Monica mine.

After all the farm activities, Monica's brothers, Will and Mike, will usher everyone to their seats. Maddy and Kayla will hand out a program of sorts to our guests just moments before the festivities begin. Josiah is the master of ceremonies.

Over the last year, he and I have gotten really close, and I'm glad he's standing up for us today. He is one tough dude. He is as kind as he is funny. Lately, he's been in a funk, and I'm not sure what that's about. Monica and I are both worried about him, but for now, he's remaining tight-lipped. I'm just glad he's here and healthy. His last check-up showed he's still in remission, and we are all happy about that. Cancer had no chance with him. Thank fuck.

At three on the dot, everyone is seated, and the air is buzzing with anticipation. Josiah and I walk up the aisle between the chairs. We stand before our guests and the group gasps. Apparently, they read their hand-out, but maybe we're not so believable. Our guests are faced away from the house and aren't privy to the spectacular view I have. Monica and her father step out their front door, and everything stops.

Monica didn't want to be super traditional today, and she did things her way, right down to the cow print Chucks she's currently wearing that make me smile. She didn't tell me about those. Tracing her tanned legs up, my eyes roam over a simple, yet elegant, white gown that makes my heart skip a beat. She's absolutely breathtaking.

Her father, who looks every part the proud country man, escorts her toward me. Dressed in his best Wrangler jeans, button-up, vest, and cowboy hat, he is ready for what's coming. They walk toward the group as quiet music plays in the distance. When they reach the beginning of the aisle, the music changes and everyone knows what to do. Our guests rise for the bride's entrance, and even though my eyes are locked on Monica's, I know some ladies are crying. Once they reach the front of the aisle, I step to them as Josiah turns to his father.

"Who gives this woman to be married to this man?" he asks.

"Her mother and I do," John says with a little waiver to his voice. He kisses Monica on the cheek and then steps away to join Kathy and the rest of the Fields family.

Taking Monica's hand in mine, I lead her over to where we are going to exchange vows and rings. This moment feels monumental. This is a life-changing experience, one I never believed was going to happen to me, and I'm excited and looking forward to what comes next.

Josiah looks at us, smirks, then speaks over our heads. "You may all be seated. Thank you for coming today to take part in this special day for Christian and Monica." Holding hands, we turn toward each other.

"Christian, have you prepared vows you wish to share today?" Josiah asks, and I nod.

Clearing my throat, I begin. "Monica, for years you've captivated me. Until you, I had never met anyone who could see me completely and accept me just as I am. With you, I never needed to pretend to be someone I'm not. It's taken me a long time to realize you wanted me, flaws and all. Thank you for always believing in me, in us, and for not walking away when that's what I deserved. I love you more today than I did yesterday, and I know my love will continue to grow as each day passes. Today, I give you all of me. All that I am and all that I will be. I'm yours, now and forever."

Sniffling sounds come from the crowd, and looking at Monica, I see tears in her eyes. As she tries to blink them away, one escapes and runs down her cheek. I chase it with my hand and wipe it away. "Hey, beauty. I love you," I whisper to her. She nods and swallows before she speaks.

"Christian, you are frustrating, stubborn, strong-willed, arrogant, and selfish." *Shit! This isn't how vows are supposed to go, are they? I thought it was all lovey-dovey, not point out all the flaws that stood in our way.*

"Amen," someone hollers. I hear chuckling in the crowd, and I know it's my boys. They all came, and now I'm wondering why I invited the assholes to the most important day of my life.

Knowing I should pay attention, I focus back on Monica, who has a smirk on her face. She apparently stopped talking and is waiting for me. *Guess I am all those things she said.* Smiling at her, she smiles back, knowing she's got my attention.

"After I discovered all those things, and considering the number of times you've been an ass—sorry, Mom—I could have walked away. But no matter what, I was still smitten. On those rare occasions where you let your guard down, you showed me the real you. The loyal, loving, caring, and giving person you don't show to many others. That's what kept me coming back.

"I knew if you stepped outside of yourself and saw what I did, you'd discover he's a better version of you. Thank you for revealing your true self to me. I love you, Christian. I am all yours, now and forever."

Josiah nods his head and pulls the rings out of his pocket. "Now it's time to exchange the rings. Christian, repeat after me. With this ring, I thee wed."

When I slide the platinum band on Monica's hand, I say the words. "With this ring, I thee wed." Monica repeats the process with my ring and then Josiah finishes with the best words.

"I now pronounce you husband and wife. Christian, you may kiss your bride."

Pulling her into me, I waste no time bringing my lips to hers. Trying to keep it PG rated, we kiss softly and then I whisper against her lips, "I can't wait to get you alone. You look stunning." Monica giggles and gives me another peck before we turn to face the surprised expressions of our friends and family.

"Surprise!" we shout at them all, and the air is filled with laughter, whistles, and hollers.

Chapter 39

Monica

We did it. Christian and I are officially married, and we pulled off an epic surprise on our friends. We obviously had to tell our parents because we held it at the farm and we needed to get Christian's parents to come from New York.

Everyone is surprised and overjoyed. After the ceremony, we take some pictures and then head over to the decorated farm building for food, toasts, and dancing. During the ceremony, one of the farm's employees handled the food arrival and setup so that my whole family could be present the entire time.

The ceremony went by so fast. Christian looked amazing in his black suit and custom Nikes. When we walk over to the reception and he removes his suit coat and rolls up his shirt sleeves, I'm about to lose it and drag him somewhere more secluded.

We sit down at the bride and groom's table while everyone finds their spots. Facing each other, he sees my desire right away. He knows I'm on the edge. And seeing that reflected at me in his eyes feels amazing.

Christian traces the dip of my dress, following it as it travels deep between my breasts. His touch is teasing, feather-like wisps that send goose bumps all over my body. I shiver and my nipples pebble behind the thin fabric. Closing my eyes. I hope my boob tape won't give me away. Christian leans into me and runs his tongue up my ear, softly blowing in it before he whispers, "You think that's hot? I've got something that will make you even hotter. Want to see?" This man is making me desperate.

Breathy and nodding frantically, I don't care who is around. He slowly lifts his pant leg up and shows me his socks. Confused, I tilt my head at him, silently questioning what he's trying to show me. I don't have a foot fetish. Actually, it's the exact opposite. I dislike feet; they're gross, and he knows that. So what is he trying to show me? Leaning over, I study his sock again, and that's when it registers: cow print. His socks are cow print, like my shoes, and we just got married on a dairy farm. Adorable. There is no doubt Christian is my other half, that's for sure.

During the garter toss, Samantha steps up next to me, wrapping me in a hug. "You're married," she squeals.

"And, to your brother," I answer back with a laugh.

"Ugh, don't remind me." She fake groans, then quickly adds, "I'm just kidding. I've been rooting for you two forever."

"Thanks Sam, that's meant a lot."

Elbowing me, she asks, "When are you going to try for a baby?"

My mouth falls open and a gasp falls out. "What? We just got married. Babies aren't on the agenda for a bit."

"I want to know when there will be some uptight mini cowboys to spoil." We break out into a fit of laughter, drawing everyone's attention. Samantha waves her hand at the group. "Don't pay us any attention. Rocco, Ace, Josh, Tristan, or Josiah, which one of you is next?" The guys all point to Coach and laugh.

"Guess we have a lot to look forward to, huh?" I say as Christian points to the cake table.

Sam hugs me again. "Guess that's your cue. Love you, Monica."

Squeezing extra hard, I reply, "Love you too."

After the dinner and dancing, we toast everyone with champagne and s'mores cupcakes. It's getting late and all the kids are getting restless. Thankfully, we encouraged everyone to grab a room at the Motel 6 in town, and they listened. No one wanted to drive the couple of hours it'd take to get back to Chicago. Plus, my parents invited everyone to come back for lunch the next day. From what I heard from Lian, he hasn't gotten enough time with the cows, and my brothers are going to help him and Sam feed the calfs tomorrow. Even though the day was long, it was everything I dreamed it would be.

Done for the night, I nudge my husband and tell him I'm ready to go. He shouts, "Night, y'all," to everyone, throws me over his shoulder, and runs to his SUV. After he settles me in the passenger seat and buckles me in, he kisses me, leaving me panting, before getting in and tearing out of the drive, giving a honking salute on his way.

We elected to stay at another hotel farther out of town, not wanting to run into any of our friends. I can just imagine what those pranksters would come up with to ruin the fun we planned on having. Christian checks us in while I cuddle into his side. The ride in the elevator to our floor is torture. Christian whispers dirty things into my ear while running his fingers delicately over my cleavage. My breathing intensifies, and in no time, my breaths are hard and edgy.

Once we're behind closed doors, I kick off my shoes and sashay toward the bed. Christian toes off his shoes and then works the buttons slowly on his shirt while standing across the room, stalking me with his eyes. He removes his shirt, drops it, then reaches for his belt.

Sitting down on the bed, I focus my attention on him. He drags the belt through its loops and drops it to the floor. Next, he unbuttons his pants and slides down the zipper. Once they fall down his muscular legs, he steps from them. When he's dressed only in his cow socks and black Calvin Klein boxer briefs that high-light all he is packing, I squeal. Swallowing, I lick my lips, eager for him.

Christian runs his fingers over himself and gives a firm squeeze. Then he stalks over to me and my heart rate picks up. I spread my legs as he nears, and he steps between them, putting his cock at mouth level. Leaning forward, I give the head of it, peeking out from his waistband, a kiss, and a deep growl comes from above me.

"Monica," Christian warns.

Feeling feisty, I want to push him a bit. I pull down his boxers, freeing him. I lick him from base to tip before swallowing him whole. Not expecting it, Christ-ian's body stills, and a groan falls from his lips. I run my hands up and down his thighs, and a shiver racks his body. His cock jumps in my mouth. "Monica. Babe," Christian says on a groan. I suck again before I slide back, letting his hard cock fall from my lips.

Moments later, when it seems Christian has gained back control, he looks down at me and says, "Dress off. Now."

He steps back, allowing me to stand and turn in front of him. He unzips the dress and helps me step from it before he spins me back around. Not bothering to look, he tosses it toward the nearby desk as his eyes eat up the sight before him.

Clothed in nothing but a white lace G-string, I've never felt more beautiful, desirable, wanted, or vulnerable. This man before me is my everything. He has been since I was eighteen, and now, at twenty-seven, he is finally my husband. Our road to each other has been bumpy, filled with twists and turns. But regardless of it all, no matter how many times I've been clipped, brought to my literal and figurative knees over him, I'll never give up on us. And he won't either.

Epilogue

Monica

It's fall again, and life is crazy. Christian and I finally got out of the city last month to celebrate our one-year wedding anniversary late. We traveled back to New York. While there, we visited some of our favorite places and made fresh memories, replacing many of the bad ones we previously shared.

Christian took me out to his parents' estate since I hadn't been back since we'd collected Samantha after the time she and Lucas broke up. That weekend, I'd been so focused on Samantha, my mind hadn't allowed me to recognize where I was. When we returned to Chicago, I realized I hadn't been out to the Foxes' house since Christian's internship party.

Looking back, I'll forever count that day as my worst. It was when Christian's arrogant asshole behavior had done its ultimate damage and completely broken me. However, it wasn't the last time he'd hurt me. Unfortunately, throughout the years, he'd done some damage.

Thankfully, we've moved past that and reconciled. Being back in his parents' house, seeing them, and visiting Jacque, their chef, was amazing. It was just like coming home after a long time away. We spent the weekend laughing, loving, and making so many happy memories.

Now in Chicago and back into the swing of school, I notice my life getting busier. No matter what I do, I'm exhausted. Often, I'm taking a nap before Christian even gets home from work. It's unusual, for sure, and after doing it for a few days, I know something is going on with my body.

I visit my internist for a checkup, and Dr. Molly runs a urine sample and collects bloodwork. Within minutes, she has an answer. I'm pregnant. Trying to absorb the news, I backtrack in my calendar, realizing I most likely got pregnant while we were in New York. Right before we left, I'd been finishing up a prescription for antibiotics. The pharmacist and doctor had both mentioned something about birth control not being as effective when you were taking an antibiotic.

Honestly, I hadn't given it much thought, and here we are.

* * *

Sitting in my car after my appointment, my mind is spinning. Before we got married, Christian and I both admitted to wanting children. We just hadn't identified specifics yet. Looks like now is the time for that conversation. Christian is turning thirty next year, so I know we would have started trying sooner rather than later because neither of us want to be those dreaded old parents.

Clutching the ultrasound picture of our tiny fox, I think about how I can tell Christian, to make it special for him. Then it comes to me. I grab my phone, pull up the Nike app, and browse through the baby shoes. I find a pair of Nike Force 1 crib baby booties— they're perfect. I select the store nearest me and purchase them. Heading there, my plan formulates in my head. Calling an order into Mateo's for delivery, I rush home to assemble my surprise.

When Christian arrives home two hours later, he freezes as soon as he enters the penthouse. "Monica," he hollers out.

In the kitchen, I giggle at the hesitancy I hear in his voice. Knowing that dinner already filled our home with heavenly scents of roasted tomatoes, garlic, oregano, and cheese, he's probably wondering what's going on. Sure, I cook often, but I never make Italian food because nothing compares to Mateo's. So, smelling what he does, he has to know something is happening.

Rounding the corner and stepping into the kitchen, Christian's eyes fall on me and a smile spreads across his handsome face. Walking to me, he glances around the room. When he reaches me, he looks me in the eyes and says, "Hey, babe. How are you?"

"I'm good," I squeak, trying to hold back my excitement. Throughout the afternoon, as the news of my pregnancy sank in, the more excited I became. I couldn't wait to tell Christian.

Sniffing at the air, he asks, "Is that Mateo's I smell?" Already knowing the answer, he laughs.

Nodding, I answer, "It is. Today is a special day. I got something for you." The color drains from his face as panic spreads through his body. He's freaking out, so I reach out to him. "Christian, it's okay. You didn't forget anything. I just got some really great news today, and I wanted to celebrate with you."

He takes a moment, lets out a few deep breaths, and his color returns to normal. "Okay."

Handing him a wrapped box, he glances at it, then looks back at me, confused. "Open it," I whisper.

Carefully unwrapping it, he sees a note attached on top. It says *We're adding to the team in March.* With the words are two adult foxes and a baby fox nestled in a pair of Nike shoes. Christian's eyes search out mine and they're swimming with confusion. He opens the box and sees the miniature Nikes and looks back at me again. Then he realizes what I'm hinting at.

With wide eyes, he questions, "Really?" His normally strong, confident voice is raspy and filled with emotion. I nod. He takes a tiny shoe out of the box and turns it around in his hand. A smile breaks out across his handsome face, calming my anxious heart immediately. Relieved, I let the tears that have been hovering all afternoon fall.

Christian looks inside the box at the other shoe, as if he's amazed. Then, when he reaches inside, I know he's found the ultrasound picture. He drags it out and stares at it, then locks his eyes on mine. "Really?" he says again, his voice thick with hope, love, and awe. Wiping away my stray tears, I again nod my head. He sets everything down on the counter and wraps his arms around me.

"I love you, Monica. I can't wait to meet our baby," he whispers against my hair. Cherishing the moment, I just hold on to him, feeling the same.

Over a delicious dinner of chicken parmesan, salad, and breadsticks, we celebrate the news. By the time dinner is done, we've talked about my doctor's appointment, what to expect, when I'm due, work expectations, delivery hopes, telling people, and our excitement. Tonight, we've made some choices for our family going forward, and that feels good.

Seeing that it's still early in the pregnancy, we

aren't sharing the good news with our friends and family until we're in the clear. We purchase a few books from Amazon that walk you through pregnancy and what follows it. And we talk about fears or concerns we have. Overall, we are incredibly excited.

Being surrounded by little people all the time, I'm ready to have one of my own, especially with the man of my dreams. Watching him interact with Sam and Lian has been one of my favorite things. In fact, he and I often snag them following Sam's peewee hockey games to give Mika and Shiloh a brief break. They still have their daughter Aurora to deal with, but she's such a laid-back baby.

In a few weeks, we are going to Sam's game, and many of the Steel players will also be in attendance. Even though Mika officially retired before this season started, he remains close to his former teammates. In fact, we all spend a lot of time together. Lucas and Samantha, Mika and Shiloh, Ace, Rocco, Josh, and even Coach Tristan. These are some of Christian's best friends, and their wives, partners, and girlfriends have become some of mine too.

I've even heard Coach has someone special he's tucked away. There are rumors that some of the guys may have met her at a charity fundraiser a few years ago, but he's keeping things really quiet. The others guys' relationships are chaotic and messy. Thankfully, they're still young and don't have to have it all figured out yet.

Until our little fox makes his or her arrival in March, I will relish the time I have with my students, my friends and their kids, my nieces and nephew, and my husband, continuing to make memories.

This weekend, I'm going to see if Shiloh will let us take Lian, Christian's favorite person, to a movie and out for dinner after his brother's hockey game. She mentioned having the entire team over for pizza, and I wonder if getting the little brother out of the way might make things go smoother. Plus, it'll give us practice for when our little one arrives.

This can't be real. Someone pinch me, please. My happily ever after has arrived. Even though I've questioned if it could be possible, I'm sitting with my husband, the man of my dreams, and I'm pregnant with our first child. This is the life I always wanted.

If you'd like another peek into the Chicago Steel world, visit my website at https://907publishing.wixsite.com/my-site and subscribe. Once received, every month the latest and greatest news in the Steel World, and you'll learn about any extra sneak peeks that will go straight onto my website.

Acknowledgments

What to say... I fucking love the Steel men and I hope you do too. Through this process of writing, certain scenes have worked their way into my manuscript and then when it comes time for my editors to do their thing, I'm told some of those incredibly adorable, swoon-worthy, super-hot moments don't move my story along. And because of this, I chose to remove them. But the good news is that they haven't been forgotten. No, those stories are making their way to my website as little sneak peeks into the futures of these amazing couples. Make sure to check them out.

There are many thanks I owe for helping me get to book three in my series.

Thank you, Karen (Feed Your Dreams Designs), for just being you. You always lend a listening ear, provide valuable advice and insight, and make me smile. Thank you for believing in me and always encouraging me.

Thank you, Shauna (Ink Machine Editing), for catching all my blunders, incorrect words, punctuation, and tense. You truly make my words shine.

Thank you, Nicole (Emerald Edits), for helping me

share the story that's written in my heart. Your direction and prodding have helped me to weave stories I can be proud of sharing.

Thank you, Darren, Zach, and Kadin, for all the love you give me. I couldn't do this without each of you. I love you three so much.

Thank you, Vader, for giving me love and reminding me to take breaks, even if it's to feed you a treat. I love you, baby girl.

Thank you to those readers who have become friends. Your support, encouragement, and laughter have kept me going. Thank you for welcoming me into your lives, I know it's a true honor. Be blessed.

World of Chicago Steel

Have you read *Hooked By You*, the first book of the Chicago Steel Series with Lucas and Samantha? If not, you can find it on Kindle Unlimited. Also on Kindle Unlimited is the second book, *Checked By You*, Mika and Shiloh's story.

Hooked By You–Chicago Steel Series Book One

Lucas

She's a goddess in heels. Absolute perfection. Well, almost.

Samantha Fox is the heiress of Fox Sporting, my new management team. As one of the best wings in the NHL, I have never shied away from a challenge, and she is definitely a challenge. But if her company representing me doesn't stop me from wanting her, the fact she's engaged should, right?

But the noticeably absent sparkle from her left ring finger makes me question. I vow to myself that I'll find out what that's all about. And if she's single, I plan to make her mine. Or at least, mine for the night. I just need one taste of the divine.

Samantha

Off-limits. That's what he is. Lucas Bouchard is the prestigious new client acquired by my family's company. From what I know, not only is he an amazing hockey player, he's a humble and generous philanthropist too. Also, he's a walking aphrodisiac.

It doesn't matter that I've just broken off my engagement to a cheating, using loser. Every time our eyes lock, I find myself captivated. But he's not for me. No matter how many times I remind myself of this, though, it doesn't compute. Plain and simple, I want him. And keeping my distance might prove impossible.

Checked By You–Chicago Steel Series Book Two

Mika

She's the uber-sexy, single mother living next door. Everyone tells me to keep my distance. But there's something about her. Specifically, her eyes. They speak to me. Drawing me in like a siren. I want to know her, but she's more guarded than Buckingham Palace. However, after one afternoon in her presence, I find myself addicted and wanting more. Willing to do whatever I have to just to make it past her defenses.

Shiloh

My next-door neighbor is an insanely hot, single professional hockey player. As if that isn't bad enough, he's a nice guy too. After spending an afternoon where he showed my son how to skate and took us out to ice cream, I want to let him in. My past cautions me to put on the brakes, but I find myself going full steam ahead, ignoring all the red flags waving at me.

Also By Jessica Buss

Chicago Steel Series

Hooked By You (Lucas & Samantha)
Checked By You (Mika & Shiloh)
Clipped By You (Christian & Monica)
Coming Soon
Speared By You
Slashed By You
Delayed By You
Tripped By You
Blocked By You

About the Author

Jessica Buss was born and raised in Anchorage, Alaska. She is married to her high school sweetheart and has two sons. Although she has both her bachelor's and master's degrees in Psychology, she stepped away from that field to be a stay-at-home mom. Now that her kids are growing up and she's getting more time to herself, she's giving this writing thing a chance.

https://907publishing.wixsite.com/my-site